NICOLE B. HICKS

Stone

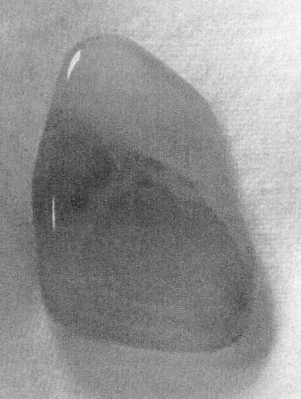

WHY THE PRINCESS ATE THE STONE

Copyright © Nicole B. Hicks, 2015

This is a work of fiction.
Names, characters, places and incidents are either the product of the author's imagination, or have been used fictitiously.
Any resemblance to persons, living or dead, businesses, locales or events is strictly coincidental.

Cover Design
Cassandra J. LaPorte
www.CassandraLaPorte.com

Map by
Amy P. Simmonds
"InkaDoodleDoo"
www.allthingsround.co.uk

All rights reserved.
No part of this book may be reproduced in any form
or by any electronic or mechanical means,
including information-storage-and-retrieval systems,
without prior permission in writing from the author,
except for brief quotations embodied in articles or reviews.

*What is the opposite of love?
If you said 'hate', you are not alone,
but read on to discover that which
I've been learning all my life.*

*For my husband, Skeeter and my son, Andrew
my parents, Tom and Jamie
my sister, Lauren
and my nephews, Edward and Daniel...
All of whom have helped me learn how to find love
in the face of its opposite.*

Thanks to:

*My beta-readers, especially Liz and Deb
for encouragement, enthusiasm
and kindness in their corrections.*

*My artists, Cassandra and Amy
for making my ideas beautiful.*

*Robin McKinley
for bringing back the magic of fairy tales.*

*C. S. Lewis
for opening the door to fantasy.*

*Tamora Pierce
for showing me so many kinds of magic.*

*And to Sir Terry Pratchett
for making me laugh for a moment,
and think for a lifetime.
#GNUTerryPratchett*

STONE

WHY THE PRINCESS ATE THE STONE

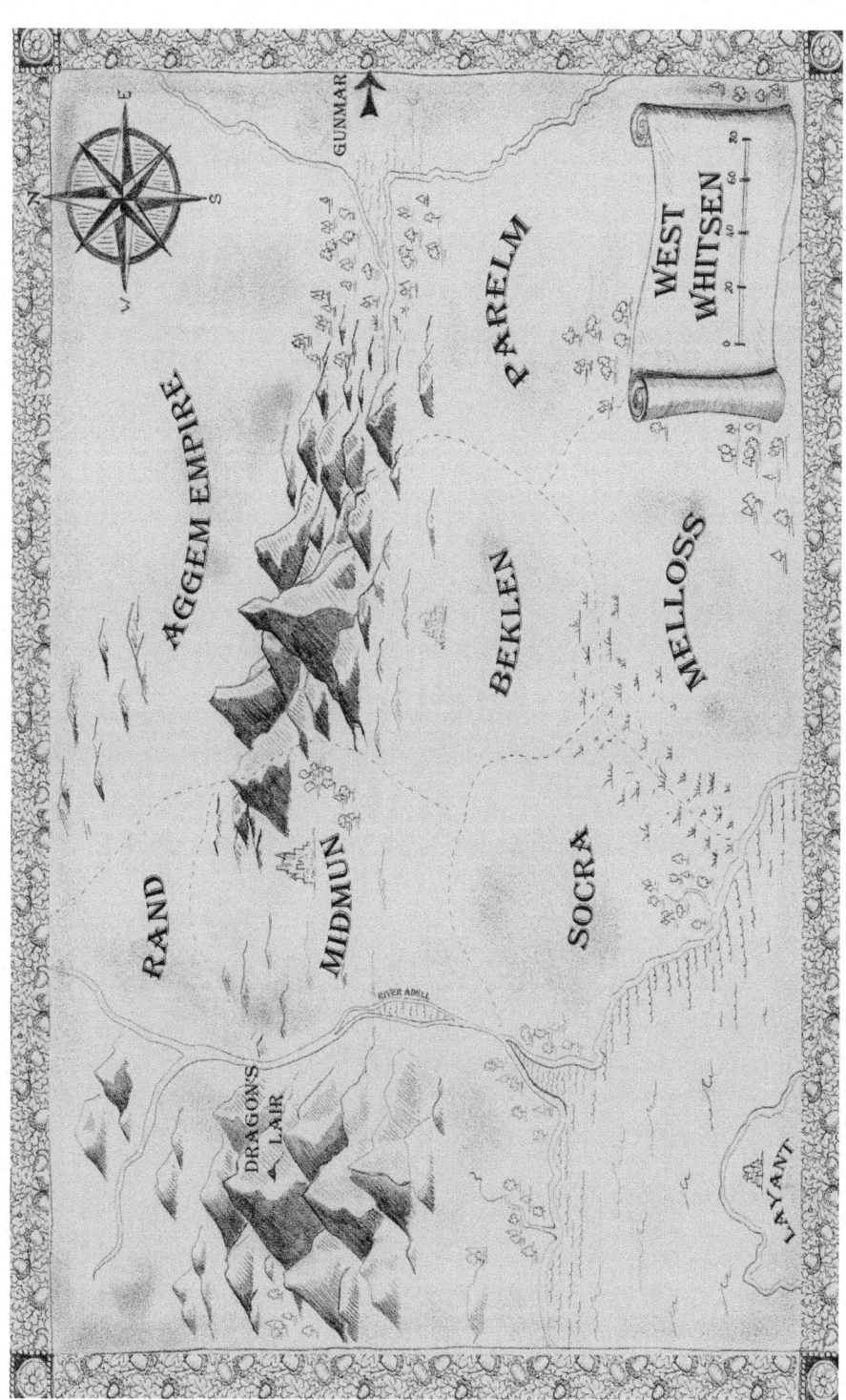

> "I WEPT NOT,
> SO TO STONE WITHIN I GREW."
>
> -- DANTE ALIGHIERI
>
> *Inferno,*
>
> *Canto 33,*
>
> *Line 49*

STONE

Section 1
Of Soup and Stone

"We are three hungry soldiers in a strange land. We have asked you for food, and you have no food. Well then, we'll have to make stone soup."
-- Maria Brown, Stone Soup

Once upon a time there was a princess named Niren. She had shining, straight dark brown hair which fell to her knees when it was not bound up in buns and braids. Her eyes were blue and her skin was fair, which means she was prone to sunburn, unless she wore a hat with a wide brim. She had a ready smile and a pleasant laugh. Her governesses had always found her studious and enthusiastic.

Niren lived in Wayhall Castle in the mountainous kingdom of Midmun, on the continent of West Whitsen. She was the eldest of two daughters born to King Thowin and Queen Jaynn. Her younger sister, Lyru, was also fair of complexion and blue eyed, but her long hair was blonde and slightly curly. Her face was a little rounder, and her lips a little fuller. The two of them each had a dusting of light freckles across their cheeks and noses.

Princess Niren, you must understand, had encountered a great many different kinds of things to eat. Local peasants brought offerings of rustic breads, and various vegetables, many of them with strange colors and amusing shapes. Foreign dignitaries gave gifts of exotic and exciting spices which turned their foods bright yellow or blazing red. Blazing could be used to describe the tastes as well. The cooks and bakers of her own castle and country competed to delight her with their creations. They presented her with fishes, fowl and field-beasts all of which were baked or boiled, braised or broiled. Every sort of cake and pie, various ices and pastries, as well as subtleties galore graced the board for dessert. Niren savored all of it with delight. Certainly, she never lacked for quantity or quality of food.

Why, then, do you suppose such a well fed, well-bred princess would eat a stone?

Chapter 1
Now Read On...

"Our love is sharpened by the stone of our challenges and strengthened by the struggles of our growth."
  -- Steve Maraboli, Unapologetically You

Niren was betrothed to Prince Misk, the second son of the king of Beklen. This marriage had been arranged at the time of her birth, between her parents and his, for the strength and prosperity of their countries. It was based on an old promise between their grandfathers. The two of them met for the first time on Niren's sixteenth birthday, and grew very fond of each other during the yearlong festivities preceding the wedding, which had been set to take place on Niren's seventeenth birthday. Balls and banquets, picnics and parades, fetes and festivals were all held in honor of the royal couple. These events took place in the small cities and rural villages of Midmun, because Niren was the heir and was slated to inherit the throne, while Misk's older brother, Jenan, would eventually rule neighboring Beklen.

The country's clerks ran a census as the royal family traveled. Queen Jaynn and Prince Misk's parents joined the progress for the last few weeks. This trip through Midmun was an opportunity for the people to become acquainted with the young man who would someday be their king. As they traveled, Niren came to know Misk, and she found herself falling in love with him. Misk was wise and winning, and he became quite popular and respected. The citizens of Midmun also tested the prince. There were jousts and boxing matches, as well as foot races, chess games and riddles. In the last village they visited before returning to Wayhall Castle, an even greater challenge was set forth.

King Thowin called Chancellor Gojen up to the podium. The advisor wore old-fashioned robes, rather more ornate than those of the king. With his long, graying blonde hair, and pale, flaky skin, he was easily recognized, and was well known to many in Midmun. Everyone in the crowd attended to him while he spoke, sharing the information which messengers had recently brought to the king.

"We have received reports from sseveral of our western villages, requesting aid. There is a dragon plaguing the border." For all his stately nature, the chancellor spoke with a slight speech impediment, drawing out and stressing his esses. "Where it came from, no one yet knows. As far as the sseers and the knight's army can tell, it is a full-grown creature, both strong and vicious. It has been ssnatching livestock and wild game, and as if that were not bad enough, in the last few days sseveral young woman have gone missing."

Fear and dismay spread like wildfire through the crowd. Women clutched their children to their sides, and several young men thrust their fists in the air in a show of defiance against the dragon, and solidarity with the king. Many eyes watched the sky for a sign of the beast.

Gojen cleared his throat and continued, once the crowd had quieted. He called the prince to the podium. Misk left Niren's side, and climbed the three steps to stand beside the advisor.

"Are you brave enough to go and slay the beast? You will win glory and honor forever, if you succeed. Moreover, you will protect your new country, and earn your place as the King of Midmun."

Misk lifted his head up high. His face shone with zeal.

"It will be my great honor to defend my new home. I will not allow this dragon to go on killing. I accept this challenge! I will fight the dragon!"

The crowd roared its approval, while Niren, who was standing next to her mother, began to weep.

Prince Misk was brave. He was honorable. He was doomed.

Chapter 2
Once Done is Twice Begun

"The unreal is more powerful than the real, because nothing is as perfect as you can imagine it, because it's only intangible ideas, concepts, beliefs, fantasies that last. Stone crumbles. Wood rots. People, well, they die. But things as fragile as a thought, a dream, a legend, they can go on and on."
-- Chuck Palahniuk, Choke

Once Prince Misk accepted the challenge, he began his preparations to journey to the west instead of returning to Wayhall. Niren, along with the kings and queens and most of the entourage, would return to the castle as planned. There, they would finalize the preparations for the wedding.

Misk decreed that he would take only his squire with him to face the dragon. No other knights, nor any of Midmun's small contingent of magicians would join them. Niren protested, but Misk stood firm.

"This dragon is only a beast," the prince said dismissively. "And this is little more than a hunting expedition. I am taking my squire because it is a great opportunity for him to learn, and for the two of us to bond. There is no need to take more than the two of us. Trust me."

The new squire was a young man whom Misk had chosen from ranks of Midmunese pages hoping to serve their future king. He saw to it that swords were sharpened and lances were balanced, while Misk inspected his work. Together with the king and his advisers, they studied maps of the western border, and read the reports which had arrived. They reviewed strategies and made their plans. Food and supplies were loaded onto a mule, and the horses were fitted with armor.

Niren felt fretful and proud, all at once. When she was a young girl, she had heard stories and studied the history of Midmun's wars. Those battles had been safely in the past, or sufficiently far away to be of little concern to her, and Midmun had been at peace for decades. The tales of dragons which had thrilled her as a young maiden now returned to haunt her.

When the time came for the prince and his squire to go, Niren clasped Misk's hand in her own. She inclined her head close to his shoulder, and whispered, "I expect you back for dinner, which will be served promptly at seven. As fish will be served, please bring a bottle of white wine."

Niren sought refuge in humor, because she was unwilling to speak of the fear and doubt welling up inside her. She was determined to send her prince off with a smile, and that he should be assured of her confidence in him.

Misk's green eyes widened. Then he smiled as he caught her humor, and laughed. He agreed to bring the wine.

"Not only shall I do so, milady, I shall bring flowers for the table as well."

Misk and Eto began to ride westward, through the last foothills of the mountains of Midmun and into the flat and desolate borderlands. Things went well enough for the first several days. At first there were outlying villages, where they stopped to rest. They gathered more information about the state of affairs in the borderlands. Misk quizzed local lords and villagers about the dragon's recent activity. Even as the distance between villages increased, there were plenty of streams to fish in, and there was game to hunt. Misk was in high spirits as they made camp.

"Won't it be grand, Eto? To return, carrying a fang or scale. Perhaps they'll add that to my coat of arms."

Eto grinned at the passion and enthusiasm in Misk's voice.

"I'm certain of it, sir."

"I can't wait to return to Niren again. Just think, we'll be returning just in time for my wedding day. I'll tell you, I wasn't all that keen on the wedding, for a long time. Most of my life, in fact. It was arranged by my parents and hers; neither of us ever had any say in it. Then I met her. I got to know her while we were on the tour. She's wonderful, and I'm not saying that just because she's lovely. She's funny too, and smart. I've landed on my feet."

"I'm sure the wedding will be grand, sir. You'll be the pride of Midmun and Beklen. I hope that someday I can do something just as grand. Fight some monster, save a lady, become a hero. All in a day's work, for us knights. Once I am a knight, that is."

Misk hooted with good-natured laughter, and Eto joined him. They slept well, and continued on their way, as soon as dawn reached the horizon. The going became more difficult as the landscape began to climb again. These were no rolling foothills but sharp, rocky protrusions from the earth. The ground was covered in slippery shale. It was clear that they had crossed the border, and there would be no villages in this forbidding place, but Misk and Eto continued, unperturbed, until darkness began to settle over them.

"Time to make camp. If you'll tend to the horses and the mule, I'll go out there and see if I can find some game."

"Of course, I'll have the fire ready by the time you're back."

Once camp had been set, a brace of rabbits was spitted over the fire, and a few small potatoes were roasting in the coals. As the young men leaned back against their saddles and watched the stars come out, Prince Misk pulled a leather wine skin from his belongings. He uncorked the wine, and poured it into two leather cups, handing one to his squire.

"A toast. To my new bride!"

"To Princess Niren!"

Together they drank, and watched the fire, and toasted, each other. They drank to Midmun and Beklen, and to each the kings and queens. The wine warmed their bodies, and they grew more and more relaxed.

"To the fall of the dragon!"

This led Eto pose the question which had been plaguing him since Misk accepted the quest to slay the dragon.

"Prince Misk, I've got to ask you something. It confused me, and I really want to understand, before we get all the way to the dragon."

As he spoke, he leaned closer and closer to the prince.

The prince smiled, and put his hand on Eto's shoulder, and slowly moved him to a more upright position.

"Of course."

He drew a second wine skin from his pack.

"This was for our return trip, but I think I'll just open it now. There will be wine when we get home. What did you want to ask?"

Eto settled himself in his blankets, and sipped his wine.

"Sir, why did we come out here alone? You could have led King Thowin's army to fight this dragon. You said it was just hunting a beast, but... What could possess even the bravest knight to go alone against the most fearsome beast in all the land? Why?"

Misk glanced at Eto, his green eyes widened in surprise. This question had never occurred to him.

"Knights fight dragons in single combat. It has always been that way, or at least it's been that way since Sir Halb. Don't you know the Legend?"

Eto shook his head, and replied, "Sir Halb? No, Sir. I don't think I've ever heard that name. Who was he?"

Misk rubbed the stubble growing on his chin.

"I can hardly believe it," said Misk. Then he conceded, "Perhaps he is not so well known here in Midmun. Most of the knights and squires in Beklen have become knights and squires because of Sir Halb!"

"I am a squire because my father was, as was his father before him, going back for hundreds of years. Lords and Ladies as far back as anyone can remember. Not one of those lords was ever a squire to a king, though. Mostly everyone here serves his father, or an uncle. It was expected of me, but I think I would have wanted this life, anyway."

"You see, Eto, this is exactly why I did not bring a squire with me from Beklen. We will be able to teach each other so much."

"I'm glad you chose me, Sir. But who was Sir Halb?"

So, Prince Misk, who had been tutored by his country's finest poets and musicians, recited the Legend of Sir Halb:

> "Generations have told this tale,
> Round fire and table, with bread and ale
> A knight, alone, must never fail.
> A solitary soul on a quest for a grail

Hear me now as I tell the plight,
Of brave Sir Halb, the valiant knight
A hero known for wit and might
Who set the country back aright

A dragon had come to curse the land
Some brave lad must make a stand
With a steadfast heart and actions grand
To save the meek and weak and bland

The king set him forth on the perilous quest
So he journeyed alone, into the west
To seek and slay the brutish pest
And prove to all he was the best

He and his horse traveled many a mile
Watching the hills, where once in a while
Smoke rose up, all foul and vile
Marking the dragon's lair and pile

Approaching the cave that fateful day
The knight knelt down, and began to pray
Asking for wisdom to find the way
To best the beast he'd come to slay

As Halb surveyed the craggy glen
The dragon smelled him there, and then
Emerged from his sulfurous smelling den
With a roar to frighten the staunchest of men

The knight stood fast, he trembled not
For here was the glory he'd always sought
With breath like acid and brimstone, hot
The time had come, and so foes fought

No mere lizard would break Halb's steel
His blood was boiling with zest and zeal
He'd come, the dragon's fate to seal
To puncture, slice, to flay and peel

They carried on, sword versus claw
Wounds and burns and punctures raw
The devilish drake, 'gainst the man of law
'Twas a sight to inspire angst and awe

At last the man, with a fearsome groan
Sliced with his sword, cleaving flesh and bone
The hillside shook with the dragons moan
And the knight was left, victorious, alone

A knight enters battle with nary a friend
His squire keeping watch around the bend
For his soul and honor he must fend
And the foul fiend, bring to an end."

As the prince finished his recitation, Eto's brown eyes were wide, and his jaw hung slightly agape, but he was smiling. He rather looked like a man who had found a lost coin, or come in sight of his home after a long journey.

"Prince Misk, honestly, if I wasn't already in your service, and on my way to a knighthood, such a tale would set me on that road. When we return to Wayhall, I'll have the bards teach everyone that legend. Perhaps they'll add a verse about you."

Misk grinned at his squire, his eyes twinkling with pleasure and merriment.

"When we were younger, my brother Jenan and I spent hours spent playing make believe. We took turns at being the dragon and Sir Halb. It's amazing to think... soon enough, we'll both be kings."

"And you'll be good kings, too, Sir."

"Thank you, Eto. Good kings are those who have good advisors, and the support of good friends. I look forward to serving Midmun.

But of course, it will be years until I become king. I've learned so much from my father. Now that I'm here in Midmun, I can get to know King Thowin, and learn from him, as well."

"King Thowin is wonderful, Sir. I am blessed to serve both of you."

Misk smiled, and concluded, "I will fight the dragon alone, because Sir Halb did, and so doing, he proved that it could be done. Where would be the glory, where the honor, if we were to overwhelm a brute, not with skill and cunning, but with force and numbers? No. We risk more, and gain more, in this way."

Misk paused, and laughed at himself.

"If I fail at my work as a knight and a prince, I will look into becoming an orator."

Eto didn't let himself dwell on the thought that if you failed as a knight, facing a dragon, you would die. He certainly didn't speak the thought aloud. Instead, he joined in the laughter, and the two of them settled into their blankets and slept well past dawn.

The prince and his squire went on the next day, scanning the land, looking for herds of deer or wild sheep that might draw the dragon. There were no real villages on this side of the border to the western wasteland, but some nomadic herders had fallen victim to the dragon's marauding, losing both livestock and two young girls.

They made their way to an area where the dragon had been nesting. The ground was scorched and torn in places. All of the wildlife appeared to have fled, and the land was silent, except for whistling of the wind.

On the last night they camped together, Eto checked every bit of Prince Misk's equipment. He sharpened blades which were already sharp enough to slice a human hair, and polished brass bits and buckles until he could see his reflection in them.

"There you are, Sir. Everything is as sharp and shining as I can make it. I think I'll turn in, and get some rest, if there's nothing else?"

Misk let Eto retire, but he sat up all night in a vigil, watching the stars. He prayed, and thought of Niren and his new country until dawn approached. He lingered over memories of his time spent together with Niren on the progress and of lessons which he had learned from his father and brother.

Misk awoke Eto as the sun rose. The squire readied the prince, buckling his breast plate in place and handing him his helm.

"Squire Eto, you have served me well, and I thank you. Wait here for me, and if I do not return from this battle, take my love to Niren, and watch over her. Serve her as you would serve me."

Eto frowned.

"Of course you'll be back, Sir. The dragon doesn't know it, but it's as good as dead."

Misk walked off, alone. Eto kept camp, watching and waiting, and never doubting that his lord would come back with a token of victory and a tale to rival that of his hero, Sir Halb. Still, he wished he was accompanying the prince to the battle.

Chapter 3
The Dragon's Den

"It is a power stronger than will. Could a stone escape the laws of gravity? Impossible. Impossible for evil to form an alliance with good."
  -- Isidore Ducasse Lautreamont

Meanwhile, in a cave on the hillside, the dragon sat and smoked and smoldered. He waited. And he hated. He hated Prince Misk and Princess Niren. He hated King Thowin and Queen Jaynn. He hated Wayhall and Midmun and everything and everyone inside those borders. And he coveted everything within the country as well. He wanted it all for himself, all the power and magic and glory, not to mention all the gold.

The dragon could smell the polish on Misk's shield over a mile away. (Never underestimate a dragon when it comes to the smell of metal.)

Each step brought the prince closer to his destiny and to his doom. At last, within a few yards of the lair, Misk stepped over some unseen boundary and the earth beneath him began to shake and tremble. Rows of boulders rose up from the ground, forming a spelled barrier, a ring of rocks from which there was no escape.

The dragon emerged from the cave with a sound somewhere between a roar and a laugh. Silvery green scales covered its enormous body, and spiraling horns protruded from its head. It was a fearsome sight, and Misk trembled, but he thought of Sir Halb and mastered his fear quickly. He pounded the butt of his spear on the ground three times.

"Dragon, I have come to do battle with you, not to run away! My honor binds me to this spot more surely than do any of your magical conjurings."

With that, he raised the tip of his spear and charged, closing the distance before the dragon could shift its bulk.

The battle between the prince and the dragon was fierce. Misk had combat skills which had been honed all his life, having been taught and trained by the masters of two kingdoms. He had courage and strength. Most of all, he had Niren to fight for. Unfortunately, the dragon had fire, talons and magic. Each wound Misk inflicted seemed to disappear, as if the wound were merely an illusion... or perhaps as if the flesh itself was the illusion.

When his spear snapped in half, Misk drew his sword. Over and over he slashed at the beast, marking the dragon's legs and belly, without seeming to have much affect.

On and on they fought. All of Misk's visions of honor and glory faded in the harsh reality of a fight for his life, replaced by dark thoughts which came, unbidden. Sir Halb must have been a myth. It was insanity itself to come and fight this dragon alone! Niren was lovely, but far away and safe. She was a cosseted lamb, naive and unaware of his sacrifice. His squire, Eto, was a child, an untested novice. Both of the kings were soft, years of peace had weakened their arms and their resolve.

With each wound, these thoughts crept into his mind, bringing despair with them. This poison must have been a part of the dragon's magic. It undermined the prince's confidence, stripping him of a weapon sharper than any sword. It also removed his faith in others, which took away his protection, more surely than melting his shield.

The dragon flapped its great, green leathery wings, creating a wind which blinded the prince. It swept Misk's feet out from beneath him with its spiked tail and while he lay reeling, it bellowed and breathed fire engulfing him.

With his final breath, Misk called Niren's name. The sound of his cry was bound by the ensorcelled ring, until the dragon released the barrier spell. As the boulders disintegrated Misk's shout echoed down into the valley where Eto waited.

The dragon rose up into the sky and flew off, over Eto's head. The stunned squire climbed toward the site of the battle, his heart filled with heavy dread. He scrambled over the shattered boulders and came upon Misk's burnt and broken body, and he wept. Silently, he wrapped the body and placed it on a sledge he constructed from saplings. Then he urged the horses to head toward home.

Chapter 4
The Return of the Squire

"Man is harder than iron, stronger than stone and more fragile than a rose."
  -- Turkish Proverb

The squire and the horses made the long journey back through Midmun as quickly as they could manage. Eto returned to one of the villages he and Misk had visited, for food and information. Several villagers had seen the dragon fly over, apparently on the day Misk had died, but not since. Dejected and exhausted, Eto set out again. The horses, still spooked by the dragon and the dead body behind them, were restless and unruly

At last, as he approached Wayhall Castle. He disregarded the main gate, and went, instead to the knight's guard house. Eto left Misk's litter behind, guarded by the resident knight, as he went into the castle proper. The guards there watched as Eto left, and stared at the litter in silent horror. A few of them followed the silent squire into the throne room.

As he approached the dais, he bowed first to the King and Queen, and then to Niren, and her younger sister. As usual, Chancellor Gojen stood behind the king.

"Your Majesties. Your Highnesses. Chancellor." Eto looked from one to the other. "I bring... I greet you, and I bring news. I bring you terrible news. Prince Misk has been... when he fought the dragon, it ... it killed him."

Sobs racked his tall, slender body, and he shook his head, unable, for a moment, to continue. He trembled, and sucked in long, ragged breaths, fighting for control.

Niren looked at the squire in utter disbelief. Suddenly, she stood from her throne, at her mother's side, and said, "Sir, that is a vicious lie!" She ran down the steps from the dais and out of the throne room.

Princess Lyru rose at once, intending to follow her sister. Before she could descend the stairs, Chancellor Gojen stopped her, laying a hand on her shoulder. Lyru looked down her slender nose at his hand, and he let go of her. Still, he insisted that she wait a moment, before she went to her sister.

"Your Highness, perhaps we sshould first hear the rest of this terrible tale, and then we will be better able to help Princess Niren to accept the fate which has befallen Prince Misk. Please, Ssquire Eto, tell us all you are able."

Haltingly, with his voice breaking, and fighting off tears, Eto told all he had seen and heard. A servant brought him a flagon of warmed wine, to soothe his parched throat, but Eto did not drink from it, even when he had finished telling the sad story.

"Your Majesties, forgive me. I would have done anything... anything to save him. He told me to wait for him, at camp. He wanted to be like his hero, Sir Halb. He told me to bring Niren his love and to protect her, if he wasn't able to return. Forgive me. Please."

Eto sunk down onto his knees, in distress and supplication.

Queen Jaynn descended the steps of the dais, and went to the distraught squire.

"My son, stand please. You have done all that could be asked of you, and now you must rest. Allow us to see to everything."

Eto was helped to his feet and led away from the hall.

King Thowin summoned Gojen to his side, and instructed him to ensure that Eto was attended to by the court healers and given anything he needed. He sent Lyru and Jaynn to Niren's chambers. Lastly he called for Prince Misk's parents to be brought to the throne room.

The audience with the king and queen of Beklen went just as poorly as you could possibly imagine. Poor Queen Margam had to be taken to the infirmary after falling in a faint. King Hastho grumbled and growled, seeking a place to lay blame, and finally wept. Once Hastho had left the throne room to comfort his wife, King Thowin went to Niren's chambers on a similar errand.

In Niren's chambers, the thick green velvet drapes were drawn closed. Niren lay face down on her bed, the covers in disarray. Queen Jaynn and Princess Lyru sat on the upholstered divan, clasping each other's hands. In the dim, cool room, the only sound was Niren's sobs, which were slowly evolving into sniffles. (Even a princess can only maintain a full out sob for a brief time.)

King Thowin sat down beside Niren with a deep sigh and spoke softly but firmly.

"Dearest, sit up. Come now. Sit up and take deep breaths. There."

Niren sat up and laid her head on her father's shoulder, brushing away the slightly gray hair resting on his collar.

"Listen to me," he said. "Your mother and sister and I will help you in whatever ways we can. Here, with us, you may feel and act just as you wish. Weep or shout or faint. I promise that we will understand. If you wish it, we will cry alongside you, and we will shout with you until the stones in the walls ring with our echoes. It will not be the first time these walls have heard such cries."

Niren's crying diminished as she listened to her father.

"In public, however, you will be calm. Sad, but calm. You will master yourself, and show Midmun that you are a fit leader. The country will be at sixes and sevens. Remember that some of our subjects have lost loved ones, as well. Everyone will look to you for strength. You must show them how to grieve well."

Niren looked up at her father, her blue eyes bleary, her cheeks red, and tracked by her tears. She cleared her throat.

"I'll try, Papa. For you, I will try, but I don't know how."

King Thowin smiled sadly, stroking Niren's long, brown hair, some of which had come undone from its braids as she wept. He brushed the strands back, away from her damp face.

"None of us know how to be strong, not at first, but we learn. You will learn, too. You are young, and this tragedy has struck early, but no one escapes grief in this world. It isn't fair, and it isn't fun, but you will find your way. There is no magic cure for grief, but you will survive it. In time, you will find joy again, though you cannot fathom it."

As Thowin fell silent, Lyru stood and walked to the washstand. There she poured water from the pitcher, and dampened a facecloth in the basin.

"Here," she said, as she handed the cloth to her sister. "Clean your face; you can't let anyone else see you like this."

Niren jumped up from her father's side, her temper flaring

"Do you think I care what people think? Right now? I don't CARE! I don't care what anyone sees or what they think! Do you think I care that my face is dirty?"

Lyru continued, despite Niren's outburst.

"Perhaps you'd better care. Papa said it, you have to be calm and strong while everyone is watching you. The people will see you, and they will care, whether you like it or not. You aren't some common girl. You can't just hide here, crying. Or at least you can't let them SEE that you've been crying."

"Lyru, I think that will be enough. This isn't the time." Queen Jaynn stood, too. "Come with me. We will check on Queen Margam and make sure she is well. Then we can begin to make the arrangements."

Jaynn kissed Niren on the forehead and smoothed her hair.

"I am so sorry it has come to this. I would take away your pain, if that were possible. Remember that you are not alone, however much it may feel that way."

The queen led Princess Lyru from the room. Lyru looked back over her shoulder, but couldn't find anything more to say.

Thowin took Niren's hand in his own. He rubbed his thumb over her palm in a soothing motion, over and over.

"Your sister is right, you know. She certainly could have been kinder and less direct, but your country will look to you. This is your loss, and it is your task to bear it well. They will, however, insist on thinking of it as their loss, too. That is because they love you, and they have come to love Misk. If you thought they were watching you while you were happy, cherishing each of your joys as their own, know that now they will redouble their efforts. They will need to see what you are made of. They will need to know your strength and resolve. Can you lead them, Niren?"

Chapter 5
The White Dress, the Black Dress

"Too long a sacrifice can make a stone of the heart. O when may it suffice?"
-- William Butler Yeats

Chancellor Gojen and Queen Jaynn saw to it that the funeral plans were made and carried out. Because Queen Margam was unable to travel, King Hastho decided that Prince Misk would be interred in the royal burial grounds of Midmun. Flowers from wedding bouquets were made over into funeral arrangements. Bright clothes were packed away, replaced by solemn grays and blacks. Wayhall Castle fairly buzzed with the hustle and bustle of readying itself for a royal funeral.

Then suddenly all the frenzied activity came to a halt. On the day of the funeral, a silent gloom settled over the castle's inhabitants.

The funeral took place in the castle's small, ornate chapel. The wooden pews were full of people who had come for the wedding, and stayed to pay their respects at the funeral. Beautiful stained glass windows lined the walls, each depicting a historical scene... but they did not shine well, because the day was gloomy and overcast. The weather suited Niren's mood perfectly.

The priest, who was to have presided over the wedding, instead conducted Misk's funeral. Both of the kings spoke of prince's courage and honor. Eto spoke of his great respect for his knight-master, and Misk's faithfulness to Niren and his new country.

Niren did not speak publicly. Instead she sat quietly between her mother and Queen Margam. After all the speeches, she greeted dignitaries, those lords and ladies whom she would one day rule. Her face was set in a perfect mask of calm and more than one person mentioned her poise.

The group of mourners made their way from the chapel to the burial plot, and there Misk was laid to rest with generations of the kings and queens of a country which he would now never serve.

At the grave site, as tradition dictated, grave gifts were laid at Misk's feet. These included silk and velvet pouches filled with gold coins and gems. Scrolls of history, poetry and religious matter came next. Thowin and Jaynn offered a fine longbow, and a leather quiver full of arrows. Eto gave Misk's sword, which he had polished till it was shining and bright, back to his knight-master. King Hastho and Queen Margam returned Misk's shield to him, newly adorned with a black bar, which signified that he had fallen in battle. Niren's gift came last, her veil and the rings which would have marked their marriage.

Through all this, Niren was stoic, remembering what her father had asked of her and wishing to avoid scornful contempt from Lyru. Finally, released from her duties, Niren fled to her chamber and wept bitterly through the night.

The stress and strain of grief wore heavily on Queen Margam. For a fortnight, she was too unwell to travel back to Beklen. Even small exertions left her feeling faint, and she had no appetite. Chancellor Gojen, using what little magic was available in the kingdom, attempted to assist the court healers. King Hastho was constantly at her side. Niren visited, at first, but Gojen asked that she stop, as it seemed to be a detriment to the queen's well-being, a sad reminder of what might have been. In this, Niren felt very isolated. She thought perhaps she and Margam could have helped each other through their grief.

Finally Margam had recovered enough to travel home, though it seemed uncertain as to whether her health would ever be as it had been. Niren kissed Misk's mother and father goodbye, and bid them a safe journey home. Since Eto was currently without an assignment to another knight, he was posted to Beklen, where he would serve King Hastho for the span of a year.

Mourning began in earnest. While Margam was still in residence, her condition was taken into consideration, but now Niren ordered the drapes drawn, clocks stopped and mirrors covered. Men stopped shaving and women wore small nosegays pinned to black bands on their sleeves.

The princess packed her trousseau away and had the trunks relocated to the attics. Except for required meetings with her father, as the future queen, she remained in her suite of rooms at all times.

Chapter 6
Emerging from the Cocoon

"Constant dripping hollows out a stone."
   -- Lucretius

    The year-long period of mourning passed in Midmun. Slowly, steadily and surely, Niren began to come out of her shell, recovering her wit, wisdom and her will to live. She emerged from the cocoon of black silk crape, donning gray and lavender, both less severe and more becoming.
    King Thowin included Niren in all decisions of policy, weighing her opinion, treating her as the first among his advisers. Her mother encouraged her to begin joining the ladies of the court as they embroidered or strolled through the gardens. Even Lyru joined the act, suggesting new styles for her sister's hair, now that it was not hidden under a black cap and veil.
    As her time with governesses had ended before the wedding tour, Gojen began to tutor the princess. He instructed her in the history and rules of magic and healing. This, at last, caught Niren's interest in a way that embroidery never had. She spent long hours in the advisor's study, pouring over books and scrolls filled with herb lore and stone craft along with uses of candles, bells and written incantations. Gojen taught her how powerful connections were made, whether by use of an image, a duplicate, or a detailed description of the person or object to be spelled. He spoke of the way mana, or magical energy, flowed between the caster and the target of the spell. All of it fascinated the princess, and drew her out of her misery.

He taught her the history of magic users in the kingdom, mostly healers of great power who received the highest honors to be granted by kings in wars, long ago. King Thowin's father, Johnel, had been a healer of great repute.

Eventually, they broached the subject of dark magics. These stories enthralled and horrified Niren at the same time. Every healing plant had a poisonous one to balance the scales. A stone to deaden, dull or destroy existed for each one that vibrated with a force for life and health and strength. In every generation, some magicians chose to work the magic of death and poison and entropy. While few in numbers, they were made powerful by their lack of scruples.

"Historically, practitioners of dark magic were hidden away, and were known only to the bands of raiders or thugs they commanded. Then, more than a sscore of years ago, one magician, as powerful as he was vile and evil, came out of hiding. Indeed, princess, he was in a position to take over this entire country."

Niren listened with horror as Gojen related the tale of her only uncle, her father's older brother.

"That man was Prince Otyk, King Thowin's older brother, first in line for the throne of Midmun. He was cast out over twenty years ago for use of vile and violent magic, sspells which were ssaid to have nearly destroyed the kingdom."

Niren frowned and shook her head.

"He was cast out? I thought Otyk was dead. I thought... I was told he had died in the Great Spell, along with my grandfather. I don't understand."

"Only a sselect few of your father's closest confidants and most trusted advisers are privy to the knowledge of how powerful Otyk had become. Very few indeed know that he was forced out of Midmun in the Great Sspell... After all, your father has not even told you, our future queen."

Gojen had spoken about all of this as if discussing the weather or crop reports, but the account shook Niren deeply. The realization of that much power and deception having come so close to the throne had terrified her.

Unhappily, she approached her father for more information. After they exchanged greetings, and she kissed him on the cheek, she asked him about Otyk.

"Father, I need to know about your brother. If I am to be queen, eventually... even if that day is far in the future, I need to understand what he did. I thought Otyk was dead. Now, I've learned that he's been cast out. What if he comes back, once I am queen?"

Thowin sighed deeply, looking suddenly much older than he had. His face paled, noticeably, and his eyes looked bleak and sad.

"Otyk is dead, Niren. He must be. No one has heard from him, or about him in all these years. He would never have just given up. Not after all he had done. He is not coming back."

"Please, Papa, I think I should be told all of it. I feel as if I need to know everything that happened. I'd prefer to hear it from you."

Thowin settled in his chair, and Niren sat across from him. He was silent for a long moment before he began the account.

"I was quite young, Niren. Younger than you are now, just about Lyru's age. I was finishing my years as a squire, and I attended court when I was not travelling with my masters. Yes, I learned diplomacy and leadership, but no one expected me take the throne, at least not here in Midmun. My brother had been sitting at my father's side, learning kingcraft since I was born. There was never any doubt that Otyk was the one who would succeed to the throne, while I would command his knight's army."

"My brother was never inclined to knighthood. His strength was not physical power, but mental prowess. He was one of the most intelligent men in the kingdom. No one ever disputed that. He was brilliant enough to hide the darkness within, like a bright ballgown hiding a gangrenous wound. But there was nothing bright or light about the magic he was working."

"Where did he learn such dark magic? Who taught him? How could he learn it, here in Wayhall, right under everyone's noses? He was the crown prince. I can't cross the courtyard without scrutiny."

"It was not the same. Back then, there was magic everywhere. The magicians kept watch over the kingdom, and the castle, and it was all the scrutiny we needed. At least that was what we thought."

"That is, until livestock began to disappear from farms and pastures. Our weather changed for the worse. It became unpredictable and dangerous. There were storms and floods. Lightning caused great forest fires. None of that prepared us for the worst, which was yet to come. Illness struck, and it caused fevers and delusions, like waking nightmares. My mother was one of the first to fall to it. You know now, to my great sorrow, how much turmoil a sudden death may cause."

Niren nodded, listening in horrified silence.

"As investigations continued, your grandfather began to suspect something dire. He became convinced that someone must have been working against him from within Midmun. Whoever it was acting against him had access to too much information to be an outsider. The saboteur knew too much, and struck too accurately for it to have been a random attack. He believed that he could not trust anyone in his own kingdom, not even his own sons. Not, I think, because he suspected either of us as a culprit, but because he thought we could be under attack as well."

"He sent a knight with a message for King Payke of Beklen, who was Misk's grandfather. Payke sent help, immediately. That, Niren, was the beginning of our true alliance with Beklen. That was the basis for your betrothal to Prince Misk."

Niren stood up and walked to the fireplace. She adjusted the positions of several baubles and figurines which were placed on the mantle, without ever seeming to really see them. When she'd come to her father for answers about Otyk, she hadn't expected to learn of any ties to Misk. Grief and anxiety bubbled back up from the place where she had buried them.

"When the Beklenese magicians and advisers came, they proved, without a doubt, that Otyk was behind the attacks and disappearances. They learned that he had killed his mentor, and in so doing, he had greatly increased his own powers. Each and every spell named your uncle. All evidence pointed to him, and to him alone. There was no choice but to cast him out. It was either that or kill him, and my father found he couldn't order his son's death, no matter what his crimes. But Otyk would not go graciously nor easily."

Thowin paused, and swallowed most of the wine from his cup.

"It was a war, Niren, albeit one that the common citizens knew nothing about. Can you imagine the panic, if the people were to find that the crown prince was at war with his father, set on destroying their king? That Otyk was a practitioner of black magic. He had already murdered his own mother, their queen, among several others. How would the people react, knowing that nothing would stop him in his haste to gain the throne?"

"Because your grandfather would not order Otyk's death, he made a plan to ensure Midmun's safety in another way. He gathered every magician, every hedge witch and healer, and, with King Payke's court advisory Dozak, they constructed a Great Spell, one that would repel Otyk from our land forever. It worked, Niren. It worked, but at such a great cost. Many of the magicians died, burned up by the spell, including my father. Others lost their vision, their hearing, or even their magic. And there was nothing I could do. We let everyone believe that Otyk was killed while working with the others... not against them."

Niren stopped fussing with the trinkets and went to sit at her father's side. She set aside her grief in order to console him. She took his hand in hers.

"Of course there was nothing you could do. Not if all the magicians in Midmun had failed. You were young, as you said. What could anyone have expected of you?"

"I couldn't help, Niren. I couldn't heal them. I couldn't do anything, because my magic was gone too!"

Thowin's face was a mask of misery, and Niren's expression reflected his.

"Oh, Papa. I didn't know that you once had magic. Why didn't you ever tell me all of this?"

"I see now that I should have done so. It's not something you tell a little girl, and when you were older, it was still too difficult. It breaks my heart to talk about it, to remember it. So many died, Niren, and I couldn't save them. So many lost so much, and I couldn't restore them, not as a healer, and not as their king. I'm sorry that I didn't tell you sooner. It isn't because I have not trusted you."

"I understand, Papa. You must have been distraught. You lost everyone, and had to take the throne too."

"And all without my magic, which was suddenly gone. Magic has never been the same in Midmun since. The Great Spell seems to have leached most of the power right out of the earth, in much the same way as it was lost to the individual magicians. Or perhaps the magic was repelled with Otyk. Scholars have never agreed as to which. As you know, small magics still work, healing or visions, but nothing more than that, and now you know why. I suppose it is all for the best. At least Otyk is gone, and the suffering was not in vain."

Niren left her father with a kiss on his cheek and an apology.

"I am sorry to have brought to mind all this loss, Papa. I never knew such sadness and sorrow had visited Midmun. I always thought it was perfect here, and that nothing bad could ever happen. I liked the fairy tale better."

As she went through the door, Thowin sighed again.

"So did I."

Chapter 7
Heart Smart

"The past is a stepping stone, not a millstone."
  -- Robert Plant

The search for a husband for Niren then started in earnest, as the law of Midmun stated that a daughter could succeed to the throne, but that she must first be married. Thowin and Jaynn began to seek information about foreign princes, sending their representatives to every country which had a marriageable son. The princess herself was not thrilled at the prospect, but there was little she could do to put it off any longer.

Jaynn discussed the information she had gathered about possible suitors with Niren, as they sat together in the queen's sitting room, working on their embroidery.

"I wish I didn't have to wed anyone, Mama. I wish the law wouldn't force this on me. How can I think of being married to anyone but Misk?"

The queen reached out and touched Niren's face, soothing away her frown, giving what small comfort she could. Then, with a little pat on her hand, she continued.

"I understand how unpleasant this must be for you to think of marrying someone other than Prince Misk, dear. Anyone would be shaken by it."

"Shaken," said Niren, considering the word. "Yes, that's a very good way to think of it. I feel like my life has been shaken to bits."

"You've lived your entire life in the certain knowledge that you would marry Misk. Life often changes, and we must change with it. It won't be so bad, you'll see. There are several princes to choose from, and your father and I will help you make the best decision. In fact, it's time we began to think of finding a proper husband for Lyru, as well."

Lyru, sitting nearby, and shamelessly listening to the conversation, gasped.

"What? Mama, no! Not yet!"

Jaynn simply smiled, and the three of them returned to their embroidery work.

Life resumed in a less emotional and more predictable fashion. Niren continued in her role as adviser and student, taking in all she could, and working hard to assure her country that she would make a good queen. She gained confidence and grew to be a lovely, thoughtful young woman. If she was more stoic, less frivolous than Lyru and the other young women at court, then that was perfectly understandable and could only serve her well as queen.

Just as Niren felt she had her feet firmly beneath her, another change came along, one which pulled the carpet out from beneath her, sending her reeling once again.

Reports began to come in about a new sickness growing in outlying villages. Court healers were dispersed and began to travel from place to place, doing their best to relieve the fever. Most people survived, some losing vision or hearing, some seemingly unaffected afterwards. In every village, one or two died.

Over the next weeks, the sickness moved from the western villages toward Wayhall Castle and the surrounding town. Two chamber maids who had visited with family on their day off returned and fell ill. One of the maids recovered well, if slowly. The other did not recover at all.

Magicians, healers and knights worked at staving off panic, but fear grew, especially in the ranks of servants. Several families fled to the homes of unaffected relatives, but they only succeeded in taking the fever with them.

Then Queen Jaynn fell ill. The fever gripped her body and haunted her mind. Gojen and the court's head healer attended to her day and night. Every herb, stone and elixir known or thought to relieve fever was brought to her. Candles were burned, bells were chimed, and incantations were spoken over her. Still her strength waned over time.

One good day would be followed by two or three where she could scarcely sit up in her bed.

Niren learned how to prepare and apply cool compresses, putting to use her previous study of herbs. Although the sickroom smell turned Niren's stomach when she visited, she rarely left for more than a few hours. She worked tirelessly, soothing her mother and others who had fallen ill.

King Thowin requested healers be brought in from all over West Whitsen and beyond, sparing no expense. These new healers and herbalists did little to change the outcomes of those suffering from the fever. Some suggested that the fever must be of magical origin. The king shuddered at the thought of another magical attack on his kingdom while he was helpless to fight it off.

Some of these newly arrived healers suggested that perhaps magic was returning to Midmun, and that any spell could and would weaken over time, and come to an end. One, Danj of Beklen, even contended that the depleted magic could have been steadily returning to the land, but siphoned off by some hidden enemy. How better to attack a country supposedly devoid of magic?

Gojen scoffed at them, and the healers native to the Midmun did the same. Thowin, in desperation, ordered Gojen to investigate the theory, but nothing came of it. No proof of magical malevolence could be found.

Then the unthinkable happened. King Thowin collapsed, falling from his throne, burning up with the fever. He died quickly, succumbing to the illness the next morning. How long had he been feeling the effects of the fever? Everyone questioned each other, but no one knew the answer. He had used his knowledge of healing, and stoically hidden his symptoms and continued to work day and night as he searched for a cure. Queen Jaynn only lasted another day after his death, giving up her fight, lost in grief and despair. The funeral for the King and Queen of Midmun was a sorrowful, somber affair, attended only by those who had already been exposed to the fever. They were buried side by side, not far from Misk's grave.

Niren met with Thowin's lords to discuss the leadership of Midmun. As she was as yet unwed, not even betrothed again, Chancellor Gojen was appointed as Regent. As such, his duties included the search for a suitable husband for the future queen, as well as governing the grief-stricken country.

Niren was thrown back into mourning. This time, there were no kind, understanding parents to help her through it. This time, it was Niren trying to guide Lyru through the process, though she herself felt as though the sun had gone out.

The princesses never fell ill, despite the time they had spent with their mother and others who had been affected. As the first weeks of mourning passed, fewer and fewer reports of the fever arrived. It seemed to have burned itself out of the land, and eventually all news of it ended. With nothing more to do, the foreign healers returned one by one to their homelands

Lyru and Niren oscillated between clinging to each other in their shared grief and pushing one another away, under this new strain. Niren stoically continued as she had under Thowin's tutelage, not unfeeling, but unwilling to show her grief. Lyru, who had once been disgusted by shows of emotion, now grew hysterical at times, lashing out at Niren, Gojen, and in fact anyone who was close enough to feel her grief-born wrath.

Niren consulted with Gojen on the intelligence he and her parents had gathered about each of the princes of a marriageable age. These princes were second or third sons with no thrones of their own. Thus they were free to come to Midmun and to take up the crown. None seemed an especially likely candidate, at least to Niren, but word was sent out for seven of them to come to Wayhall and meet with the princess.

As these invitations went out, Niren felt the old panic begin to rise up inside her. How could she face marriage and the prospect of another loss? Her mother was no longer here to set her mind at ease. Her father was not going to be able to help her choose wisely.

At last, she sought council from the Chancellor.

"Gojen, please. Tell me there is something you can do to protect me. I'm so afraid of what will happen when the princes arrive."

Gojen quirked his left eyebrow.

"Protect you from what, Your Highness? I'm afraid I don't understand. Ssurely you don't fear an attack from one of the princes?"

Niren frowned, and sighed. Her mother would have understood what she meant.

"No, not an attack. I understand that I must marry one of these men. I will do what I must, to be queen. Marriage is one thing, but I've been hurt enough. I don't want to feel anything for them. I don't wish to fall in love. I'll choose the prince based on what is best for Midmun, not for me."

"What is it that you want me to do? Ssurely I cannot prevent you from feeling any emotional connection to these princes."

"But you can! You taught me about the principals of magic, the law of opposites. Everyone knows about love potions. Can't you concoct a potion to prevent love, as well? Please, Gojen. I cannot face another loss."

Gojen watched the princess for a moment, with his fingers steepled against his chin.

"I will ssee what I can do for you, Your Highness. It may take ssome time."

After several days of study, Gojen told her he had come upon a solution. It would take time to prepare, but he had found a way to do as Niren had requested. The work would be ready before the first of the visiting princes was expected in Wayhall Castle.

Chapter 8
Unromancing the Stone

"A fool can throw a stone in a pond that 100 wise men can not get out."
    -- Saul Bellow

Gojen's preparations took over a week to complete. During this time he did not meet with the future queen at all, which freed her to spend more time with her sister. This was wearing on Niren, but clearly Lyru was not coping at all well with the loss of her parents. Each day brought tantrums in public and unrelenting despair in private.

Slowly, Niren coaxed Lyru out of her hysteria, taking her for long walks in the gardens, inviting resident duchesses and countesses along. Later she listened to Lyru amuse herself by verbally tearing apart the ladies' fashion sense and personalities, in the privacy of the royal suites. Lyru wasn't exactly hateful, just woefully insecure. For the time being, Niren reasoned, she could be allowed this small, private pleasure. Before long, though, it would have to come to a stop. At some point, Lyru would have to take control of all these negative emotions, and begin her life anew. She would need to find friends amongst the young women she scorned.

Finally Gojen summoned Niren to his workroom. His preparations were complete, and he was ready to show her his answer to her request. She arrived looking anxious and even paler than usual.

"This is blue chalcedony, Your Highness."

He held a small, smooth stone in his gloved hand, about the size of an almond. It was a smoky, waxen blue, the color of cornflowers, with flecks and streaks of brown.

"Chalcedony is from the quartz family, which is mined in the west. It is a sstone known for protection of the heart. It absorbs negative emanations, and promotes emotional balance. It will do as you asked of me. You will not need to worry that you will care deeply for any of the princes, even the one you sselect."

Niren nodded, listening intently to Gojen's explanation.

"How do we set it? Do we use gold, or silver? I do hope you will be capable of doing the work, I do not wish to involve a jeweler, or anyone else in this."

Gojen laughed softly, not at all an attractive sound. He shook his head.

"Were the sstone to need a ssetting, Princess, I would have sseen to it. You cannot wear this sstone, not for the sstrong effect you sseek."

Niren made an impatient, dismissive gesture with her hand, clearly frustrated.

"Gojen, you are being deliberately vague. Say what I must do with this stone, this blue chalcedony, at once."

"Of course, Your Highness. It has been ssome time ssince I have worked a magic ssuch as this. I was not certain that anything like this could even be accomplished, here in Midmun, or that I had the sskill to carry it out. You must sswallow it."

The princess could not have looked more shocked. Her eyes were wide, and her pale cheeks flushed.

"No, highness, don't look at me in ssuch a way! This sstone will not choke or bind you. Once you have sswallowed it, it will bide next to your heart. It will sstop you from ever again feeling the pain of the death of one you love deeply. It will be just as you wished."

Niren still looked incredulous.

"Tell me more about this spell. I too was unsure that such magic could be worked, once I'd thought about it. I'd like to know how you accomplished all this. It's a little frightening."

Gojen pressed his thin lips together.

"It was not an easy task, I assure you. Perhaps no one else in Midmun could have accomplished it at all. I have access to the library of books and sscrolls collected after the Great Sspell. I would show you the sspell, but it is not written in Midmunese, but in the old tongue. I do not believe you sstudied that with your governess?"

"No. You're correct. However, I don't need to know the specific language for you to explain the spell to me."

Gojen nodded and continued with his explanation.

"You asked for a potion. I could find nothing in the sscrolls which would ssatisfy your requirements. Women can create love philtres, but the effects are sshort lived. Any attempt at an opposite sseemed to create outright hatred. I feared that would cause more problems than it could possibly ssolve. Next I researched jewelry, and the use of gemstones. That led me to this sspell. It will not cause hatred, but will protect you from sstrong feelings prevent and emotional pain."

Niren listened to Gojen's explanation, but was clearly still not satisfied.

"I don't see why it cannot be set as a ring or pendant. Is it not a bit extreme, to swallow a stone?"

The magician shrugged.

"You could try it, Your Highness, but I believe that you would find that the effects were not as powerful as you wish them to be. I would have to sstart again, from sscratch, and the first of the princes is due to arrive very ssoon. I may not have enough time, or enough mana, to finish the task."

Niren fidgeted with the long braid hanging over her shoulder while she tried to decide on a course of action. Gojen carried on with his instructions as if her hesitation was of no importance.

"You must trust me, Your Highness. Hold out your right hand. I have not once touched this sstone. It must bind only to you, or the magic will not take hold."

She held out her hand, taking the pebble, feeling its cool smoothness on her palm. It instantly began to warm against her skin. Gojen noticed her reaction, and smiled.

"Ah, there, you ssee. You can already feel the power in the sstone. That is because I have prepared it especially for you. I can ssee the recognition of it in your eyes. Now, while the sstone bonds to you, you must repeat these words--"

Niren's face reflected her panic, again.

"Magic words? I have to do the magic for myself? I thought you had finished this task, Gojen! I don't have any magic of my own, as you know perfectly well."

"The sstone is prepared. Everything is ready for you. But it is your protection, and it will require your voice, your will, your desire and your energy. I will enhance all of these with my ssmall magic. There is nothing to fear. I will not let this sspell fail."

Niren sighed and agreed.

"Then tell me the words I must say."

Gojen placed his hand over hers, and recited the spell.

"Vitrify, ossify,
Crystallize and harden,
Temper the ssteel,
Fossilize the garden!
Induratize, fortify,
Make fast the gates
Sspell this sstone to ssafely sstop
All pains from loves and hates!"

Niren repeated the phrases, carefully, precisely. Then she placed the stone on her tongue, and swallowed.

As she left, still flushed, Gojen slipped an exact replica of the stone from his left hand into a pocket in his robes.

Chapter 9
Stoned

"When arguing with a stone, an egg is always wrong."
  -- African Proverb

Niren retreated to her chambers, and did not emerge for days. She ate little, and grew increasingly detached from her life and her duties in the castle. Gojen managed all business matters, and instructed the castle staff to let the future queen rest.

Princess Lyru grew more and more agitated. She finally barged into her sister's room uninvited, on the third afternoon on which Niren did not seek or summon her.

"Where have you been? Don't you understand how alone I am? How can you be so cruel to your own sister? You finally decide, for a few days, that I am worth your time, and then you're gone again. You're as fickle as the autumn wind!"

Through all of Lyru's tirade, Niren sat in her armchair, looking out the window. She hardly blinked as her sister let loose her fury. She was wearing the same dress as she had the day before.

"Niren! Don't you have a single thing to say to me? Some reason for ignoring me, an excuse, or better yet, an apology?"

Niren turned, then, and looked at Lyru.

"You mentioned the wind. Certainly you have become as loud and as bothersome as a hurricane. There are others with whom you can spend your days. And certainly there are others to whom you can elect to spill your vitriol. Go and choose some duchess or countess as your companion. I'm sure that she will think it is a great boon to be your friend, for a little while at least. Or... don't. Go back to your chamber, and wait for me to summon you. All of those princes are due to start arriving here any day. Perhaps you can have one of the ones I haven't chosen. In any case, go away. Just go away."

Lyru stood by the door, her mouth drawn in a sour grimace, as she stared at her older sister.

Then Niren turned to her and smiled, just slightly. Her pretty face looked vicious in the afternoon light coming in through the window.

"Wipe that look from your face, Lyru. Gather your wits. Don't you remember what you told me when Misk died? People will see you, and they will care."

Lyru fled, slamming the chamber door behind her. Niren started then to rise from her armchair, but after a moment she sat again, with a heavy sigh, spreading her skirts out around her and returning her gaze to the palace gardens.

Section 2
Seven Deadly Princes

"So when they continued asking him, he lifted up himself, and said unto them, "He that is without sin among you, let him first cast a stone at her.""
-- Jesus Christ, Gospel According to John 8:7

Chancellor Gojen spent most of the next week in his workroom, getting ready for the arrival of the princes. He painstakingly prepared a small, personal gift for each of the princes who would soon arrive. He used all the information he and Queen Jaynn had gleaned about them to ensure that the gifts would suite their personalities and passions.

Meanwhile, he left Niren alone in her chambers. He knew that the magic of the stone would need some time to fully take hold, and he had no intention of letting his plan go awry. Soon the stone and the magic would fully encase Niren's heart. She'd never fall in love, he was certain.

Would his spell be strong enough to stand once all the princes were in place?

Chapter 10
A Not So Irresistible Force vs. An Immovable Object

"Anger is as a stone cast into a wasp's nest."
  -- Pope Paul VI

Niren sat on her throne, looking down from the dais as the first of the princes approached. Lyru was supposed to have been there, with her and Gojen, but she appeared to be off somewhere, sulking. Niren couldn't find it in herself to have her sister summoned to the throne room, and then be forced to the task of dealing with her melodramatic behavior.

"Prince Ergan of Rand. Bow before Princess Niren, the future Queen of Midmun."

Prince Ergan did so, as the herald announced him. As he rose and approached the throne, Niren got a good look at the newcomer. He was tall, with dark blonde hair cropped close to his head. Most of his face was hidden behind a thicket of a beard. He had deep set, shadowed eyes and ruddy complexion. He was more rugged than handsome, but Niren did not think he was unattractive. He wore simple dark brown leggings, and a deep red tunic, but over this he wore a luxuriant fur coat, even though the weather of Midmun was temperate.

The prince walked quickly and quietly as he approached the dais. Every movement he made was fluid and efficient. Drawing a red fox stole from his pack, he started up the steps toward Niren. She cleared her throat and shook her head. A guard stepped forward and stopped the prince.

"You may hand that to my lady-in-waiting."

The appropriate young woman stepped forward, and he handed her the stole, looking less than pleased. The lady-in-waiting was grateful that the stole was not of the sort which had the head and feet still attached. It felt soft and supple in her hands, and it was just a little heavier than she'd expected. As she laid it on a small gilded table to the side of the dais, the prince spoke to Niren for the first time. He had a rather thick accent and a deep bass voice.

"Your Highness, I had high hopes that you would appreciate my gift. I assure you that this is a very fine specimen. You will not find its equal; there is no animal with so vibrant a color as the Randish fox."

With a distant look in her eyes, Niren paused. The room was silent as the prince, and all the gathered nobles waited for her response.

"That may well be, Prince Ergan, and I do appreciate the gift. That said, I am certain that in Rand there are rules of etiquette, and that princes are expected to be well versed in them. If they so vastly differ from our own, I will allow my former governess to tutor you in decorum. Until then, do not approach our person without our leave."

Ergan's face drew tight in a scowl, and his ruddy skin reddened further.

"Rules? You speak to me of rules and decorum and leave? I have come all this way to court you, to give you a gift, made from a beast which I have hunted and prepared with my own hands?" Ergan's voice grew louder. "Princess you may be, and Queen you may become, but I think perhaps it's you who must learn some manners!"

Gojen listened for a moment, then stepped forward, taking charge and stopping the argument before it could go any further.

"Your Highnesses, I am certain the two of you can become better acquainted at dinner this evening. You have sso very much to learn about one another and the countries and cultures you represent. Tonight, we will celebrate the auspicious arrival of the first of the princes."

Niren settled back into her throne, and nodded, replacing the sour look on her face with one of bored acceptance. She pinched the bridge of her nose, trying to fight off the beginnings of a headache.

"You are dismissed, Prince Ergan. All of you are dismissed. I want to prepare for the evening meal. Yes, you as well, Gojen. Go, now, and please see to it that Princess Lyru does not miss the wonderful opportunity to dine with Prince Ergan."

Ergan grimaced at the sarcasm in Niren's voice, and the flippant dismissal. Gojen escorted Ergan to the chambers which had been prepared for his visit. He stopped at the doorway to show the prince a gold-hilted dagger, set with a bright red ruby in the pommel.

"Please excuse Princess Niren. Sshe is ssimply overwhelmed by ssuch an impressive gift, and by meeting you, the first of sso many princes who are coming to court her."

Ergan's sour expression was proof that Gojen was simply fanning the fires of his indignation.

"Many princes? This is the first I've heard of that. How many? Too many archers spoil the hunt, you know."

"Only a few more. You'll have sseveral days before any of the others arrives. For now, please allow me to present a gift for you, from our country. Of course it would be wholly inappropriate for the future queen to present you with a gift sso early in your acquaintance, but we in Midmun wish to sshow our eager hope that you will remain with us, and become part of our kingdom. Please don't allow a poor beginning to sspoil your time with us here. Don't be put off, when you could be sso close to becoming our king."

The prince smiled, somewhat mollified. He examined the dagger with a critical eye, then he smiled as he weighed it in his hand.

"This is good steel, with a nice, sharp edge. I am glad to know such quality exists in Midmun. Perhaps we can arrange a hunting trip. Arrange a time for me to inspect the kennels, and the stables, and the armory."

"I will adjust the agenda. Now, I will leave you to your privacy until the dinner being held in your honor, while I ssee to your requests."

Once in his workroom, he took a replica of the dagger from a locked cabinet, hidden in the stone wall. After unwrapping the white cloth wound around it, he chanted a verse over it.

"*Dagger cut, like vicious wrath*
Ssever friendships in your path
However viewed in Niren's ssight
You believe that might makes right

Sstormy temper, loud and tough
Sshe will ssee you as rash and rough
Uncouth, unkind, unwanted too
Sshe'll never make a choice like you."

Then he took the dagger and wrapped it again in the spell-protected white cloth. Now that the spell was in place on the pair of daggers, he was satisfied that he could manipulate Prince Ergan from afar.

The welcome dinner that evening was an unparalleled disaster. Princess Lyru, having been sought out and sternly reprimanded by Gojen, was sulky and sarcastic. With each course and every comment, she made it known to all that she would far rather be in any place but this.

Niren, who would normally be able to coax and cajole Lyru into a better mood, just sighed and frowned at each display. Neither of the princesses really paid the least bit of attention to Prince Ergan, who in turn was cold and arrogant. He drank more than was seemly and made harsh statements about the quality of the meat served. He grew steadily less likable with each course.

The noblemen and women in attendance noticed all of this. They glanced at one another with growing dismay. Where were the charming princesses of old? How would either of them ever manage to make a marriage in this fashion?

Lady Risole, one of Queen Jaynn's dearest, closest friends did what she could to maintain conversation and keep the peace. Gojen did nothing to assist her.

All of these interactions did not go unnoticed by Prince Ergan. He thought he'd soon have these people, including the princesses, behaving as they should, once he was king. By the end of the meal, he had drawn his new dagger from his belt. Rubbing his thumb over the ruby he stood, and walked out of the dining hall, scarcely pausing to bow to the future queen.

All of the participants of the meal suffered from a certain degree of indigestion, and none but Gojen slept well that night.

Chapter 11
Pride Goeth Before a Fall, and Taketh Greed with It.

"Men of genius are often dull and inert in society, as the blazing meteor, when it descends to earth, is only a stone."
 -- Henry Wadsworth Longfellow

Several more meals and meetings progressed in much the same manner. A partnership between Niren and Prince Ergan became increasingly unlikely and unattractive to either party. He spent as much time as he could with the hunting dogs in the kennels, preferring the company of the hounds. This continued until the arrival of two more princes, come to try their suite.
The herald announced the each of the newcomers, in turn. "Grand Duke Depri of Socra. Duke Edger of Socra."
Upon the arrival of these two new princes in the Great Hall, Prince Ergan made a mockery of a bow to Princess Niren. He sneered at the newly arrived brothers, and took his leave.
"I wish the two of you the very best of luck with this princess, and her court. Believe me when I tell you, this country isn't nearly rich enough to pay for the privilege of being married to her."
Momentarily shocked out of her seeming indifference, Niren stood and ordered Ergan escorted from the hall, the castle and the country. The castle guards hurried to obey her. Seeing him gone, she settled back onto her throne, allowing the stone's effect to leach away her brief anger.
As he travelled back toward his home, Prince Ergan was as badly behaved with his mount as he had been to the princess. He drove the horse hard and fast, and was not at all sparing with the whip. While Ergan made camp, about halfway back to Rand, the horse pulled its

picket from the ground and ran off, with all of Ergan's money and most of his possessions, including the ruby dagger. The prince had to finish the journey home on foot, and often in the rain. As he walked, his mind cleared, and he began to question himself and his actions in Midmun, wondering why he'd gotten quite so enraged.

Meanwhile, the brothers were shocked by Prince Ergan's harsh words and rude demeanor. After a moment, they recovered themselves, and bowed to the princess.

Grand Duke Depri, the elder and taller of the Socran princes, was richly dressed in shades of violet. His crushed velvet coat was adorned by satin piping and lace ruffs at the throat and wrists. His hose ended in knee high leather boots, with brass buckles, and elevated heels which exaggerated his height. His long, auburn hair was coiffed perfectly over his green eyes. His beard, a deeper shade of auburn, was short and neatly trimmed.

The younger prince, Duke Edger, was blonde and amber-eyed, with a sallow complexion. He wore his blonde hair set in tight curls. His jaw was clean-shaven, but he had a fussy little mustache which had been waxed to keep its shape. He wore a yellow doublet over matching hose. Even his pointed shoes were yellow, however impractical they must have been for traveling. Both brothers wore an astonishing number of gold chains, and Edger had a gold hoop in one ear.

Just as Prince Ergan had done, both of the Socran princes had brought courting-gifts for Niren.

Depri presented a beautifully jeweled egg, the facets sparkling brilliantly in the light. A lady-in-waiting stepped forward to accept the egg, and took it to Niren for inspection. She took the gold leafed, amethyst-set trinket in her hand and examined it closely. The egg was enameled in a deep purple, with crisscrossing bands of gold leaf encompassing it. At each intersection of the bands, there was a tiny, brilliant amethyst. Once she would have sighed with delight at such a beautiful, well-crafted object, she now smiled her distant smile, the one which never quite reached her eyes.

"Many thanks, Grand Duke Depri. This is a lovely gift, and we shall treasure it."

Though her words were correct and courteous, they rang a bit hollow. Depri didn't seem to notice, as he launched into a speech about the egg.

"A beautiful object for a beautiful princess. My people hope that you will treasure it, as I will treasure you when we are wed. The royal jeweler makes fewer than a dozen eggs each year. He spends a month or more creating them, and each design is unique. They are the envy of every person in Socra, and beyond, but only elite have even been invited to the royal museum to see the entire collection. You should consider yourself blessed to receive such a treasure; not many outside of my homeland have ever possessed one, and this one is particularly fine."

Once Depri finally fell silent, Duke Edger stepped forward. He summoned one of servants from his personal entourage. The servant carried a bolt of yellow silk wound around a wooden core. Another of Niren's ladies-in-waiting took it, struggling a bit with the weight of the fabric.

Princess Niren stopped the young woman with a wave of her hand before she could bring it up to the dais.

"We thank you, Prince Edger. We will see to it that such lovely cloth is put to some good use. Galma, please see it taken to my sewing solar."

The lady-in-waiting curtsied and hurried away, happy to be relieved of the heavy, lustrous silk.

Prince Edger looked put out for a moment. Then he arranged his features into a smile for the future queen.

"I assure you that you will not find this silk lacking in any way, Your Highness. Any garment you have made from it will feel luxurious and rich against your fine and delicate skin. I find it well suited to royalty, as it would likely snag on skin roughened by any hard labor. I will look forward to seeing what you will have made from it."

Gojen stepped forward from his place beside Niren's throne.

"Good Princes of Ssocra, allow me to have you sshown to your chambers, sso that you may take ssome time to recover from your journey. We sshall all dine together this evening, if you are of a good will. I know both princesses will be delighted to sshare in your company."

After the princes were escorted to their chambers, Gojen paid a visit to each. At Depri's rooms, he received a gracious welcome.

"My Lord, Grand Duke Depri, I very much wish you to understand that, while Princess Niren cannot yet ssay this, sshe very much admires your charming gift. Every young woman wishes to be wed to ssuch a great man as yourself, from your prosperous and generous country. Princess Niren is no different. As ssuch, we would like for you to have this token of her affection and intention."

Gojen handed the visiting prince a small, silver looking-glass. The ornate, twisting, braided handle split to wrap around the sides of the mirror, and then came together again, forming a loop at the top.

"This is not just any looking-glass, Your Highness. If you sspeak the words which I sshall teach you, it will sshow you images of your future here in Midmun, no doubt as a great and powerful king. Allow me to mention that I believe our beautiful princess will look quite fetching on your arm, a handsome accessory to your ambitious and far-reaching reign."

Gojen taught Prince Depri the few simple phrases that would call images into the looking glass. The vainglorious prince seemed happy enough using it as a mundane mirror before he invoked the magic. Gojen watched over Depri's shoulder for a moment as a scene of a battle unfolded, with the prince leading a victorious charge.

Leaving Depri smiling as he was entertained by the glass, Gojen went to visit Prince Edger's chambers, where he was accepted with significantly less grace and charm.

"Tell me, Chancellor Gojen, does your lovely princess have no clue how valuable the gift which I brought her is? I had that silk imported from the Far East, where I am told a thousand worms must spin and toil to produce the fibers. I could have left it in the vaults at home, and would certainly have done so, if I thought it would be so easily dismissed."

Gojen smiled his oily smile, and soothed the prince at once.

"Your Highness, I am ssorry you think sshe did not appreciate your gift. Both of the princesses are even now in the ssewing room, pouring over your ssilk with gloved hands. They are imagining the fine gown it will be made into, and how radiant Niren will look in that lovely sshade.

Sshe will be the envy of ssunshine and daffodils, once sshe is sso adorned."

The princesses, of course, were doing nothing of the sort, but the prince was easily mollified, especially when Gojen brought out the gift he had brought for him.

"And now, allow me to present a gift for you from the kingdom of Midmun. This gift is to express how much we value you, and look forward to the future, in which we earnestly hope you will sshare in the ruling of this land."

Gojen opened a leather pouch and poured the contents, several uncut yellow gemstones, out into Duke Edger's open hand.

"Tourmalines from our ssouthern mountains. These are a rare find, because this brilliant amber is far less common than pink or green sstone, or even red ones. These are considered especially fine and if I may ssay sso, they ssuit you very well. I have left them unset and unpolished, sso you may use them as you ssee fit. We have only just begun mining these. Perhaps you can tour the area, and with your keen eye and guidance, we can begin to produce more of these sspecimens. Lore sstates that these sstones will make the bearer fearless."

Gojen left Edger to pour over the gemstones with an eager grin on his face, and returned to his workroom to finish his projects before that evening's meal. He took two parcels, each wrapped in white cloth, from the vault in his wall. After unwrapping the mirror's twin, along with another pouch of gems, he examined them carefully.

He took the looking-glass, with its intricate, twisting gilded frame, and completed the spell which would allow him to control everything Prince Depri saw within the mirror he possessed.

> "This mirror bright, within your hand
> Will sshow you ruling Niren's land
> Her king must be of the less proud kind
> That which you sseek, you'll never find
> But while you watch, your ego grows
> Sstroked by the things the fair glass sshows
> Till you believe you'll be her choice
> And allow her neither vote nor voice"

Gojen watched the images form and dissolve on the glass for several moments before he wrapped it in a spelled cloth, satisfied. Then he turned to the bag of gemstones, smiling at the ease with which his plans were advancing.

"*A greedy prince is not becoming*
Ssuch avarice will ssend her running
Become entranced, as these gems glow
Increase your cravings, feel them grow
Covet, hunger, wish, desire
The need within burns like a fire
Consuming you, with each day, more
Niren ssees you as a bore."

Gojen contented himself with the thought that these budding love affairs had thus been ended before they could begin. He was nothing if not a shrewd judge of character. While he could not change a person's basic nature, he could exploit their weaknesses and call their vices to the forefront of their thoughts and actions. This was the same magical skill he had used to ensure that Niren would never be satisfied with either of the Socran princes.

That evening's meal certainly went more smoothly than the first with Prince Ergan had. Both Socran princes were set on outdoing the other, being as solicitous and winning as possible, at least they were charming to the princesses. Between the two of them, there were jabs and jokes at each other's expense.

As the week progressed, there were many meetings, as well as tours of Wayhall Castle, and the surrounding lands. Both princes asked intelligent questions, reflecting their interests and leadership strengths, and of course, Gojen's influence over them.

Prince Depri was curious about Midmun's military strength and leadership. He found Niren to be surprisingly well versed and well spoken, and mentioned his approval to Chancellor Gojen.

"She has an impressive understanding of the military, for a woman."

Prince Edger quizzed Niren and Gojen, and even Lyru, about mining operations, storehouse capacities, taxation and trade relations with surrounding countries. Again, Niren was well spoken, if unenthusiastic about these subjects. When he spoke about such things to Lyru, she stormily refused to participate in the discussion.

"I don't know anything about finance or trade. I don't care to know."

"I am certain, that with time, I can teach you the intricacies..."

"I Don't Care, Duke Edger! Don't you listen? I don't care about any of that!"

Each evening, after the meal and entertainment, Prince Depri retired to his chambers and watched the looking-glass show him great military victories and social gatherings where he was more sought after than the beautiful queen who was the real, rightful ruler of the land. Each morning he arrived at the throne room, more confident, bolder, and more determined to win Niren and Midmun.

Likewise, Prince Edger spent his evenings in contemplation of his prized tourmalines, and his plans to make Midmun a force to be reckoned with in international finance and trade. He was certain that nothing could stop him. Spread out on his desk, near the ledgers he was studying, the gems seemed to glow brighter than the lamp should allow. At every opportunity, he spoke of such things as embargoes and tariffs and distribution of assets. Even the court treasurer, Barin, found himself unequal to the task of keeping up with the prince, but Edger continued to seek him out as a dining companion.

With the brothers continuing on this tack, Niren was lulled even further into her stone-induced indifference. Princess Lyru continued to skip meals and meetings, finding new places to hide, from time to time.

Chapter 12
Sloth Broth

"Like a stone rolls down a hill, I have come to this day."
-- Ishikawa Takuboko

The fourth prince sent word that he would be two days later in arriving than had previously been arranged. When all was said and done, he was four days later than expected, and even then, he did not arrive at Wayhall Castle until late in the afternoon.

Court had convened earlier that morning, and ended for the day, but the key players were hastily summoned back to the throne room to greet the tardy prince.

"Prince Stohl of Layant, bow before Crown Princess Niren of Midmun."

As the herald announced him, the heavyset prince slowly ambled down the aisle, bowing slightly, not nearly as deeply as protocol demanded. Even this caused him to fall short of breath. Thin, wind mussed hair fell into his eyes as he rose, and hung there, making him blink rapidly as he spoke.

"I've brought a gift for you, Your Highness, if that boy hasn't lost it on the way." His voice was higher than one expected from a man of his size, as well as thin and reedy. He clapped his hands twice. "Boy, bring that package to me, at once!"

A young servant brought forth a large, flat rectangle, wrapped in oilcloth. One of the nearby ladies-in-waiting accepted the package, and unwrapped it at Niren's request. Her work revealed a beautiful watercolor depicting two swans, drifting on a cool, blue lake. A nearly full moon was reflected in the dark water.

Niren, who had always appreciated art and beauty, actually shook off the effects of the stone, and stood with a smile to see it more closely.

"Oh! Prince Stohl, this is exquisite. Your brushwork is superior, I can see the swan's feathers, even from here. The colors are so soothing, and peaceful. I will treasure it."

The prince cleared his throat, and managed to look just a little embarrassed.

"Your Highness, I must beg your forgiveness, but no. I must apologize for the misunderstanding, but I cannot allow you to think I created this. I was uncertain as to what gift I should bring for you, so I asked my dear mother for advice. She selected this painting for you. Mother can have more made for you, as many as you like. I am so pleased that you like it so much. The artist is --"

Niren interrupted him, sitting back on her throne with an exasperated sigh, and a sweeping gesture of her hands, dismissing the prince and his explanation.

"Perhaps you can tell me all about it at the evening meal. I am certain you will wish to refresh yourself before then, after spending such a long time on the road. Chancellor Gojen will show you the way to your chambers."

Gojen led the prince and his servants to the guest suites, with the prince dawdling abominably, pausing to look at each suit of armor, sculpture and painting. His servants were clearly well used to this behavior.

When the group finally reached the designated chamber, the prince flopped down onto the divan, and at last brushed his thin, sandy colored hair from his hazel eyes. His pale blue tunic was slightly stained with sweat and dust, but he showed no intention of changing into something fresher. The servants hurried about the room, setting things to rights. Gojen watched from the doorway, smiling to himself.

"Don't just stand there, Chancellor Gojen. Come in, and sit a while with me. The servants will bring us refreshments. Now, tell me all about your princess. She is fetching, isn't she? I might consider commissioning a painting of her. Indeed, she is a lovely young woman. It's a terrible tragedy, isn't it, about her parents, and of course, that other prince. Misk, or some such name? I meant to write a letter of condolence, really, I did, but you know how it is."

Gojen entered, and bowed, and sat down on a nearby armchair.

"I am certain that Princess Niren forgives the lack of a letter from you, after all... sso many others wrote to her. How many letters could sshe need? Sshe is very fortunate that a prince ssuch yourself would come all this way for the opportunity to meet her. As a ssmall token of welcome and thanks, we would like you to have this gift."

Gojen handed a beautifully crafted flask to one of the servants, who took it at once to the prince. The leather was carved and dyed with the image of a tall green tree, which bore not just apples, but pears and peaches, and many other varieties of fruit, together. There was a leather-capped cork in the mouth, as well as a carrying strap attached to the shoulder.

"This flask is filled with a ssweet nectar. I am quite certain you will find it to your liking. More importantly, it cannot be emptied. You must only tap the cork three times, and the nectar will refill it at once."

Stohl opened the flask and took a long sip, and then another. Finally, he tipped his head back and drank deeply, smacking his lips when he had finished. Then he corked the flask, and tapped the cork three times with his pudgy finger. When he opened it again, he found it full.

"This is delightful! What a wonderful gift! Ah, Chancellor Gojen, you've no idea how I must harp on the help to keep even the smallest amount in my glass. You see it, don't you? They haven't even brought the refreshments I requested. It's not as if it were a difficult task. Yes, yes, I can see I will enjoy my time here."

With that, he settled further back into the cushions on the divan.

"Now, Chancellor, if you will excuse me, I'd like to rest my eyes for a short while before the meal. They're full of grit from the road, you know. It's very irritating."

With a nod and a murmur of understanding, Gojen excused himself as the prince's eyes drifted shut.

Once alone in his workroom, Gojen began the familiar ritual of setting the gift to his purposes. He took the flask's twin in his hand and recited his spell:

> *"This ssplendid nectar tastes the best*
> *While encouraging your well-earned rest*
> *Let others do the work at hand*
> *You're too important, understand*
> *You desire ssweet, quiet peace*
> *This nectar puts you at your ease*
> *Sservants exist to do each task*
> *While you ssit and tap the empty flask"*

Once satisfied that Prince Stohl would never lift a hand to woo or win Niren, he wrapped it in the spelled white cloth. Then he turned his attention back to the looking-glass, sending new images of military escapadebalas and triumphs to Grand Duke Depri. Duke Edger was so dreadfully boring, consumed with finance, and so disinterested in Niren, Gojen almost regretted wasting any magic to make him seem unsavory. Still, having come this far, after so many years of waiting, it wouldn't pay to become sloppy. Every detail of his plan must be perfect, so he renewed that spell, as well.

At the evening meal, Grand Duke Depri monopolized Niren's attention, speaking as though he were certain that no one else was as worthy of her time. Duke Edger more or less ignored both princesses, engaging instead in conversation with Lord Darin, the court treasurer, stroking his own mustache as they conversed. Prince Stohl was late. When he finally arrived, he fidgeted endlessly with the leather flask which he had brought with him. He hardly reacted to the talk and activity around him. In this, at least, he seemed to make a perfect match for Niren.

Princess Niren struggled to appear polite, but those who knew her well noted her lack of spirit. She remained aloof and distant and unreachable.

What Niren lacked in spirit, her younger sister made up for. Lyru glared at everyone around the table. She was beginning to feel panic rise up in her mind. What would become of Midmun with rulers like these? She didn't know how Gojen could even allow these three princes near the throne or her sister. What in the world had happened to Niren and why was she so different now? Why was everything so different now?

Prince Stohl excused himself early, just after dessert, citing exhaustion from the road. This left Lyru paired once again with Duke Edger. He didn't even notice when she slipped from her chair while the quartet of musicians played a beautiful piece written in memory of the king and queen, crying softly as she went. Her sister didn't notice either.

Chapter 13
Letters to Another Queen

"I would happily help to turn the stone being thrown at me into a boomerang."
   -- Peer Steinbruck

The future queen was somewhat surprised by a request, asking for an audience. The source of this request was Squire Eto, who had returned from his year of service to King Hastho of Beklen.
   Eto entered the throne room, and bowed deeply.
   "Your Highness, it is my honor to return to the service of Midmun. I was deeply upset to hear of the passing of the king and queen. I now swear my fealty to you, and ask you accept my oath, and to assign me to a new master."
   Niren blinked back a few tears at the site of Prince Misk's squire. At the stinging sensation behind her eyes, she swiped her hand across her face.
   "It is a matter of course that we accept your oath and fealty. You have ever been in service to Midmun, and we thank you for your dedication in your further service to the king and queen of Beklen. Chancellor Gojen will see to some suitable reward for you."
   "Your Highness, please, I don't want any reward. If it pleases you, I do carry messages from King Hastho and Queen Margam."
   A lady-in-waiting stepped forward and accepted a small sheaf of letters, wrapped in a ribbon. Niren excused everyone, and went to her chambers to read in privacy.
   The letter from Queen Margam started with an apology for not having written sooner. It revealed the difficult time she'd had traveling back to Beklen... it took much longer than the usual journey, for they

often had to rest several days at a time before she could continue. Now that she was home, she had settled into a very quiet lifestyle. She didn't seem especially ill, but her will and desire to be with people had diminished greatly since her return.

King Hastho wrote of his continued wish for friendship and alliance, and asked that Misk's grave be tended and honored, for Hastho was certain he would never return to Midmun. No one in Beklen blamed Midmun for Misk's death... although it took some time to convince his elder son, Jenan, the future king, that there was no cause nor any place for hatred between Beklen and Midmun.

In a more personal letter to Niren the queen wrote that she and the king wished her a life full of love and joy. Misk had clearly loved her, and known that she cared deeply for him. Despite his sacrifice and his death, nothing could change the year of joy they had shared, and the alliance between countries was only strengthened. She wrote, too, that she should never hesitate to call on Beklen for aide.

Niren read the letters, and then stared at the stack of parchment lying on her desk, and waited. She waited to feel relief, or anger, or sadness. She felt none of these things, only a cool detachment, as if they had been written to some other woman named Niren, to some other queen. She sighed and shook her head, unable to dispel the vague feeling of a desire for connection. Then she packed the letters away in the desk, and went to bed.

Meanwhile, Gojen prepared a reward for the returned squire. From his stores, he selected a long sword with an intricate hilt.

"A ssword to cut your oath and ties
Mistrust the truth, believe the lies
Poisoned by the flowering doubt
Until it forces all faith out
Lead astray, upset the sstance
Give no quarter, allow no chance
Ssever and sslice, with every sstrike
Unbalance man and mind, alike."

Gojen approached Eto the next afternoon with a beautifully crafted sword. Eto protested several times that he did not require any reward, but Gojen was firm and insistent, and refused to take it back.

"Please allow Princess Niren to give you this ssword. Think of the guilt sshe feels, having ssent you to face a dragon. Why, you could just as easily have been killed with Prince Misk. And then sshe ssent you away for a year. Sshe will feel better if you keep this ssword. I, for one, believe your deserve it."

Because he was still unassigned to any knight master, the young squire spent his time in the training halls. He helped other squires and sparred with them, eager to keep his skills sharp. All this training and sparring he did with his own sword, finding the one Gojen had given to him to be too pretty for a working sword, as well as lacking the proper balance.

Princess Lyru had taken to hiding in the galleries overlooking the training hall. No one bothered to look for her there, as she had never expressed any interest in sport before. Truthfully, Niren often forgot to have her sought out, and the chancellor had no desire to waste his time and energy to find her and force her into attendance with the future queen.

After several days of watching Eto train, having grown desperate for some human contact and some conversation that wasn't about her poor manners, Lyru approached Eto when he was alone in the hall.

Eto bowed deeply, brushing the sawdust from his tunic.

"Your Highness! What a great honor, to have you come to speak with me."

Lyru acknowledged the squire with a smile.

"I have seen you here, practicing and sparring and training the pages and younger squires. I wished to tell you that I admire you for spending your time helping others. I hope you will not mind if I continue to observe."

"Princess, you hardly need to ask a squire for permission, but I would be honored to continue with your audience. I enjoy helping the younger boys, and it gives me something to do." Eto sighed. "I still have not received a new assignment. I am thrilled to have you in the gallery, as long as you won't find it boring."

Lyru continued to return to the gallery to watch the squire and the other young men as they practiced. It became her one hour of peace and happiness each day.

Chapter 14
He'll Flirt with Any Skirt

"What would it profit thee to be the first?
Of echoes, tho the tongue should live forever,
A thing that answers, but hath not a thought
As lasting but as senseless as a stone."
  -- Frederick Tennyson, Isles of Greece -- Apollo (l. 367)

Gojen had ensured that all of the princes were so entangled in their own thoughts and desires that they only interacted with Niren and each other in negative ways. Even if Niren were capable of feeling anything more than apathy, she would never agree to be married to any of these cads.

Into this growing circle of negativity came Imperial Prince Ulst, second son of Empress Hetmi of Aggem.

Upon being announced, he bowed. Then he approached the throne, stopping at the foot of the dais, and bowed again. As he stood, he brushed his long black hair back from the shoulders of his sapphire waistcoat. He appeared to be fit, neither too thin or at all fat, and he was quite tall. His face was handsome, with full red lips, and smoky blue eyes. The long, thin line of a scar ran the length of his left cheek, carving its way over the cheekbone and into his beard. The scar did little to detract from his attractiveness. In his hand he held a small glass bottle.

"Your Highness, I have brought you a gift from my homeland, Aggem. This oil is scented by a rare orchid. A drop, or two, will help to enhance your beauty and loveliness. The bottle is small, but it will last, for the scent is very concentrated. And of course, should you and I be wed, we will have more brought to you each year, when the orchids in our hothouse bloom. In addition, my beautiful princess, allow me to present one of our treasured orchids, as a token of the friendship that begins to grow today."

He handed both the oil and the orchid to a lady-in-waiting and bowed once more. Niren smiled politely as she instructed the woman to take the gifts to the royal suites.

"These gifts are unique and lovely, and we thank you for them. Please instruct Chancellor Gojen in the proper care of the plant. He will see to it that someone of the staff is also properly instructed."

Gojen stepped forward to receive the instructions and show Prince Ulst to the guest wing of Wayhall.

Ulst smiled and bowed to Niren again, then to Lyru. Surprised by this attention, Lyru managed to smile back. Prince Ulst had quickly managed to intrigue both princesses. Niren found herself paying attention to him, despite the effects of the stone. He seemed so different than the princes who had come before him.

As they made their way toward the rooms set aside for Prince Ulst, Gojen drew a long silver chain from the pocket of his robe. As he allowed it to dangle from his fingers, an amulet set with a large sapphire slid to the bottom of the chain.

"Please accept this ssmall gift from Midmun. A token of our esteem for you and your country, and a mark of the joy and affection we hope you will sshare here in our land."

With that, he handed the amulet to the prince, who examined it with a smile on his lips. He lifted the chain over his head, and let the pendant slide down the chain and settle onto his chest.

They spent several more moments together, discussing the care of the orchid, and details about Ulst's journey into Midmun. After a pause, Prince Ulst changed subjects.

"Tell me, Chancellor, for the reports we received were really rather vague. Did the dragon die of the wounds given it by that other prince? Misk. Or is it still about? It's a terribly romantic story, but a bit concerning, isn't it? If there is a chance I must face that dragon, I'd prefer to be well prepared."

Gojen regarded the prince critically.

"The dragon isn't dead. Prince Misk's ssquire reported that it had flown away from the battle, ssemingly uninjured. It has been sseen from time to time, but never very near Wayhall."

"A lucky squire, then, that the beast did not kill him. And lucky, too, that there have been no sightings near the castle! But of course that has been a great relief to you, what with the fever. You've been very busy."

Gojen nodded, looking a little out of sorts.

"These last two years have been difficult for the princess and for all of us in Midmun. You would do well to avoid these painful ssubjects with her. Sshe won't thank you to bring thoughts of the dragon to her mind. Now is the time to look to the future, and to a partnership between Midmun and Aggem. Charm and ssoothe her, Prince Ulst. Bring her joy and delight. Lighten her burden, and sshe will love you for it."

Agitated, Gojen returned to his workroom and struggled to soothe himself. After several minutes of pacing and muttering under his breath, he finally grew calm enough to think about the situation. He had grown complacent when none of the other princes had asked about the dragon. He had not prepared for inconvenient inquiries.

Once he was certain that his emotions were in check, he selected the spell cloth containing the amulet's twin. He then set about ensuring that Ulst would not be able to trouble him with more questions adjusting the spell he had in mind.

"Enamored of each face you ssee
You flirt with them, and they with ye
Niren, Lyru, courtiers too
Even sservants interest you
Charismatic, cool and charming
The princess you'll avoid alarming
With the amulet beside your heart
Your questions never make a sstart"

That evening's meal was a merrier event than any which had been seen in that hall for a very long while. Prince Ulst, even unaided by the amulet, was the kind of person who made everyone feel important and special. While Depri took Niren's attention, Ulst worked his magic on Lyru, charming her. Then, somehow, without causing a fuss, he managed to edge Grand Duke Depri away, and spent a while becoming more closely acquainted with the future queen. When Depri tried to interrupt, Ulst cleverly included him in the conversation without letting him take over.

Niren and Lyru each went to bed feeling hopeful, each of them feeling as though she could face the next day. But a good start, one enjoyable evening, one pleasant dinner, doesn't make for a marriage. Ulst continued to pour on the charm, like honey over crepes, making everything a bit more palatable. Then, that which had started out as a refreshing change became a stifling, cloying distraction. In fact, he was a distraction to almost everyone at court.

He roamed the halls and passages, gently flirting with the maids and cooks and ladies-in-waiting. When Princess Niren was not available, he dallied with the resident noblewomen, or Lyru, when he could find her. Charming as he was, the other princes soon came to loathe him.

At first, Lyru was very taken by Ulst's friendly charms. At almost fifteen, she was discovering her interest in the opposite gender. She blushed and returned his smiles, until she saw that he also shared his smiles with every other young woman in the castle. Then the Imperial Prince became just another person for Lyru to avoid.

Chapter 15
Subduing the Sister

"See how
Even the smooth stones ache
With stories of their own
In the shuddering light of day."
  -- Scott Hastie

    As her infatuation with Ulst faded, Lyru returned to her sulking and scowling. Once Gojen had been willing to see this as a childish reticence, but he began to notice a look of shrewd assessment in her eyes. She was swift to look away, or to direct attention to Niren or one of the princes, but not quick enough to completely avoid Gojen's notice. In his workroom, he prepared a stained glass rose with a spell to control the younger princess. He had noticed her penchant for disappearing when she was supposed to attend to her sister and the princes, as well as her recent trick of trying to divert attention from her when she grew uncomfortable. He constructed a spell which would be sure to keep her out of his way.
    "Like this glass, both ssmall and bright
    Clear as crystal, fades from ssight
    Transparent as a veil of air
    A wisp of memory, barely there
    What you ssee, you cannot tell
    Your voice has dwindled down, as well
    Ssecond place and ssecond best
    Niren rejects you, with the rest"
    Gojen had the rose delivered to Lyru with a note fallaciously signed by Prince Ulst. The note apologized for any offense she might

have felt. "I am friendly to a fault, my dear Lyru, but be assured that if you were eldest, or even a bit older, I would wean my affections from all but you. Please accept this token of my great esteem."

She took the sentiment of the note with a grain of salt, but the rose was a lovely thing, and she felt the pain of mistreatment ease a little. She hung the bauble in her window, where it glinted in the sunshine, each morning.

Often the princess skipped official meals, and went to the kitchens to get her food. None of the cooks paid her any attention, but she felt that was because they were busy doing their work, not ignoring her. Occasionally, she was forced by Gojen and Niren attend meals in the dining hall. While at the long, crowded table, she picked at her food with little appetite. Other than an occasional half-hearted smile from Prince Ulst, she was more or less ignored and left to her own devices. Niren ate in silence. The princes made up for that fact by being much more talkative than the best manners would dictate.

Lyru spent most of her days avoiding people. In the early morning, she could stroll in the gardens, because none of the princes were early risers. Each afternoon, she retreated to her hiding places, often passing the hours in the galleries overlooking the training hall. Most of the time, she simply hid, watching Eto train, sometimes with other pages and squires but often alone. It was soothing to watch him practice his footwork. No one else ever came to those galleries, and no one noticed her there.

Eventually, she was overcome by her loneliness. She approached the squire again, when he had taken a break from his training. She offered him an orange which she had brought from the kitchen.

"Have you ever had an orange? They don't grow in Midmun. We have these imported from Layant. I find them very refreshing, and I thought perhaps you'd enjoy one. You've been working very hard."

"Thank you, Your Highness. You are incredibly kind."

Eto bowed, then led Lyru to a rough wooden bench. When she was seated, he joined her, and peeled the orange. He pulled the first segment out, and offered it to the princess. She thanked him, in return, and popped the piece of orange into her mouth. Her face lit up with delight, and Eto noticed for the first time how lovely she was when she wasn't frowning or scowling.

This unlikely friendship grew as Lyru continued to visit and to bring small gifts, oranges and small loaves of bread, and soft cheese, which they shared while they sat together on that same wooden bench.

"My old governess would be scandalized if she knew we were here without a chaperon. These days, there's no one who much cares where I am or with whom I spend my time."

"I don't believe you'd be doing it, if it were wrong, Princess. I'm only surprised you aren't bored, watching a squire do drills, and eating bread and cheese on a small bench. You've got all the castle to roam, any food you like to eat, and all of the princes to entertain you."

Lyru's face darkened.

"Squire Eto, I hate the princes. I hate being anywhere near them. I know it's quite shocking for me to say such a thing, but it's true. I avoid them, whenever I can. The company here is much better."

Eto looked surprised, but very pleased.

Lyru was silent for a moment, then she seemed to come to a decision. She dropped her voice, although there was no one nearby.

"Eto, I think I can trust you, and now I think I must. I have no one left to whom I can turn. Something is terribly wrong. Will you meet with me, later, in the garden? After the evening meal? I can't talk about it here, where anyone could walk in."

Eto was a bit taken aback by her request, but agreed at once to meet her at the garden pavilion.

Lyru fidgeted and squirmed her way through the meal. Even Niren noticed that something was amiss, and frowned at her sister's antics. As soon as she was excused from the high table, she made her way to the garden. She found the squire waiting for her in the pavilion, near the reflecting pond. He bowed and they settled themselves on a bench. The pavilion sat at an intersection of four garden paths, and Lyru took a moment to check each of them before she confided in Eto.

"Eto, why is it that you are the only one who seems to notice me? At times I feel I am fading away, growing transparent... or even invisible. No one ever seems to notice me."

Eto laughed, gently, when she told him this.

"Perhaps it's because you hide from everyone but me. You're no more transparent than I am Your Highness. It's only that your sister and Gojen are so busy, and everyone else is busy with them. They still haven't found me a knight-master. How will I complete my quest and vigil? But never mind, that's my worry, and you've got plenty of your own. There is another prince coming tomorrow, I heard. Perhaps this one will be just right, and things will get back to nor--"

"Normal? Is that what you think? Do you think it can ever be 'normal' again, without Mama and Papa? With Niren behaving as she is?"

"No, Your Highness. It won't be much like the old normal. You'll all have to work to make a new normal, in your new life. But you'll grow into it. It won't be so bad, after a bit."

Lyru smiled a little, though her cheeks were still wet with tears.

"You sound a bit like Papa, when you speak that way."

"Well, then, my work here is done. It's kind of you to compare me to the King. Don't hide from them, princess. Your father wouldn't want that. Go and show them that you're stronger than they think. We'll find some way to get this all sorted. Don't allow them to think you're invisible, and they'll soon notice you. I don't know how they can help it."

So Lyru went and endured another meal in the company of her sister, whom she scarcely recognized, Gojen, whom she did not trust in the slightest, and the four princes, all of whom she loathed.

Chapter 16
Like a Dog with a Bone

"Envy sees only the sea, not the stones in it."
 -- Russian proverb

The next morning, as expected, the sixth prince arrived. He wore a long dark green robe, wrapped around him and belted with a wide sash of silk brocade. His skin was dusky, and his eyes and hair were very, very dark. His hair was cut long and shaggy, framing his high cheek bones and narrow chin.

"Daegun Vyne of Gunmar," announced the herald. "Bow before Princess Niren, the future Queen of Midmun."

Vyne did so, and as he rose, he looked around the throne room. His eyes lighted on the other princes, and he did not appear to be pleased at the sight of them. The expression on his face settled into what would become a familiar frown. Then he turned his attention to the dais, and the princess waiting there.

"Your Highness, may I present a gift from the people of Gunmar? This is a Jade Dog, an iconic symbol of Gunmar, carved by a skilled artisan in our capital. His father and grandfather also carved jade. Jade is known for luck, and the dog for protection. My people, and of course, myself, wish you prosperity and peace. In order to guarantee the best luck, make sure the dog is facing east, toward the rising sun. Never allow it to become wet, or the jade may lose its luster. Always ensure... what is wrong Your Highness?"

Taking his eyes from the gift, and looking at the princess to ensure she understood his instructions, he found that Niren had stood, and suddenly looked furious.

"Why do all you suitors bring me gifts with conditions? With lists and requirements? With... expectations? These aren't gifts, they're... chores!"

"Princess Niren, I can hardly be held accountable for the gifts these others have given --"

"We don't hold you accountable for them. But you come in here with these rules... who gives a gift with rules attached? There are too many rules! And too many princes! Didn't your mother teach you anything? Did any of you ever have a mother?"

Overwhelmed by the pressure she felt, Niren choked back a sob, and ran down the stairs and out of the throne room. Princess Lyru and several ladies-in-waiting followed her. In the meantime, Vyne and the other princes all stood looking at each other, dumbfounded and uncertain as to what to do next. Gojen stepped forward, armed with a concerned smile.

"Esteemed princes, I beg your pardon. The future queen is under a considerable amount of stress. She is feeling the strain of all that is expected of her, and I ask that you forgive this outburst. Perhaps she is suffering from a headache, or some other small discomfort. I will see to it that she will be more herself this afternoon. I invite you all to take tea with us at that time, in the Room of Roses. And now, Daegun Vyne, I would be honored to show you to your accommodations."

Gojen took Vyne off to the suitor's suites, while the other princes each went to spend their morning pursuing various hobbies and activities.

"Daegun Vyne, again... I apologize. I have never sseen ssuch behavior from the princess. I hardly know what to think. I assure you it won't happen again."

Vyne looked around his suite, clearly agitated. He fidgeted with a small cloth packet which hung from his wide belt.

"I say, I did expect a much better welcome than that. I am of half a mind to go back to Gunmar immediately. Is this really the best suite you have available for me?" He walked to the window, and his frown deepened. "It seems a bit drafty, if you ask me. Just how long have those other princes been here? It's quite a distance from Gunmar to this place, and it took an age to arrive, but as I say, I have half a mind to return, at once."

Gojen smiled calmly, and reassured Vyne in his most conciliatory voice.

"I ssaved this room especially for you, as it faces east. I believe that is considered auspicious in Gunmar? Please, I beg you to sstay, I have been looking forward to your visit. Pay no mind to the other princes, none of them has fared at all well with our future queen. I doubt any of them will fare as well as you stand to do. As a matter of fact, I believe I can aid you, if you will accept this gift, and keep the nature of it a private matter, between just the two of us."

Vyne stopped what he was doing, walking around the room, adjusting items, turning them this way and that. He reconsidered, thinking he could always go home once he had received the gift, and he found himself unable to ignore Gojen.

"A gift for me? Of course, I am certain you've given each of those other fellows their own gifts, and probably something better. I say, you should have sent the invitation to me first, seeing how far I had to travel to reach this place."

Gojen forced himself to conceal his irritation.

"Daegun Vyne, again, I assure you that no sslight was intended. And, perhaps you have heard a phrase that is common, at least here in Midmun. We save the best for last."

Before the prince could lodge another complaint, Gojen produced a small, rectangular box, made of ivory. Each panel was carved with the images of leaves and flowers, connected by running vines.

"A puzzle box, Your Highness. There is an intricate sseries of movements which will open the lock, and reveal the charm in the chamber. I have ssensed powerful magic inside this box, but I dare not use my own ssmall art to find the ssolution, for fear of disrupting that which lies within. I knew at once, when you accepted the invitation that this treasure was meant especially for you. A man of your cunning, and one so in tune with the energies and cadences of nature will surely find the key with haste. None of the others could begin to appreciate or understand ssuch a rare treasure... They would have no chance of opening it, and even if they could manage it, I don't think any of them deserves such a fine sspecimen. I cannot help but believe that possessing ssuch an item will help to lead you to the rulership of Midmun."

Vyne turned the box over and over in his hands, fascinated.

"It is a fine thing. Alright, I am curious, you've caught my interest. I'll stay, for now, but can't give me any clue on how I can open the box? I say, that hardly seems sporting. And ... you assure me... none of those others has one of these? With a head start?"

"Once and for all, Your Highness... the trinkets I have allowed the others are reflective of their base natures. Each received ssome ssimple object, and each thinks it a great boon, but none of those is equal to your puzzle box. Not one of their gifts has ssuch a unique ability to aid them in their pursuit of Princess Niren. None of theirs has any magic. I do adjure you to keep the true nature of this a ssecret from the others, lest they become overwhelmed by jealousy. You know they're likely to resent you. Let them think it a pretty, but useless, a trinket like their own."

Vyne was instantly drawn in by the lure of having something the others would covet. He went and sat at the desk chair, his fingers stroking and poking the box, turning it this way and that. Clearly, Gojen had been dismissed, so he returned at once to his workroom. On his way there, intent on starting the magic that would constrain the future queen once more, he did not notice that the door to a storage room across the hall was ever so slightly open.

From his secret panel in the wall, the magician drew several items. First, he addressed the newly arrived prince. He hastily assembled the twin of the puzzle box, bereft of any magic, save that which he had put there. As he worked, Lyru slipped out of the storage room, and watched through a crack between planks in the door. No one saw her there, for Gojen did not encourage visitors to this wing of the castle.

Listening quietly, scarcely daring to breathe, Lyru overheard Gojen's chanting.

> *"You sseek advantage, fortune, luck*
> *Though you lack both nerve and pluck*
> *Jealous of each gift and treasure*
> *Till your own brings you no pleasure*
> *Twist and turn, repeat, revolve*
> *An empty box, you cannot ssolve*
> *As a dog chases its own tail*
> *You are destined, now, to fail"*

Setting the puzzle aside, he turned to the small, blue stone laying amidst the folds of white cloth on the work table. Lyru wasn't able to see what he was looking at, the angle was too severe, and the stone too small.

"Vitrify and vilify
Watch Niren's heart harden,
Make brittle her ssteel,
Ssow rot through the garden!
Induratize, demoralize,
Trust not to fate
Sset this sspell to prevent all joy
And transform love to hate"

As Gojen wrapped each of the spelled artifacts and returned them to his safe, Lyru slipped quietly back into her hiding place, across the hall, waiting for Gojen to leave his workroom. Once he had done so, she made her way to find Eto in the training rooms, with a look of fierce determination on her face.

Chapter 17
Not Your Queen

"Life is mostly froth and bubble,
Two things stand like stone --
Kindness in another's trouble,
Courage in your own."
　　-- Adam L. Gordon

　　The next time Lyru met Eto in the training room, she was forced to wait to approach him, as he was sparring with another squire. As soon as he was alone, she rushed to him to explain what she had seen and heard in Gojen's chambers.
　　"Oh, Eto! It's bad enough that Gojen is casting spells on these horrid princes. But now he's set his magic on my sister too! Why? I can't understand why he would do such a thing. I have to go and tell her! I can't even think what made me come here first, except... except that I am afraid. She hasn't listened to a word I've said in weeks. Why would she believe me about something as bizarre as this?"
　　"You're right, Princess. I don't know much about magic... none of us who were born in Midmun does. I never thought we'd see magic like that, happening here. He's set on making sure she never falls in love... never marries and never becomes Queen. A spell to prevent joy and promote hate. He wants her to hate the visiting princes? It feels..."
　　Eto paused, and Lyru finished the sentence for him.
　　"It feels... Dark. Dark and cold and hard. Just like Niren. At least, like she is now. Eto, I need your help. Niren, and all of Midmun need your help."
　　The squire paced the floor as he thought.

"Of course I will help. It's my duty, and I want to help you and your sister, but who can we go to? How far do Gojen's spells reach, and how many are under his spell? Who can we trust? Princess, think about it. You can tell your sister what you've heard. She won't listen. She won't be able to listen. I wonder..." Eto's worried face grew darker with dread.

"What is it? What else?"

"I wonder if Gojen had a spell on Prince Misk, too. Perhaps that's why he wouldn't take more help with us to fight the dragon. He said it was because of Halb, he wanted to live up to the legend. I wonder if there was more to it, than that."

Lyru trembled at the thought. She covered her face with her hands for a moment, and took long, deep breaths, working to calm herself.

"We all trusted him. Papa trusted him, made him Chancellor. How could he turn on us? Niren has never hurt anyone, let alone him. It doesn't make sense unless... Oh! Oh, Eto. I've just had another thought..."

Lyru drew another deep breath to steady herself, and stood to her full height. She lifted her head, and squared her shoulders. She'd had enough of going unnoticed.

"Squire Eto, I am not your queen." She paused. "That being said, your future queen is in no position to grant you a quest, so I am going to do just that, in her name. I cannot leave Wayhall to find help, but you can. Niren needs you to find help, Eto. I think that perhaps Gojen had something to do with the fever. What if he killed my parents? What if he decides to kill me and Niren? Or worse, what if he's keeping us alive so he can make us his concubines. None of the princes would stop him. He'd name himself king."

"I won't let that happen! You have my word on it. But where do we go for help? Perhaps there's someone in the market who can help, or can direct me to someone with enough power."

Lyru was skeptical, but she could not think of any better solution.

Chapter 18
Too Much of a Good Thing

"Virtue is like a rich stone, best plain set."
-- Francis Bacon

"Princess, now that we know how dangerous Gojen is, we have to be more careful. We can't let him see either of us as a threat. If he notices us together, or if a servant says something about us, we'll be his next targets. He'll kill me, and perhaps do far worse to you."

Lyru shuddered at the thought, and agreed, sadly.

So the princess began to search again for another hiding place. She haunted many of the halls and passage of the castle. One afternoon she was leaving her own suite when she heard voices and footsteps approaching. Quickly, she darted into Niren's room, sure that no one else would dare to enter. She waited silently and breathed a sigh of relief as the voices' owners passed by the door without pausing.

Lyru wandered around the room, curious and lonely and longing for a connection to her sister. First, she opened Niren's wardrobe, and wistfully poured over the beautiful, 'grown-up' dresses there. Lyru had one more year until she began to wear the floor length gowns which marked her as an adult, rather than the simpler dresses which came to mid-calf.

She opened the jewelry chest, and held several beautiful pieces up to her neck and ears. Each of the sisters had inherited some of Queen Jaynn's jewelry, but most of it was considered too mature for Lyru. Niren was of age to wear it, but rarely did so.

After returning the jewelry to the proper place, Lyru sat at Niren's desk, and opened the center drawer. Lying there amongst the stationery and sealing wax, she found the letters from Beklen. She read each of them, and there she saw King Hastho's pledge to Niren that she could always call on him for help. A flood of relief washed over Lyru. Surely, the same would apply if Lyru asked for help in Niren's name.

At their next meeting, Lyru told Eto about the contents of the letter.

"Now I feel like a bit of a fool. Of course King Hastho will help us. I should have thought of it at once. I can leave at dawn tomorrow."

"You? Why must you leave, Eto? Isn't there someone else we can send?"

"Princess, who else can we trust? I know the way there. And more importantly, perhaps, the king knows me. He'll believe me, and that will save time. I'll bring help as quickly as I can, but until then, be careful. Don't give Gojen any cause to accelerate his plans, or to pay more attention to you."

Lyru agreed unhappily. Eto left the following morning, finally on a quest that could win him his full knighthood.

That same day, Sheikh Lyttogun of Melloss arrived. He was the last of the princes invited to compete for the hand of Princess Niren. Gojen, standing behind Niren's throne had to restrain himself from laughing with satisfaction as he saw the prince approach Niren and bow to her. Everything he'd learned of this man convinced Gojen that this prince would never meet Niren's standards. Looking at the Sheikh now, he grew even more certain of his assessment.

The tall, heavy prince strutted toward the throne, with his head high and his shoulders back, as if he were already the king. He swaggered. A bright orange turban crowned the sheikh's head. From beneath the fabric, hanging down into his pale brown eyes, and brushing the collar of his garment, were wisps of dark hair, the tips dyed a bright crimson. His oversized robe ranged from amber at the neckline, and deepened through bright tangerine at the waist to carnelian at the hem. The robe was belted tightly around the prince's large stomach. He carried a staff as a walking stick, gilded and set with fire opals in a ring around the knobbed top. He used the stick to propel himself down the aisle. *Click* *Click* *Click* The staff sounded on the flagstone floor, and echoed against the walls and ceiling.

After the Sheikh of Melloss bowed, his servant brought forward a small wooden chest with several tiny drawers. Opening the largest of those small drawers, Lyttogun withdrew an orangish gold necklace. The pendant was an open oval with an ornate letter "N" at its center. The outside of the oval was a series of scallops.

"Your Highness, this jewelry is made from gold mined in my homeland. Only in Melloss does one find it in this glorious shade of orange. Don't you adore the color? SO bright! So... striking! I took the liberty of having a full set made for you... rings, ear-bobs, bracelets, and of course, this pendant. Should we wed, a torque will be added, to mark you as a noble of Melloss. A fully matching set to match your beauty. You will honor me and my country greatly when you wear these treasures."

He bowed once more, with an elaborate flourish of his right hand.

Niren nodded, and offered her thanks then instructed that the jewelry be taken to her dressing room for the evening. Her eyes did not light up. Her smile was like one painted onto her pale face. Gojen practically crowed with delight as he showed the most recent visitor off to the suite set aside for him.

"Your princess is a quiet one, isn't she? Still, I can't say as that wouldn't come in handy. A quiet queen, yes." As he spoke, he stroked his dark, crimson dyed goatee.

Gojen assured Sheikh Lyttogun that the princess was quiet until she became more acquainted with those around her, and always very well mannered.

"Sshe is sso well mannered, in fact, I am ssure sshe was loathe to praise your lovely gift before the other princes. None of them brought her anything like as lovely as the necklace. And like any young lady, sshe does love jewelry."

"Good, that is good. I had wondered, since she didn't appear to be wearing any jewelry, today. Women at home wear ever so much. Sometimes I wonder that they can walk about, what with the weight of it! And, as I said, she was very quiet. I am not used to quiet women, they're all too outspoken in Melloss. I believe I will grow to like it here in Midmun, where I can get a word in edgewise."

"And we in Midmun are certain we will like having you here, too. We believe it will be magnificent to have you as our king! To sshow you how much we appreciate you, we have prepared a gift, especially for you."

Gojen presented a large bronze dish, which was surrounded by silver filigree work. Opening the ornate lid, Lyttogun found an aromatic selection of candies. Each cube shaped piece was a warm yellow, orange or red, and was dusted in fine white sugar.

"This is Lokum, my lord Ssheikh. There are sseveral variations of it here; orange, lemon and rose. I have had it imported from the far ssouth, especially for you. Rose is my favorite, but I am certain you will enjoy each variety. There is nothing quite like this delicacy. Even if you've tried it before, I guarantee it will not have been the equal of this. I will leave you to ssample it and to rest before the evening gathering."

As had become her habit, Lyru hid across the hall, and listened as Gojen brought out the dish's twin, and spoke the spell over it.

"Ssilver dish, with candy bright
Zesty and ssweet, a true delight
Though larger than life in all you do
Niren will take no notice of you
Every gesture and deed is great and grand
But Niren flinches at each demand
Consume, ingest, destroy, devour
The bones on the plate are those of your power"

Lyttogun arrived at the evening meal wearing another of his ostentatious orange robes, this one bright, with irregular black stripes, like those of the large cat living in the eastern countries. His voluminous black breaches were gathered at the ankle, and he wore leather sandals with orange gold beads.

Gojen had seated him between princes Vyne and Stohl. Prince Stohl paid very little attention to the newcomer, preferring the company of his flask, but Daegun Vyne hung on his every word. Lyttogun turned the conversation to hunting, and Vyne invariably reported that he had killed a bigger beast, or a more dangerous beast, or more of the beasts in question. These grandiose tales made both Niren and Lyru frown with distaste, and push their plates back.

Grand Duke Depri, seated across the table, joined in the conversation. Talk turned from hunting to swordplay, and Depri challenged the sheikh to a 'friendly' duel, an exhibition of skill, to take place the next day. All through this conversation, Duke Edger continued to accost Lord Barin with a barrage of questions and comments about the financial stability of Midmun, ignoring all of the other princes and both princesses.

In a rare moment of sisterly camaraderie, Niren whispered to Lyru that she was glad there were no more princes coming, and Lyru nodded. In her heart, though, Lyru wished for another, one more worthy of her sister and of Midmun. She feared that any of these fellows would destroy her country in no time.

A multitude of questions kept Lyru awake and fretting all evening. How far away was Squire Eto, and was he safe? Was help coming? What more was Gojen plotting? If he was done spelling the princes, would he turn more magic loose on Niren? Or would Lyru herself be the next target? The long night passed as she tossed and turned in her bed. She finally slept just before dawn. She remained asleep through breakfast, waking just in time to go and witness the sparring match.

Chapter 19
An Exhibition of Skill, and Something Else

"As creeping ivy clings to wood or stone, and hides the ruin it feeds upon, so sophistry cleaves close to, and protects Sin's rotten trunk, concealing its defects."
  -- William Cowper, The Progress of Error

Grand Duke Depri and Sheikh Lyttogun were on the dueling court, preparing for the exhibition when Lyru arrived in the gallery overlooking the room. She quietly joined Niren and Gojen where they were seated, slipping into place beside her sister. Prince Ulst was sitting behind Niren, commenting on the preparations. Niren tried to divide her attention between the spar and her companions, but she found it difficult to attend to either with any enthusiasm.

Duke Edger stood as second for his brother, looking bored and quite put out. Depri wore a metal helm, and a chain mail hauberk over a padded shirt and breaches, which were dyed the color of an eggplant.

Gesturing to his garment, he declared, "I always spar in this color, so that the stain will not show when my opponent bleeds on me." His laughter grated on Lyru's nerves.

Sheikh Lyttogun wore rust colored leather armor from head to toe, despite the fact that this was a spar, and not a true duel. Vyne, acting as his second, supervised the Mellossian prince's squire as he buckled and fastened each piece in place.

Prince Stohl arrived, late as usual, and slipped into place beside Ulst. He was seemingly disinterested in the spar, and came only because the steward directed him here after breakfast. He slouched on the bench, occasionally tapping the cork of his flask. The sound of the tapping was a bit distracting to those seated in front of him.

When all was ready, Niren rose and signaled for the spar to begin.

The princes made several passes, getting a feel for their opponent's timing and strategy. With lunges and thrusts, parries and retreats, they tested one another. Since this was a friendly spar, and not a true duel, neither became aggressive very quickly.

Though each was well trained, the difference in style was easy to notice. Depri was quick and agile. He slipped through when the sheikh was too slow to block him. Lyttogun, who was much larger and heavier, relied mainly on his reach and strength.

Prince Ulst commented on each strike and defense as if none of them had ever seen any swordplay before. Lyru rolled her eyes and thought that the courtiers sitting on the rows of benches behind the royalty were far better behaved than Niren's suitors.

On the court, Depri feinted left, then swept at Lyttogun's legs. Taking a swift step back, Lyttogun swung his sword high, and knocked the helm from Depri's head.

The audience gasped, and then suddenly began to laugh. Chuckles and titters spread throughout the gallery. For there on the floor, beside his helm, was Prince Depri's hairpiece. The auburn wig lay on the sawdust like a dead animal. Even Niren had to hide her face in her handkerchief. Lyru's shoulders shook with the effort to reign in her laughter. Ulst roared with mirth, but Stohl just seemed confused.

From his place at Lyttogun's bench, Daegun Vyne smirked. Sheikh Lyttogun took several steps back and away from the grand duke.

Duke Edger checked to see if his brother was hurt. Ascertaining that he was unharmed, Edger picked up both helm and hairpiece, and offered them to Depri. After refusing to accept either, Depri stormed, red-faced, and shiny-headed, out of the arena. The others followed, now that the morning's entertainment was spoiled, or in the opinion of several, greatly enhanced, but now ended.

The next morning, Depri and Edger met with the future queen. In truth, both princesses thought that Depri looked just as handsome without the wig, but he was mortified and inexplicably furious.

"My suit will never be taken seriously. I am the laughingstock of this entire country! I cannot stay! I am going back to Socra at once."

Niren blinked a few times as Depri's fury breaking through the stone's spell momentarily. She smiled kindly.

"We are so sorry to hear that you feel that way, Grand Duke Depri. I don't believe Midmun is as unpleasant as that. Is there nothing we can do to convince you to stay?"

Depri mistook the smile for a smirk, and his anger and embarrassment swelled.

"Nothing! There is nothing that can allay this humiliation. And to think that you would invite seven princes, when clearly I would have done! Or if not me, then certainly my brother would have made a suitable substitute. Surely, you cannot be thinking of marrying Stohl of Layant! It's an insult, having so many of us here, bowing and scraping as if we weren't royalty too. Yes, I certainly will be leaving, and my brother is coming with me. There is nothing for us here."

"Is this so, Duke Edger? We would like to hear your sentiments on this as well, as one of the six -- that is -- five remaining suitors."

"Yes. Yes, exactly. Five remaining suitors. I have always been a man of numbers. The odds do not add up at all well in my favor. With your leave, I will go back to Socra with my brother. I believe it will be more expedient and economical to travel together."

"We grant our leave to both of you. We would by no means wish to oppose expedience and economy. We wish you traveling mercies, and pray that Socra will always be our ally and our friend."

As the princes made their way from the throne room, the echoes of laughter from the court followed them.

Gojen couldn't have been more pleased with his progress. With three of the seven princes gone, he was well on his way to a place where Niren would never marry. He would only have to content himself with the title of Regent for a short time more.

Of the four remaining princes, Gojen was certain he had nothing to fear from Stohl. The prince began coming late to each meal he attended, and skipping many meals entirely. The elixir in the flask sated his appetite, and he ate sparingly, losing weight. He spoke very little. One could scarcely imagine why he'd come, or what he thought to accomplish by remaining in Midmun. The magician wasted little of his mana on Stohl, other than ensuring that the spelled flask continued to perform its function.

The time and attention Gojen saved on Stohl were taken up by Daegun Vyne, who began to plague him, pestering him for aid or advice in the solving of the ivory puzzle box. Gojen made a show of performing 'passive' spells on the trinket, telling him that anything more powerful would damage the magic within. These spells lit up select areas of the box, and Gojen advised Vyne to concentrate on these. Thus, the prince of Gunmar was set to an activity akin to a dog chasing its own tail. Gojen was satisfied that while Vyne wasted his time on the box, he was making no progress in the wooing of the princess.

Prince Ulst continued to charm and delight, cutting a path of bruised and broken hearts throughout Wayhall Castle. Gojen only had to renew the spell on the amulet infrequently. Because Ulst's flirtatious nature was so close to the desired result of the spell, the magic did not drain quickly.

Lyttogun seemed to be gaining the weight that Stohl was shedding. He often sent a servant to Gojen for "More of that delightful Lokum." Gojen rationed it out to him, never refusing, but sending less as time went on. He sent warnings that his supplies were not unlimited, pleading with Lyttogun to constrain himself from eating more than a piece or two each day. Finally, the prince stopped sending the servant, suspecting that the lesser amounts were a result of pilfering. Gojen hemmed and hawed, and finally produced a few 'extra' pieces of lokum for Lyttogun.

"You must make this last. It may be some time before another shipment arrives."

The princesses themselves were considerably more intractable than the imported princes. Niren went for several days at a time, safely ensconced in the effects of the stone, until suddenly something would jolt her from her languor. Each time Gojen respelled the chalcedony in his workroom, he met with resistance. He had expected that after this amount of time, Niren would have acquiesced to the magic, but her will and passion continued to assert themselves, the last thorn in his side.

Chapter 20
To Beklen...

"Roads go ever ever on,
Over rock and under tree,
By caves where never sun has shone,
By streams that never find the sea;
Over snow by winter sown,
And through the merry flowers of June,
Over grass and over stone,
And under mountains in the moon."
   -- J.R.R. Tolkien, The Hobbit

Eto began his journey to Beklen in high spirits, thrilled to be doing something useful, at last. He was also happy to be out of Gojen's sight, though he was worried about Lyru, and of course, Princess Niren as well.

He traveled quickly on the road to Beklen, making good time. He stopped only when his horse needed to rest. He bought food in villages along the way, rather than taking the time to hunt. He was driven to reach King Hastho as soon as possible. This time, as a questing squire rather than an honor guard to an ailing queen, he arrived at the castle gate much more quickly than he'd expected.

King Hastho was surprised but pleased to see the young man again. That pleasure dropped away from his face once Eto presented the request for aid from Princess Lyru. The squire privately gave the king the letter from Lyru, and answered several questions about what he had seen in Midmun. The king called for a small meeting to assess a strategy to stop Gojen.

That evening, while he waited in the council chamber, Eto stared at the wooden door. Carved in relief, it depicted a lion with a great mane springing up at a dragon. The sight of it filled him in equal measures of both hope and dread.

Those whom King Hastho had summoned began to arrive, and quietly took their places. The king sat at the head of the long table, with Prince Jenan on his right and Eto on his left. Sir Ytef, head of Beklen's military took a place half way down the table. The royal quartermaster arrived with his arms full of scrolls, and took his place at the far end of the table. A scribe with parchment, quills and an ink pot sat on a stool before a sloped table. Lastly Danj, adviser and magician, sat beside Prince Jenan.

"Many of you will recall Eto of Midmun, who was Misk's squire. He has brought a request for aid from Princess Lyru, acting in her sister's stead. It seems that Niren, the future queen, is bespelled."

King Hastho relayed what Lyru had written to him. He told the council of the spells the younger princess had witnessed. He reminded them of the fever which had killed Midmun's king and queen. He then paused for a moment to let his advisers adjust to this disturbing news.

"Beklen will, of course, come to Midmun's aid as we have done in times past. We will honor this request, and our friendship with Midmun. Were it not for his death, it would be Prince Misk to whom we would send help. We will act as if he were there, for he is there, in his final resting place."

Several of the men at the table began to speak at once, but Danj, the magician, held his tongue. He studied and scrutinized Eto. His silence stood out, and after a moment the others quieted. With the king's nod of permission, he began to speak.

"In the reign of His Majesty King Payke, a similar request for aid came from King Johnel of Midmun. Magic was as common in those days in Midmun as is still is in Beklen and Parelm. Each village had a healer or hedge witch, a midwife or minor magician. Since the Great Spell, twenty-five years ago, Midmun has been nearly devoid of magic. Small charms, herbal elixirs, and vague visions have remained, but any spell more powerful than these either fizzles out, or backfires. The mana, or magical energy, simply fails to endow magicians. Now there are a few herbal healers who can add a bit of potency to their potions, and a few seers with a better than even chance of predicting the weather or the gender of an unborn child."

"Every magic user of the last two generations has studied the effects of the Great Spell, as it is called. It was the masterpiece of a generation of gifted individuals, working together. I can tell you are wondering, young squire, why this spell was necessary. I understand that much of what I am about tell you is not common knowledge in Midmun. I believe there is a need for you to understand these things, so I will share what I know."

"Yes, please. I think you're right, I need to know. Thank you."

"At that time, someone in Midmun had been casting spells on the land. Illnesses spread. Livestock started to disappear. Weather grew unpredictable and dangerous. When the Midmunese court magicians could not bring these spells to an end, the king called on Beklen for help... much as you are doing now."

"Sir, forgive me for interrupting. Why is all this a secret in Midmun?"

"It is a secret because King Johnel ordered that those involved keep it so. When King Payke sent his adviser Dozak, who was my father, he discovered that Crown Prince Otyk was behind these terrible magics. The fever killed his own mother, the queen. He was guilty of matricide and regicide. King Johnel was grieving on all fronts, and he was mortified. Otyk was ill-content to wait his turn, and thus willing to use any means available to him in order to take the throne."

Eto listened to Danj, looking stunned.

"Dozak was aided by King Johnel, who had a healing gift, and all of his most trusted magic users to construct a spell to drive Otyk out of Wayhall and Midmun. Johnel wasn't willing to execute his son, so they constructed the spell to banish him forever. The Great Spell worked, but it took a great toll. One of two outcomes arose from participation in the spell. Either the magic was burned out of the user, or the magic burned them up. My father returned, but without his magic. He did not live much longer. It was he who told me all of this, lest you doubt me. Most of the celebrants of the spell were consumed by it, including King Johnel. At the same time, all the magic was seemingly burned out of Midmun. That is why all of this has been kept a secret."

Eto nodded, dumbfounded, looking from face to face to see if anyone else at the king's table was as shocked as he was. It seemed that all of those gathered knew this tragic story.

"And now, it seems that Gojen has found a way to bring magic back, and to use it every bit as maliciously as Otyk did. History is said to repeat itself. The few magicians remaining in Midmun are too weak in their art to notice the influx and effluence of mana."

King Hastho thanked Danj for sharing the information.

"And now we must come to an agreement as to whom to send and how best to help. Prince Jenan, your thoughts?"

The prince stood. He waved the others back into their seats, as they rose with him. He paced the length of the floor as he spoke.

"We mustn't send a scribe to do a knight's work, as the saying goes. However, in this instance, I feel it's the reverse which may be true. If we send an army against him, too many innocents will fall in harm's way. Danj, with his magic and knowledge, is our most powerful weapon against this scoundrel. It seems to me that we must ascertain how much mana is available to Gojen, and whether our magicians can access that mana, as well. If not, can we produce and spell objects to store the mana available to us here in Beklen. From there, we will proceed."

Prince Jenan reclaimed the seat beside his father.

King Hastho smiled approvingly at Jenan's summation.

"I concur with most of what you have concluded. I think it may be too soon to rule out any military involvement, though it must be our last course of action. Sir Ytef, ready a small force with knowledge, understanding, and, most importantly experience in working with martial magic. Work with Danj, and be prepared, should we need you."

Sir Ytef agreed with a nod and a bow, as the scribe at the corner table continued to record the conversation and instructions.

Danj sat with his fingers steepled against his chin, deep in thought. Then he turned and addressed Eto once again.

"Squire, I am curious as to why Gojen has not spelled you, and the younger princess. I would think him likely to try to control everyone in proximity to the throne."

"I believe that he tried to put a spell on me. Princess Niren told him to see to it that I received a reward for my services to Midmun and Beklen. I kept telling him I needed no reward, but he insisted. He gave me a sword. I disliked it from the moment I touched it. It is much too fancy for a squire, or for anyone who intends to fight. It's not a weapon, it's a parade piece... an ornament. And the balance was just as wrong as wrong can be. It seemed to pull me along after it. It was the most uncomfortable feeling."

Eto shuddered at the memory.

"I don't know about Princess Lyru. Perhaps he doesn't think he needs to do anything about her. No one there seems to think she's very important. She even told me she thought she was becoming invisible, slipping past everyone's notice."

Danj nodded, and appeared to have come to a conclusion, lifting his head and sitting forward in his chair.

"That perception of transparency sounds like a spell effect to me. Most likely, he cast a spell to exaggerate something she was already feeling. That sort of magic is very effective, and is slightly less costly than creating an effect from scratch. I will certainly have to investigate it. I am certain that the sword you were given is spelled to control you in some way. Have you brought it with you?"

Eto shook his head, with a frown.

"I couldn't bear to bring it. I hate the sight of it. I left it back in Wayhall, in my room, wrapped up at the back of my wardrobe."

"I thought as much. In truth, had you tried to bring it with you, you may have been waylaid or attacked, or perhaps changed your mind along the way. We can hope that Gojen was not aware of your absence right away, but we cannot assume that it has continued to go unnoticed. If he has any inkling of your mission, we must move swiftly to counteract him when he takes the next step."

The young squire paled.

"The next step? I am afraid to think of what he'll do next. I'm afraid he's only waited to kill the princesses so he can make them his concubines."

King Hastho spoke next, looking shaken.

"Gojen is the regent and only two people now stand between him and the throne. Taking those two as concubines would lend some ...

legitimacy to his claim to the throne. And should they prove uncooperative, it's another fever, or a fall down a flight of stairs. He'll stop at nothing to be king. My poor, innocent son..."

Prince Jenan looked up, doubly concerned.

"No, not you. You're safe enough, here. But Misk never had a hope against the dragon. Nor do any of the visiting princes have a chance to succeed. Spelled, or not, none of them is capable of winning Niren, not whilst she is under Gojen's influence. He's seen to it that she will never marry, and never become queen."

Chapter 21
... And Back Again

"Roads go ever ever on
Under cloud and under star,
Yet feet that wandering have gone
Turn at last to home afar.
Eyes that fire and sword have seen
And horror in the halls of stone
Look at last on meadows green
And trees and hills they long have known."
    -- J.R.R. Tolkien, The Hobbit

Danj led the preparations for the journey from Beklen to Midmun. The initial traveling party was limited to just Danj and Eto, for several reasons. Firstly, if Eto returned and newcomers were noticed, Gojen would surely know something was afoot. Secondly, with a small party, Danj could magically accelerate the return trip, at least as far as the border. This, he felt would misdirect Gojen further, throwing off any thought that Eto had sought help in Beklen, having returned in far less time than such a trip would normally take.

Each morning the two of them would rise with the sun, and break their fast. They walked steadily until afternoon, when they stopped for a meal. When Danj was rested, he would chant the spell over the campfire.

"This fire is sweet to those who roam
But we need one nearer Niren's home"

After reciting the phrase three times, he withdrew ash leaves and comfrey from his pouch and tossed them into the fire. As the smoke rose, it began to curl and twirl around them. Each time Danj performed this rite, Eto found that he was momentarily blinded by the smoke. When the air cleared, they would be at a new campsite, fire already burning. Eto recognized them as sites he had used on his previous journeys to and from Beklen. There he and Danj would rest again until morning, and begin anew. Because of this magic, they traveled on foot, their horses and the bulk of their supplies being brought along in a more mundane fashion by those who followed.

Eto, worried about Lyru, and about Midmun at large, pressed Danj to complete the journey by magic. Danj refused.

"Magic cannot do everything. Magic works best as an aid. Think of it like this, young Eto... A man with a limp may walk faster and more securely with a stick, but the stick can never do the walking for him. Or that same man may ride a horse, but he must constantly guide the horse, or it will go astray. Perhaps the horse may even run itself to death, or worse, plunge over some unseen, unnoticed cliff, taking the rider with it. Magic is full of holes. We will use magic cautiously, or not at all. I will not risk my life and yours along with it."

Eto apologized, chagrined.

Danj sighed, clearly very weary. He settled himself in to his blankets, leaning against a fallen log.

"Besides all of that, making this journey in one large step would use up a large portion of Mana... magical energy, and there is a strong chance that Gojen could detect it, even from this distance. Please, don't feel badly, I don't expect you to know these things. Midmun has set aside the study of magic for your generation, and done so to your detriment. Even in Beklen, where magic is as it always was, most squires would only know a very little about such things. Why teach more than basic theory to someone who is not born with access to the art, and will likely never see it in use? A midwife or mother can often tell at birth if a baby has been born with the ability to gather and manipulate mana. If not at birth, it usually becomes clear within a few weeks' time. They see to it that such a child receives the proper education and training."

Eto drew his own blanket close around his shoulders, warding off the evening chill.

"How can they tell, sir? I'd like to know more about that, if you aren't too tired to tell me."

Danj smiled at the squire.

"The quest for more knowledge is well worth a few minutes of my rest."

Shifting his blanket, he exposed his left hand. He held it up to the fire, allowing Eto to notice for the first time that there were six fingers on it.

"Those of us born to the art are often physically different. I am one of the lucky ones, my anomaly is not too startling. At least I was not born with a second set of eyes."

Eto looked startled at the thought, and Danj laughed.

"There are tales about such things, but I have never seen anything quite as startling as that. Perhaps those stories are true, or perhaps they are old wives' tales. It may have happened, but only once or twice. Sometimes mothers claim such a trait, expressed in the ability to see what mischief her children are up to behind her back."

Eto laughed then too.

"My mother always seemed to know everything I was doing."

"I suspect that mothers always do know, and that is a different form of magic entirely. Perhaps it manifests because the two shared one body for so long. You see, the body, its shape and form, has much to do with the magic you become skilled in."

"I won't trouble you by taking off my boot, but I have an extra toe on my left foot, as well. This is why I am adept at the transportation spell we are using. My extra finger lends itself to the crafting of charms, and the growth of the herbs which I use in those charms. Often, those who are born blind are subject to visions and interpretation. Those with eyes of differing colors can sometimes manipulate the weather. Only women can produce any sort of elixir to create or strengthen love, but most women respect both love and magic too much to do so. Men are more skilled at spelling weaponry for specific effects. That may be a matter of physique, or one of interest and attention. When creating a spoken spell, it is not essential for it to rhyme, but it seems to help some casters to focus the mana, not to mention to remember the correct phrasing."

Danj poked at the fire with a long branch and watched the sparks rise into the night.

"None of these are hard and fast boundaries. Those with ten toes can perform teleportation. These are simply indicators of natural talents. Nor are all magicians born with any mutation. If Gojen had any such visible trait, I am certain that someone would have made note of it. I have met the man, I went to Midmun when the fevers were as their worse. Although I was not looking for it, I did not notice any obvious magical mark on him. Not every magical mark is easily noticed, and some can be hidden. Still, be watchful. Such information would be an invaluable asset in defeating him."

Danj yawned expansively.

"I will be more than happy to answer any more questions, provided you are willing to ask them tomorrow. I must bid you good night, Squire Eto."

"Good night, Danj."

The next morning afforded little opportunity for questions or discussion. A thunder storm came up behind them. Danj was mostly occupied with pushing it away from the small traveling party. He explained briefly that this was a learned spell, not one that came naturally, and it took more concentration because of this.

Surprisingly, Eto and Danj were not the only people on their way back to Midmun. As Grand Duke Depri and his brother got further and further from Wayhall Castle, and from Gojen's magical influence, he grew more and more embarrassed. Finally, Depri called his horse to a halt, and turned to Duke Edger.

"What was I thinking?"

"What do you mean, Depri?"

"I mean that I've made a complete ass of myself."

Edger arched one perfectly plucked eyebrow, and gave him a sideways glance.

"What, have you? Again? So soon?"

Depri scowled at his brother.

"Alright then, Edger, have your fun. When you're done laughing at me, think about it. I've just walked away from an almost certain chance to be king. None of the others stood a chance. What competition did I have, there, really?"

Edger raised his eyebrow once again.

"Yes, I'll concede that you were competition for the kingdom, but never for the queen herself. Surely she's seen that you're less than interested in her. I stood a fine chance. More than fine, really."

He paused, and raised his eyes to look back toward the distant capital.

"I'm going back. Come back with me, and when I am king, I will make you Lord Chancellor of the Exchequer. You may have that man, the treasurer, Barin, in whichever role you desire."

Edger considered, stroking his mustache thoughtfully.

"When I could be king, myself, Depri? I could win the job, if I set my mind to it. A marriage needn't have love to be successful. I rather doubt her ability to fall in love, no matter which prince wins out. I haven't embarrassed myself, as you have. If you want her to consider you at all, you'll need my full support. So... Lord Chancellor of the Exchequer, as well as a marriage to the younger princess. That way, I can keep up appearances, and after all, the younger princess won't be needing any heirs. Besides, our dear brother Ashlor won't be pleased to see either of us return to Socra, I think."

Depri assessed his calculating younger brother, and agreed with a handshake.

"Why not? No one else wants the younger one. And perhaps you're wrong about Niren. Perhaps I can make her fall in love with me. She wouldn't be the first to do so. There's something about her... I wouldn't mind if she were the last. Besides, she will bear me such beautiful babies."

Chapter 22
Courting Disasters

"I prefer rain -- sometimes I feel sunlight will turn me to stone -- perhaps I'm a Troll."
-- John Geddes, A Familiar Rain

Depri and Edger returned to court, and were announced by the herald. Gojen appeared to be furious, his face red and scowling at the sight of the brothers. Princess Niren was calm and cool and decidedly distant.

"Perhaps I was mistaken, Grand Duke Depri? I do thought that you and your brother were set on going home, and here you are again. Enlighten me."

"Your Highness, give me another chance. What can I say to persuade you? I am a man of passion, and I was caught up in a moment of embarrassment. Every man has his pride, and a prince doubly so. I was mortified. I deeply regret my words and my actions. Allow me to attend you once again?"

Niren was silent for several moments. Her lips were pressed together in displeasure. The court remained silent as well. Finally, she nodded.

"One final chance, then. And you, Duke Edger? Have you found it to be expedient and economical to return to Midmun? Or do you do everything your brother does? Have you any motivations of your own?"

"Your Highness, I ask you, isn't loyalty between siblings something to applaud? Depri's passions are somewhat contagious, and I was swept along with them. I found it well worth my time to be considered for a marriage here. We will prove our worth to you."

Niren excused the court and went to her room. She sat by her window, watching a storm roll up through a valley. Suddenly, Lyru entered the room, unannounced. The older sister looked at the younger, surprised.

"Why are you doing in my room? What do you want?"

Lyru fidgeted for a moment before she stilled her hands. Of course, she hadn't known that Niren would be in her rooms. She had come to look for more information... and perhaps to go through Niren's jewelry again, but she could hardly say that.

"I'm sorry, I should have knocked. I've missed you. I thought perhaps we could stroll in the garden? I'd like to spend more time with you."

"Don't be ridiculous, Lyru. Can't you see it will be raining any moment? Look at the clouds. It's almost as if a giant hand were pushing them toward us."

"I am not ridiculous, Niren. Please don't say such things about me. And don't say no, not yet. We can go out for our stroll, after the rain, when the gardens are damp and fresh and green. No one else will have ventured out into them again, and they will belong just to us."

"They always belong just to us. We are the princesses here."

"Exactly, Niren. That is exactly what I mean. Wouldn't it be lovely to act that way again? To stroll through the gardens as princesses and sisters and friends. And to spend the afternoon without any of those dreadful princes hanging about. Please? I'll sit with you until the sun comes out..."

"You are kind to me, Lyru, and more loyal than I deserve."

"Don't say that, either! Please, Niren. The sun will be out soon, I'm sure."

"I almost prefer the rain... but an afternoon without the princes does sound rather restful. I cannot believe that Depri has returned. I thought at least my decision about him was over with. He and his brother. What do you think changed their minds?"

"You did, Niren! Of course they came back for you, for another chance to be your husband. Why wouldn't they?"

Niren sighed, and indicated that Lyru could sit in another armchair.

Feeling very pleased, Lyru ran down the hall to her chambers to retrieve her embroidery basket. When she returned they sat quietly, working on their samplers. Niren clearly didn't wish to talk, or to listen to Lyru's chatter. Lyru was content for the moment, simply to be with her sister, not turned away.

Eventually, the storm passed. The princesses put on their walking slippers, and went out into the garden. Once out in the sun, Lyru noticed how pale and thin her sister had grown. The future queen walked very slowly, dragging her slippers along the path, scarcely lifting her feet. After they had walked in the fresh air for a while, Niren began to lift her face toward the sun, and her footsteps grew ever so slightly lighter.

Lyru felt hopeful that whatever magic Gojen was using against Niren, they could overcome it, together. Besides, help was on the way, and Eto would be back soon.

Chapter 23
The Pot Meets Mr. Black

"He who lives in glass houses should not throw stones."
  -- English Proverb

Gojen was furious about the return of the Socran princes. It had been days since he'd renewed the spells on the mirror and the tourmalines, and they'd almost certainly been out of his range, anyway. He tapped his finger on his cheek, trying to assess the damage to his plan. Meanwhile, he respelled everything he still controlled, strengthening the magic on the pile of objects accumulated on his work table. The glass rose seemed to be making little impact on Lyru, but he cast the spell on its twin, once again. He respelled Eto's sword with no resistance at all. Niren's chalcedony continued to need to be recharged, and he did so with the sourest of looks on his face. Frustration distracted him for several moments before he turned his attention on the princes.

He manipulated Vyne's puzzle box spell so that it would convince the prince that the box was closer to opening, allowing a few more panels to slide back and forth. Gojen rubbed almond oil mixed with ground cinnamon and coriander into the sapphire amulet's twin, thus ensuring that Ulst's flirtations would become more forceful. Worn out by these spells, Gojen quickly checked on Stohl's flask and the supply of Lokum he had prepared. He fidgeted with another cloth package, checking the contents, and rewrapping it. With that, the magician went to bed, muttering under his breath that there was no rest for the wicked.

He slept until early the next morning, when he was woken by a commotion in the courtyard beneath his window.

Daegun Vyne was sitting on a bench, studiously twisting and turning his ivory box, using the bright sunlight to examine each seam and panel. Lyttogun stormed out of the nearby doorway, furious and shouting. He wore an embroidered satin vest in apricot. Over this, his matching tailcoat was cut in military style, with twin rows of copper buttons. His sword hung at his side in a leather scabbard. As always, while he spoke, he punctuated each question and exclamation with a thud of his gaudy walking stick on the hard-packed ground of the courtyard.

"Vyne! How dare you! How dare you enter my suite? Do not bother to deny it! I have a witness who saw you leaving! I know you took several pieces of Lokum! I know exactly how many I had! What gives you any right? This invasion of my privacy, this theft, this betrayal of basic trust is unforgivable, and I demand satisfaction!"

Vyne slowly looked up from his puzzle, clearly unimpressed by the taller prince's bluster. He stood, equally slowly, and adjusted his pine green robe, dusting some imaginary dust from his sleeve with the back of his hand.

"I say, Lyttogun! What's the bee in your bonnet? Or should I say turban?" Vyne laughed at his own joke, before continuing. "Yes, yes, I went into your room, It wasn't even locked. I only went in there to see if you happened to have a box similar to mine. It was only a bit of idle curiosity. When I couldn't find a puzzle box, I noticed that there was a dish of your candy. I sampled a few pieces, since you're so keen on it. It isn't as if you've ever offered a single piece to any of the rest of us. I say, you are selfish! I mean, it's candy. Just candy! It's a bit overly sweet, if you ask me. I didn't even care for it, honestly. Accusing me of theft is a bit much. It isn't as if I took anything with any real value. I certainly won't bother you or your sticky candy again."

Lyttogun's face was roughly the same color as his turban. Slowly, he lowered his right hand and reached across the girth of his stomach. He grasped the orange-gold hilt of the scimitar at his left hip then he drew it several inches from the ornate scabbard, allowing Daegun Vyne to see the sharpened steel. He plunged the sword home again, turning on his heel as he gave his last warning.

"See to it that you don't. I don't know how you punish thievery in Gunmar, but in Melloss we would remove your hand, and that is for the first offense. Another theft brings death. Out of deference to the future queen's delicate nature, and the current laws of Midmun, I will refrain from exacting the punishment, this once. I promise you, I will not warn you a second time. Stay out of my room!" With that, he stormed away, his ridiculous walking stick clicking and thudding as he went.

Vyne returned to his bench, and closed his eyes. He laid the backs of his hands on his thighs, fingers pointed toward each other. Deep breaths, in through his nose, and out again with a hum. It was only a moment before his meditation was broken by thoughts of the box. He began to try to solve it once again, questing for the secret he believed to be locked within, just beyond his reach. He didn't give the sheikh another thought.

Lyttogun walked back toward his room, intending to get a piece of Lokum, to soothe his troubled spirit. As he turned the corner, he chanced to see Ulst leaving his own room. The sheikh frowned. Surely, if he had any competition for Niren's hand, it was Ulst, walking away, down the corridor in the opposite direction. Lyttogun slipped into the newly vacated chamber, and looked around, snooping through the contents of the wardrobe, chest and desk. Atop the desk was a small silver tray, upon which were a comb, scissors, hair oil, and a razor. Beside the tray was a small pouch of mint leaves for the freshening of breath, and a glass bottle labeled "Cinnamon Orchid." Lyttogun squeezed the bulb atop the bottle, spraying the scent the air. He found himself instantly drawn to the scent, so he sprayed it up and down his body. He found nothing else of much interest, so he returned to his own chamber, where he indulged in several pieces of Lokum.

Several minutes later, Prince Ulst returned from his errand. He stood in the hall for a moment, sure that he smelled the distinctive fragrance blended for him by his chemist. Allowing his nose to lead the way, he went and knocked on the door to of Lyttogun's suite. When the door was opened by a servant, all doubt was resolved. The chamber reeked of hothouse orchid, the spicy aroma told Ulst that Lyttogun had not only sampled the scent, but had likely used three times the needed amount. For a moment, anger welled up in Ulst's chest, but he chose not to act on it just yet.

After the herald announced him to the noisome dandy, Ulst made polite conversation for bit, inquiring about courting customs in Melloss. While Lyttogun rambled expansively on the subject, Ulst quietly seethed, and plotted the fop's downfall. His mother, Empress Hetmi of Aggem, had high expectations of her second son, and she would not accept excuses. Ulst had grown tired of competing with the others, as well as pouring on the charm, thick and hot, while the princess all but ignored him. True, she didn't seem to favor any other princes either, but the time had come to start eliminating his competition. Lyttogun, all unknowing, had just volunteered to be his first victim.

Through all this, and breakfast as well, Prince Stohl slept. Even Daegun Vyne, who envied everything about the other princes, found nothing about this fellow to feel jealous over. Depri and Edger noted the tension between Vyne and Lyttogun and Ulst, and smiled at one another. Depri offered to walk with the princess after breakfast. When she declined, the smile faded from his face.

"Princess, what would you have me do? I made a mistake, and I have apologized. Could I not be what you are looking for? I think I could, if you would give me a chance. I came back to try to win your hand and your heart. Your parents were beloved, not just here in Midmun, but far and wide. Their love and leadership are legendary. I would appreciate a chance to follow in their footsteps, with you."

Niren bit her lip at the mention of her parents. She hadn't thought of them in quite a while. She blinked back a few tears, and wondered how she had slipped from raw grief into this dull ache.

"Surely you can make a name for yourself at home. You must be beloved there. You must be every young man's hero, and every young woman's infatuation."

"You would think so, but I'll be honest. There is little for me in Socra. If I return, I will likely be wed to some noblewoman, and then be sent off to war. If no war can be found for me, I'll be sent off to one of our estates, well out of my brother's way... like a thoroughbred stud, put out to pasture. He won't allow me to stay near the throne, he thinks I'm ambitious. Well, I am. I want to be king, but I'd prefer to do so as your husband."

"So, I am a means to that end. You speak of wanting me to consider you, but I assure you, this is not endearing you to me!"

"That isn't what I mean at all. I mean that if I stay in Midmun, with you, I can make a difference. I can make a name for myself. I could be good for Midmun, and I could be good for you. I want to be good for you. You've captured my attention. With just a little bit of encouragement, you could capture my heart. And then, together, we can make Midmun great. Greater!"

Niren laughed, then.

"I see. Midmun deserves the best, and you are the best!"

"I might be. How will you know, unless you at least consider me as an option? You keep shutting us out, but you will have to choose one of us. I know that none of us are your first choice, but if you don't choose, Chancellor Gojen is sure to choose for you. I think, even from the distance you've created between us, I know you well enough to guess that isn't what you want. So, consider me. I want to be the best choice, for Midmun, and for you."

Depri looked sincere, as he bowed.

"What harm is there in walking with me for an hour, while the sun is shining and the birds are singing? I cannot make the choice for you, but I can, perhaps, make the choice easier for you. Princess, will you walk with me, please?"

The novelty of Depri saying please for anything was enough to shake Niren from her lethargy, and she agreed to walk with him. She was quiet as they strolled, but she did her best to make it a comfortable silence. Happily, Depri had what he wanted, for the moment, and was content to do enough talking for both of them.

Afterward, Niren and Lyru sat in Niren's sewing room, embroidering quietly. Gojen's supply of mana continued to weaken, spread too thin, like a pennyworth of butter scraped over a pound of bread. He still hadn't found a way to respell Depri and Edger.

Chapter 24
Magic Once More

"Grain by grain, a loaf; stone by stone, a castle."
-- Yugoslavian Proverb

    Once they had arrived in Wayhall Village, Eto led Danj to the old Thaumery. While Midmun was the magical center of the continent, West Whitsen, this building had been the heart of the magic in Midmun. Market days had been held on the grounds, where adepts sold their charms and potions, while meetings and classes were conducted within. It was also the building where the Great Spell had been crafted and enacted a quarter of a century past. While the Thaumery was not strictly abandoned, few people frequented the sad relic of a place where their king had died and magic had been purged from the land. In more recent times, the small amount of magic which still worked in Midmun was practiced from home, herbal elixirs and charms were sold in booths and stalls in the market square. One elderly caretaker saw to the cleaning and repair of the main hall, but the rest of the large building went untouched for months at a time. The people of Midmun treated the building with respectful distance, as if the magicians had gone to the sea for a month, and would return to resume their duties. As time passed, they stopped expecting the return, but no one ever went so far as to repurpose the building.
    Danj took up residence in a former classroom at the back of the Thaumery, far from the main hall. He swept away the dust and cobwebs in the corners, disturbing a small cluster of spiders. He prepared a sleeping area, warding it against intruders and insects. Eto went to the market and brought Danj a loaf of bread, several cheeses,

and a platter of sliced, smoked meat. A bottle of wine and several jugs of water completed the provisions.

While Eto was off on his errand, Danj had prepared his work table. He placed his crucible on a small and smokeless fire, and he began to search for mana. Small purple spots of light rose from the crucible, and floated in the direction of the castle. Not one spark in fifty moved in any other direction. When Eto returned, he saw the back wall of the cell shimmering with cool purple fire.

"This is exactly as I suspected. Mana has returned to Midmun, and all of it, or as near as makes no difference, is being used inside Wayhall Castle."

Eto watched the sparks as they began to fade, leaving the wall looking dingy and forlorn. He sniffed, the musty scent of the room irritating his nose.

"Can Gojen tell you're here and that you've done that spell? You told me that he might detect magic, on the road."

Danj smiled, looking calm and relaxed. He shook his head.

"No, this is a small magic, and a very passive spell. It would be far more notable if I allowed smoke to rise from this long abandoned chimney. When we begin a serious attack, he will know I am here, but I believe our secret is safe for the time being." He gestured to his bedroll. "Now, I think you should get back to the castle. I am tired, and unless I miss my mark, there is a young princess waiting to hear from you."

Chapter 25
Reunion and Revelation

"A diamond with a flaw is preferable to a common stone without one."
   -- Chinese Proverb

Eto sent a message to Lyru that he had returned, and she met him the next morning in the galleries overlooking the training hall. As she approached him, she shook her head, making her blonde curls bounce, trying to dislodge the feeling of dread which had settled over her. She frowned as he bowed and greeted her. He noticed the difference in her at once.

"What's wrong, Princess? Has something happened? Are you well?"

Lyru shook her head, again. She seemed distracted, and almost disoriented.

"What's wrong? Nothing. Nothing else. Nothing new. It's just that I feel... Never mind how I feel, that isn't important. I'm not important..."

"Of course you're important, Princess."

Lyru ignored his protest and continued.

"I didn't expect you so soon. Did something go amiss? How could you have made it all the way to Beklen and back so quickly?"

Eto's face remained set in a concerned frown. He shook his head as well.

"I will tell you about my journey in a moment, but first.... I rather think we should mind how you're feeling. Something is wrong. Please, tell me."

"It's nothing, Eto. Really, it's nothing at all. I must have had bad dreams last night. I have been having nightmares, and they've been worse since you left. Don't ask me to tell you what they were about, I never really remember them in the daylight. I wake up each morning, feeling dreadful. It always passes after a while."

"Has Gojen given you anything since I left? Danj, the court magician, thought Gojen might have put a spell on you."

"No, he hasn't given me a thing. He hasn't put a spell on me. He doesn't have to. What harm can I do to him? He wouldn't bother to waste his time. Now, please tell me about Beklen. How did manage to you get back so soon?"

Reluctantly, Eto dropped the subject. They sat together on their usual bench in the gallery, sharing her breakfast rolls, and he told her much of what Danj and King Hastho had told him. The princess was shocked by the tale of her Uncle Otyk, and his role in the deaths of her grandparents, as well as the fall of magic in Midmun.

"I can't understand why people are like that. Gojen and the princes, all so greedy for the throne. If I were willing to kill Niren, Midmun could be mine to rule, but... what brings you to a place where you could ever do such a thing."

Eto looked thoughtful as he answered.

"It's greed and impatience and jealousy. It's being unwilling to accept who you are and what you're given, and to make the best of those things. Such people must never have a moment's peace... not to speak of any true happiness. Even if and when they get what they want, I imagine they move on to wanting something more. It isn't the kind of life I'd ever wish for."

Lyru turned on the bench to fully face her companion.

"Eto, what is the life you'd wish for?"

He slowly turned and faced the princess as well.

"Of course I want the same things I've always wanted. I hope to be a knight, and to serve Midmun, and the queen. But now I wish for more, as well. I'm not certain it's proper to speak of the other things I have come to hope for. I think, in your heart, you already know those things. And when the time is right, I will speak them, to you and to everyone else as well. Once I am a knight, once Princess Niren is Queen of Midmun, I will be free to do so."

Lyru smiled and all the fear and dread fell away. Her face shone with real joy for the first time since he mother and father had died.

After a moment of silent but shared contentment, they turned back to the task at hand. While Gojen stood against them, none of their dreams could come to fruition.

Lyru told Eto about the surprising return of Depri and Edger.

"I'm sure that complicates Princess Niren's decision. As if it weren't already difficult enough."

Eto went on to share what he had learned from Danj about the nature and use of magic. He told her about the magic-aided journey, and about the detection spell in the Thaumery.

The princess sighed. "It's such a lovely building, and such a sad, sad place. I would have liked to have seen the wall of magic. It sounds as though it was beautiful."

With that they agreed to meet again the next morning. Eto left the castle to check on Danj, and Lyru returned to her room to smash the glass rose which she believed had come from Prince Ulst, needing no token of affection from anyone but Eto. She spent the rest of the afternoon avoiding the princes with Niren.

Chapter 26
The Rose Blows

"Revenge is like a rolling stone, which, when a man hath forced up a hill, will return upon him with a greater violence, and break those bones whose sinews gave it motion."
     -- Jeremy Taylor

    Daegun Vyne had grown increasingly weary of being snubbed by the other princes and ignored by Niren. His consuming jealousy had only worsened since the Socran brothers had returned. The help he had received from Gojen had gotten him no further in the solving of the puzzle box. Frustration had taken root in his soul, and like tree roots growing near a stone wall or walkway, it soon began to tear apart the surrounding structure.
    Leaving the castle walls behind, Vyne went through Wayhall Village to the market place. There he sought out the few women and men who still plied their trade in magic. Of course, with mana being as scarce as it was in Midmun, these were mostly charlatans who supplemented their art with chicanery and shams. Over the next week, several of the magicians milked Vyne of both gold and hope. Each of them promised him a solution, and then offered a string of excuses as to why it would take more time, and more gold, to solve the puzzle box.
    "It's delicate, it's complicated, it's powerful and I must ward it carefully..."
    When Gojen next respelled the box, he noticed a small disruption. The flow of power which returned along the channel he had opened to the box felt a little different than it had, but he didn't have enough

mana to spare to track down the source of the discrepancy. The other objects spelled for the princes showed no such variation. He was concerned that his grip on Vyne might be slipping, and he made a mental note of it without investigating any further. He tried, once more, to renew the spells on the looking glass and the tourmalines, but he could feel that the effort was pointless. The gifts remained unaffected, the channels were closed, blocked by time and distance spent outside his range of influence. He would have to rely on the princes' inherent vices and the effects of the stone on the princess to keep her from selecting one of the Socrans.

The bulk of Gojen's time and effort was still invested in keeping Niren incapacitated by the stone. Her willing participation in the beginning had aided in his success, but this was steadily ebbing away. It was even possible that the original spell, the one Niren had spoken and believed was attached to the stone she had swallowed, was interfering. Certainly, the two were in opposition. This was complicated work, and a lesser magician would already have failed, he was certain. He renewed the spell, and pain radiated back to him along the magical conduit. She would pay dearly for this pain, when the time came.

He had noticed that she and her sister were spending more and more time together, showing that his spell on Lyru was failing as well. Gojen grimaced, and attempted to renew the spell on the glass rose. As he spoke the spell poem over the replica, the glass began to overheat. Before he could stanch the flow of mana into it, the rose exploded, embedding shards of glass in his face and hands. Gojen screamed in pain, both from the magical rebound and the physical wounds. Only by the width of his fingers did he avoid having his eyes ruined. He was not in attendance at that evening's meal nor at breakfast the next morning.

Chapter 27
Upon Deaf Ears

"Even the stone you trip on is part of your destiny."
  -- Japanese Proverb

After a series of disappointments and failures in the marketplace, Vyne's research led him at last to a sorceress named Debran. She did not have a shop in the market, she lived and worked outside the village, just at the edge of the forest.

The main room of her little cottage was filled with shelves. Not bookshelves, but shelves full of bells. The smallest of the bells was no bigger around than an acorn. Bigger bells hung on hooks below the shelves. The largest of all, a brass bell with a rim the size of a rain barrel and a clapper as big as your forearm, stood in the corner, seeming to watch over all the others as a grandmother might watch over a room full of her descendants.

Daegun Vyne knocked loudly on the door, which was answered by small boy with dark hair and merry eyes. Seeing the green silk robe the visitor wore, and the golden, beaded crown on his head, the boy bowed. Before the boy could rise, Vyne began to scowl at him and launched a series of questions and demands.

"Who are you, boy? Is this the home of Debran? I must see her at once!"

"I'm Jobias. You can see her if you want, she's right there, but you can't 'talk' to her. Well, you can talk all you like, but she can't listen. She's deaf."

Daegun Vyne stamped his foot in a fit of bad temper, like a child who had been denied candy.

"What! Deaf? I say, why did no one tell me? No one tells me anything! How is she supposed to do anything for me if she's deaf?"

Jobias backed up a few steps, and gestured for the prince to come into the cottage.

"There's no need to shout, Your Highness. I'm not deaf. I can hear you just fine. Shouting won't help her to hear you. No, see, it works like this... You come in, and tell me your troubles, and then I tell her. Then she'll have a go at it with her bells."

Vyne eyed the little boy suspiciously.

"Is it quite safe to come inside? I say, I have no wish to lose my hearing to some illness. I find this country to be very unlucky as well as unhealthy, what with all the fevers. Just how do you tell her, if I can't? What does it mean to 'Have a go at it'? I am not a commoner, and I don't understand such base slang."

Jobias sighed and rolled his eyes, clearly unimpressed by foreign nobility.

"Look sir, Gran and I have our ways. You can come in, and she'll use her magic to see what she can do for you, or you can go on back to the village. I think you know how that will work out for you. They don't know what to do with the little bit of magic they do have. She doesn't maybe have much more, but she knows what she's doing. She helps everyone around here, when she can. But it's your choice. Anyway, there's no sickness here. She lost her hearing in the Great Spell, a long, long time ago."

Daegun Vyne finally got control of his temper, and followed Jobias into the cottage. The older, heavyset woman he found waiting inside curtsied as soon as she saw them come in. Vyne nervously looked around at all the bells. Jobias began gesturing, his small hands forming complicated shapes which disappeared as quickly as they came. Vyne couldn't make any sense of it, but Mistress Debran nodded, and looked at the prince, expectantly.

Vyne began to speak directly to Debran, arrogantly refusing to continue speak directly to the child. He showed her his treasured puzzle box, gripping it as if one of them was going to wrest it from his hands. Jobias rapidly translated all this into hand signs.

Debran held up her hand to stop the prince. After a few quick gestures, Jobias nodded.

"She said to ask you, what's inside the box?"

"Some magical relic, something powerful, and rare, of course. Some charm, or perhaps a potion. The person who gave it to me was a bit vague. But anything protected by this much magic must be potent. He was reluctant to do more magic on the box, because he didn't wish to disrupt that which lay within. I say, you aren't going to do anything which might harm it, are you?"

With assurances that she would start by seeing and seeking, without acting upon the box or its contents, Debran held out her hands. When the prince handed the ivory box to her she began to examine it. She turned it over and over in her hands, and slid a few of the panels back and forth.

Vyne watched for a moment, tapping his foot impatiently.

"I say, when are you going to do some sort of real magic? I can fiddle about with it. I have done exactly that, for weeks now."

Again, Jobias relayed the impatient prince's message. Debran began to move around the room, selecting seemingly random bells from their hooks and shelves. Now Vyne noticed that they were not all made of the same material. There were several different metals, each with a unique sheen or patina. Some of the bells were made of wood or china, and some of glass and even what appeared to be animal horn.

As she took down each bell she handed it to her grandson, who placed it, in the order received, on a quilted cloth on the table. Both of them moved so carefully that not one of the bells chimed in the process. Anyone other than Daegun Vyne would have been impressed by the little boy's poise and care.

At last she stopped and walked to the table. She placed the ivory box on a short porcelain pedestal in the center of the table, and began to ring the bells directly over it. As each bell sounded, she either nodded or frowned. She then put that bell back down, or handed it to Jobias to return to its shelf or hook. Then she started again with the next one.

As Vyne watched this bizarre behavior, he grew increasingly exasperated.

"I say! What is this foolishness? I will not be mocked! Is she deaf or not?"

"Of course she's deaf! I don't tell lies. The bells are magic, sir, and she hears the magic. She could always hear magic, the Great Spell just made it so that's all she can hear. So she hears magic while you just hear the bells."

"And just what good will ringing a magic bell over my box do? Is it going to open, or not?"

"I couldn't say, sir, but that's what you came to find out, isn't it?"

Debran had stopped ringing bells, watching the two talk.

"Then tell her to get on with it. I say, I hope this does not prove to be yet another futile experiment."

The sorceress started again, ringing bell after bell over the ivory box. Nothing outwardly appeared to happen to the box. No pieces shifted or disappeared. None of them lit up, or turned a different color. Finally, she shook her head, and began to gesture to Jobias, again.

"It's no good, sir. She says she's very sorry, but there's no lucky charm or potion in there. There's nothing magical inside the box, at all. What little magic there is... well, it's all laid on the outside of it. It's like it was painted on, after the box was made."

On Daegun Vyne's face a series of emotions vied for position. The greedy, needy expression which was usually on display faded, and was replaced by disbelief, fear and wrath.

"NO!" He howled. "No! That cannot be! What about that big bell, in the corner? Tell her to use that!"

After a series of hand signs, accompanied by the shaking of both heads, Jobias spoke again, looking a little frightened.

"My Gran says it would do no good, sir. None of the bells can show magic that just isn't there. And she's sorry, we're both very sorry..."

Vyne's face was pinched and pale, reflecting his green robe, making him appear ill. He slapped the coins of his payment down on the table, and snatched the box from the pedestal, and sped out the door and down the road toward the castle.

Chapter 28
Bits and Pieces of the Puzzle

"Stone, steel, dominion pass,
Faith too, no wonder;
So leave alone the grass
That I am under."
   -- A. E. Housman, More Poems

Lyru spotted Vyne storming his way through the castle. Curious, she followed him at a distance, as he made his way toward Gojen's workroom. She stopped just short of Gojen's corridor, watching and listening from around the corner.

The prince nearly took Gojen's door off its hinges in his haste and fury, pounding on it with both fists. Gojen came to the door, and Lyru caught sight of the curious wounds on his face.

"Daegun Vyne. What is it you want?"

Vyne stared at the spots of blood, both dried and fresh, in Gojen's beard. He took a deep, shuddering breath, and his anger overcame his horror.

"What I want is for you to tell me, once and for all, what is in this infernal box. I want you to help me solve it at last. I want you to finally tell me the truth! There is nothing in this box, and there is no magic, save what you have used to make a fool out of me! You aren't the only one with magic around here, whatever you may think! You certainly stink of it, but I've caught a whiff of it in other places, too. I've found someone else, and she's told me what you've done!"

With that he forced himself the rest of the way into Gojen's workroom, and slammed the door behind him. Lyru crept closer, to watch through a crack between the wooden planks. Vyne slapped the puzzle box down on the table with such force that the inkwell toppled, and spilled on a parchment.

Gojen snarled at the Gunmarine prince, furious at the destruction of his documents.

"You want me to perform magic on this box? Sso be it!"

As Vyne watched, Gojen held one of his hands over the box, not quite touching it. The other hand clasped a small object wrapped in white cloth. Chanting in some sort of sibilant hiss, his hands began to glow, surrounded by flames.

"*This box is empty, its magic null*
A fruitless sskin, an empty hull
Your greedy ssoul could never tell
You, like the box, a barren sshell
You sseek your fortune, you're out of luck
Twist and turn, writhe and buck
Fire, hot, burns the box away
And soul-linked as you are, you'll pay"

The box reflected the flames coming from Gojen's hands for a moment, and then began to absorb the heat, slowly charring. Suddenly, Vyne clutched at his chest, and screamed. He turned toward the door and fell to the floor, clearly dead, eyes frozen wide open in terror and pain.

Lyru continued to watch, trembling with fear and disgust. While she had always thought that Daegun Vyne was an unsavory nuisance, no one deserved such a death. Gojen wrapped the prince's body in a length of white cloth. As he approached the door, Lyru retreated across the hall. Gojen dragged the wrapped body toward a stairwell at the end of the corridor. The wounds on his face were bleeding freely, staining Gojen's gray beard and giving him a monstrous appearance.

Once Gojen had slipped into the stairwell, Lyru quickly crept back across the hall. She shuddered at the smell of char and blood in the air as she entered the workroom. On the table, next to the scorched ivory box, the scroll was nearly ruined by the spilled ink. She could, however, make out parts of some of the spells, including the beginning of one with Niren's name on it. Fearing Gojen's return, she ran back to the gallery above the practice arena, where she found solace in Eto's company.

Chapter 29
Magic Like a Magnet

"If you are a stone, be magnetic; if a plant, be sensitive; but if you are human be love."
   -- Victor Hugo, Les Miserables

After the evening meal, at which the continued absence of Gojen nor Vyne was noted, Lyru snuck out of the castle, dressed as a servant of high station. No one was likely to pay much attention to such a woman as she came and went. Eto followed at a distance, watching over her. When she had told him of Daegun Vyne's fate, the two of them had decided it was finally time to for Lyru to meet Danj.

As she had been instructed, she entered through a side door, recently unlocked so Danj and Eto could come and go unseen by the caretaker. She waited quietly just inside, until Eto joined her. From there he led her through the dark building to Danj's room. They were both surprised when they found a middle-aged woman and a young boy seated on wooden chairs, across from Danj.

When Lyru removed her head scarf, and revealed her blonde hair and the silver circlet on her head, all three rose in order to bow or curtsy. Eto introduced Lyru to Danj, and Danj in turn, introduced the other two. All the while, the boy's hands were moving, the woman's eyes following him rather than looking at Lyru and Eto.

"This is Debran. She is an adept at magic. She lost her hearing and voice as result of the Great Spell. Jobias is her grandson and translator. She came to the Thaumery after she was approached by a foreign prince with a spelled box. She has noticed changes in the flow of mana here in Midmun. I believe that she will be a great help to us. I have explained what we know thus far, and what we fear may come."

The princess greeted each of them warmly, and nodded as she sat on one of the chairs. The others took their seats as well. Jobias sat across from his grandmother, and translated for her.

"That prince was Daegun Vyne of Gunmar." Lyru shivered at the memory. "I followed him to Gojen's workroom, and watched Gojen kill him. They argued about the puzzle box. Vyne was ranting and raving, demanding that Gojen tell him the truth about it. He said that some magician had told him there was no magic in it. And then.... Gojen killed him. He started chanting, and the box went black, and Vyne dropped to the floor, and I could see that he was dead. There was nothing I could do. I was so afraid."

Danj consoled Lyru by telling her that she was correct. He assured her that there was indeed nothing she could have done to stop the magical murder. "You would only have put yourself in harm's way, with no chance of changing the outcome for the prince. Gojen is far, far more powerful than anyone had dreamed."

"It's not only that. There is something the matter with him... with Gojen. His face was bleeding, dreadfully, even before Vyne went into the room. I can't understand why he hasn't done something to heal the cuts. He hasn't been at meals. It frightens me to stay in Wayhall with him, but I can't leave Niren."

"He may not be able to heal them, Princess. Magically inflicted wounds are perverse in nature. If, somehow, it is your magic which inflicts them, then your own magic will never be able to cure them. I was taught that it is something like the negative ends of two magnets. The more forcefully you push on them, the more forcefully they repel one another. You need someone else's magic, the positive end of the magnet. In a way this is encouraging. It seems he has no one to aid him, that there is no one he can trust or turn to for help."

Eto spoke up, seeking reinforcement from Danj.

"Gojen is getting more desperate, and more dangerous. Danj, please help me convince the princess that it is not safe for her to continue to spy on Gojen. If he finds her, I'm sure he will kill her. I wish I could stay with her, but that would only draw more attention. I don't know how to protect her, and she won't listen to me."

Lyru scowled at Eto.

"Of course I listen to you. I've heard every word, every time you've asked me to stop. I just don't obey you, there's a great deal of difference. I know that he's dangerous, but someone has to watch the regent, to know what he is doing. Where would we be if I hadn't seen what he's done? We'd know nothing! Who else can do it? Who else can go where I can go, without being questioned? Gojen would recognize Danj, and he'd be suspicious of you, and there is no one else we can trust. My sister's life may be in my hands, and I won't trade her safety for my own."

"I agree it is not safe for you to watch Gojen."

Lyru began to protest, but Danj held up a hand, indicating that he had more to say on the subject.

"I also agree that it is useful, and perhaps essential to our success. I will craft a charm to help to keep you safe. Before I do that, I need to know more about the dread you had been experiencing, and the feeling that you were disappearing?"

Lyru pressed her lips together, remembering the despair.

"I don't know what to tell you. It isn't very clear, and it's so hard to explain. The feeling was always at its worst first thing in the morning. Have you ever woken up with a cold in your head? You feel ill and achy and muzzy."

"Muzzy, Princess?"

"Yes. Muzzy. I don't know any other word for it. Muzzy. Unclear and uncomfortable. Just... heavy and dull and miserable. Or, I felt that I had spent the night tossing and turning, as you do when you have a fever, and having the worst dreams. There was never once any dream I could recall. I never fell ill. Once I forced myself up and into my day, I felt a little better, until the next morning. Anyway, all of that ended when Eto returned from Beklen with you. I feel perfectly well now, although I am still terrified by what I saw."

Danj considered all that Lyru and Eto had told him.

"Princess, will you consent to let Debran and I test you, using our magic to find the cause of your dread? It will not harm you. I feel strongly that you must be connected to Gojen's magical accident."

"Can Eto stay with me while you do the spell?"

Danj assured her that Eto could stay, and Lyru consented at once, feeling both nervous and excited.

First Danj took the kettle from the fire, and poured the boiling water into his crucible. He stirred slowly as he added herbs from his pouches. As he did this, Lyru could see the sixth finger on his left hand.

"These are dried petals of cicely flowers and the leaves of the angelica plant. These will aid me in my visions of the magics surrounding you. Visions do not come naturally to me, so I must enhance them with herbs."

As the sweet, green scent of the herbs rose in the steam, purple sparks rose into the air, as well. For a moment the sparks formed a stream, and wrapped themselves around Lyru. She gasped and smiled in delight. The sparks rose and fell, moving from her head to her waist several times, swirling around her. Suddenly the sparks flew away from Lyru and surrounded Eto. After a moment, they broke away from the squire, and moved back toward the princess, but before they reached her again, they fell to the ground and faded entirely. Danj quirked an eyebrow.

"That is curious, indeed. I did not factor Squire Eto into this spell..."

As Danj spoke, in the same spot where the sparks had faded, they suddenly rose up high and bright, vibrated violently, then dispersed again, fading in the air. Danj actually took several steps backward, in his surprise. He turned to Debran, who shook her head looking mystified. Jobias watched quietly, on his best behavior and finding himself a little in love with the princess.

"Now I am much more than curious. Clearly the magic involves you, and you have somehow dispelled it. It has something to do with Eto, as well. It tried to reach you again, and could not do so, because the spell was broken. There was some barrier it could no longer pass."

Lyru's eyes were wide with astonishment. She found her chair, and sat down, hard. She blinked several times, still a bit dazed by the purple sparks.

"I haven't done anything magical, I couldn't possibly have. I wouldn't even know how. I don't have any magic!"

"That may not be strictly accurate, Your Highness. Given your ancestry, it is entirely possible that you were born with the affinity for magic. Because of the depletion of mana after the Great Spell, you never learned to use or recognize it. Your father had a powerful gift for healing, before the Great Spell. It is quite likely you inherited some form of his gift. None of your generation has been instructed in the use of magic, even in theory. I mean to explore this further, with your permission, but first I would like Debran to see what she can discern, if you will permit another experiment."

Lyru agreed to allow it, and Debran rose. With her grandson's help, she unpacked a variety of bells. Jobias explained the process to Lyru and Eto. Standing behind Lyru's chair, Debran rang a large wooden bell over Lyru's head. Lyru jumped a bit at the sound, though she was trying to sit as still as she could. The clapper made a hollow sounding thud, then Debran set it aside. Next she chimed a bronze dinner bell and a brass hand-bell, neither of which seemed to satisfy her. The steel bell also failed to produce a magical resonance over Lyru, but on a hunch she sounded it over Eto's head as well. This time, the bell made music, rather than producing a dead clang. Jobias translated as Debran signed that this was because Eto's vocation was to do with steel. He was born with an affinity for weaponry and armor. Finally, she brought out a tiny glass bell. The fragile looking item fairly sang when she rang it over Lyru's blonde curls.

Jobias launched into the translation as the sound of the bell faded.

"Gran says that whatever magic Gojen used on you, and whatever magic you have, it's most likely something to do with glass. Glass is pure, and reflective and transparent. That might explain the feelings of being unnoticed. My Gran says she can't tell more until she gathers all her glass bells. She has about half a dozen more at home."

Jobias grinned and bowed.

"I'll show you when you come there."

Lyru rose from her chair, her face lit up with realization and horror.

"OH! I see now! It must have been that rose! It wasn't from Prince Ulst at all. I should have seen it at once. I understand it now. It even explains why I felt especially dreadful in the mornings."

When she noticed by the confused looks on their faces that this explained nothing to those in the room with her, she went on to explain about the stained glass rose and the note which had come with it.

"He knew exactly how to manage me, didn't he? He made sure that I would need the thing he'd sent to me. He made sure I'd want it, that I would look at it, and touch it. I was so lonely, and just for a moment, when the rose arrived, I didn't feel like I was fading away."

Eto looked disappointed, but the princess continued.

"The same day you returned, I went back to my room and there it was in my window, the red glass rose. It didn't look so pretty, any more. I couldn't stand the sight of it, all of a sudden. I knew then that I didn't need a silly bauble from a distasteful man. Prince Ulst could never win my heart, and he didn't deserve it. That became clear once I'd spoken to Squire Eto. I threw the rose onto the stone floor. It was so thrilling to watch it shatter! I thought I felt better because Eto was back, and he'd brought help, and of course that's true as well... But could I have destroyed Gojen's spell, just by shattering the rose? Is it really as easy as that? We could find whatever he's using to spell Niren, too."

"Yes, Princess, it seems that his magic shattered with the rose, at least, the part of it he had attached to you. He is investing objects with his magic, a rose for you, a sword for the squire, and a puzzle box for that poor prince. I must ask you to bring any other gifts you might receive to me for testing. It isn't always so easy to dispel magic. He may or may not try that tactic again. It appears that his intent is to eliminate or incapacitate each prince. Obviously, you and Niren are his primary targets. You must send word to us at once, if anything changes."

After conferring with Debran, Danj took several clear glass beads from his supplies. He strung them together on a ribbon, and lowered it over Lyru's head.

"This is the charm I promised. It's a small thing, meant to deflect magic. Gojen won't notice it, and he'll find it difficult to concentrate on you. It will be as though you are standing behind a mirror. You will blend into your surroundings, so long as you do not draw attention to yourself. Don't wear it at meals, or public meetings, only when you must pass unnoticed. You see, Princess, that magic can work both ways. Now, I think Squire Eto had better escort you back to the castle."

Chapter 30
Cream Rises and Shines

"He who throws a stone above him may have it fall on his own head."
  -- German Proverb

Now that Lyru understood more about the magic being used against them, she concentrated on trying to find the object that Gojen had spelled to control Princess Niren. Like her sister, she seemed to have some innate capacity to fight the spell on her. Unlike Lyru, however, the charmed item was still in place and causing harm. Even after spending hours searching Niren's chambers, Lyru had still not found anything that seemed to match the spell which she had overheard. Still, there were moments when the 'real' Niren shone through, like a beam of sunlight on a cloudy day. Each day, Lyru invited Niren to stroll or to join her as she embroidered. The invitation was accepted perhaps one day out of four, or twice a week. Each acceptance was a triumph for her younger sister. Refusals, while more common, were still painful.

Gojen was absent from meals and meetings for two more days. On the third morning, he breakfasted with them. His face bore multiple daubs of some thick, white ointment, obscuring the wounds. He claimed that he had suffered from an outbreak of a rash which arose when a servant brought the wrong herb to him from the market place. Niren remembered her lessons about magical herbs, and looked perplexed.

"Why didn't you counter it at once, Gojen? With your stores of herbs and ointments, I would think such a minor thing as a rash would have been unlikely to get the best of you."

Then, almost as quickly as she had snapped to attention, Niren subsided back into her acquiescent state, going back to her breakfast, eating slowly. Gojen did not answer, and Niren troubled him no further on that subject.

Lyttogun looked up from his enormous plate of sausages and potatoes and eggs. His outfit consisted of a robe adorned with the images of persimmons, orange ovals with green leaves. The sight of the robe, wrapped tightly round his big body was enough to put Lyru off her breakfast of fruit with cream, and toasted bread.

"Well, now you're back and perhaps you'll be good enough to tell us where that disagreeable thief, Vyne has got to. I haven't seen him for days. Not that I miss him much, but it's best to keep an eye on him. Did I tell you he came into my room and stole some of my Lokum from me?"

Prince Ulst, sounding enormously exasperated, took it upon himself to answer for all who shared the table with them.

"Yes, Lyttogun. You have. Several times, now."

Gojen carefully listened to the exchange between princes, noting the strain in Ulst's voice, before answering.

"It sseems he was very upset by your accusation of theft, Ssheikh Lyttogun. He came and told me that he must return to his homeland to cleanse himself of the sstain of your incrimination against him. Apparently, ssuch a ritual can only be achieved in certain Gunmarine temples. I am certain that all of you have noticed how terribly ssuperstitious he was."

Princess Niren looked up again from her cup of herbal tea, and scowled at Gojen.

"You allowed him to depart without my leave? You have overstepped your bounds. You may be our regent, but this was a matter of my courtship. Daegun Vyne was here for me. See to it that you remember your place in such matters, henceforth."

Gojen blinked back his surprise at this outburst.

"Your Highness, I meant no disrespect to you. Vyne was determined to return home, especially ssince he felt he sstood no chance of winning your hand, against the likes of the other princes, such as Prince Sstohl, attending to you."

At the sound of his name, Prince Stohl jerked awake. He had actually drifted off at the table, his meal untouched. Grand Duke Depri sneered at Stohl, and his brother sniffed disdainfully.

After shaking his head at the bespelled prince's unseemly display of yawning and stretching, Gojen turned back to Princess Niren, and continued.

"Again, Your Highness, I can assure you that I meant no disrespect to you. I only ssought to ssave each of you from being embarrassed. I would have explained all this ssooner, had I not been inconvenienced by my illness."

Niren finished her tea, still frowning. Upon noticing that Lyru was also ready to leave the table, she rose. As the others rose with her, she set her face sternly.

"See to it that you do not allow any such thing to happen again. While we were not overly fond of Daegun Vyne, it was, at the very least, our duty to give him a courteous farewell. If any of you others feel a need to return to your homelands, I would very much like to know before you depart. We can only hope that our future relations with Gunmar are not damaged. Lyru, will you join me in the garden?"

Lyru, incredibly pleased by being invited, agreed and dropped her napkin over her unfinished fruit. The princes began to follow, looking to join the girls in the garden, but Niren waved them off. Gojen only rose partway from his chair, sitting again before the future queen was fully through the door.

Chapter 31
Gluttons for Punishment

"You must not throw your stones into your neighbor's garden."
  -- French Proverb

Relations between the remaining princes grew more fraught and tense, now that Depri and Edger had returned, and were working together to present Depri as the best possible choice for Niren. He was quietly attentive and respectful of the future queen. He continued to try to persuade her to stroll or dine with him. Edger put himself forward only when Lord Barin was in attendance.

With Vyne gone, Lyttogun turn his abrasive attention toward Ulst, who grew more and more annoyed by him. Lyttogun strutted around Wayhall Castle as if he were already king. Everywhere he went the clicking of his walking stick preceded him. He entered rooms uninvited, and spoke loudly and at length to anyone in earshot about how grand it would be once he was wed Niren. While he was in the gardens, he made a point of jangling the wind chimes which hung from the trees. Ulst found that his ability to like and to be liked by all had failed him when it came to this popinjay. Lyttogun eventually approached Ulst, and offered to buy the cinnamon orchid scent from him.

Ulst stared at the sheikh in distaste and disbelief.

"Why in the world would you wish to use the same scent as I use?"

"Oh, Prince Ulst, you have misunderstood me. I would buy all of your scent. And then you would smell like me. Or rather, you wouldn't, because you'd have none of it left. I have never been one to share what I liked."

Ulst refused, flatly.

"Have your own scent made up. Surely, Melloss with all its orange gold, can afford a chemist for you?"

Ulst turned on his heel and stormed away. Lyttogun was furious at the dismissal. He was used to getting all he wanted, without question or argument. Soon every meal and outing was an all-out competition between the two of them. There was much verbal sparring and jibing. Edger and Depri agreed between them that Ulst and Lyttogun were doing a fine job of eliminating themselves from contention for the throne.

Stohl of Layant was too far gone, sunk deep down in the effects of the flask to be anything more than a mild nuisance. He followed the others around, tapping his flask, rarely speaking, rarely eating, and showing no interest at all in wooing the princess.

Chapter 32
The Mother of All Interruptions

"... and their coming was like the falling of small stones that starts an avalanche in the mountains."
    -- JRR Tolkien, The Two Towers

After breakfast one morning, while Gojen and Niren were hearing weekly petitions from Midmunese citizens, with the visiting princes in attendance a great commotion was heard at the gate. Without waiting to be announced, a large, ugly woman wearing a blue dress, overwrought with lace and ribbons, sailed down the aisle toward the dais. Everyone in the throne room appeared a bit shocked by this behavior.

Gojen, exhausted and exasperated, scowled and muttered under his breath.

"Who is this troll?"

The woman didn't hear the regent's comment, but Prince Ulst, sitting nearby, certainly did. He jumped up, very much agitated.

"That 'TROLL' is my mother!"

Prince Ulst realized what he had said, and how loudly he had said it, as gasps and giggles sounded throughout the throne room. Niren and Lyru stared at the prince for a moment, until the newcomer's behavior drew their attention.

"Troll? Troll! Ulst, how dare you? What has happened to you in this wretched country? I will not allow you to speak of me that way, even if you are about to become a king in your own right."

The large woman stomped her foot, as a toddler in a tantrum might do. As she did so, courtiers could see that instead of wearing slippers and stockings beneath her dress, she was wearing dark, heavy boots, much the same as foot soldiers might wear. Duke Edger laughed out loud when he saw the boots, and then fell into a fit of coughing. Depri glared at him.

As she fumed, Ulst moved to her side. The tall prince appeared to shrink in her presence, perhaps because of her ridiculous headpiece. It seemed to be made of twigs and berries and was wrapped round with lace netting. The twigs reached at least a foot over her head, forming neither crown nor bonnet but some frightening hybrid. All of it was a bright blue which very nearly matched her dress, without quite managing to do so. The effect was quite jarring.

"Princess Niren, please allow me to present my mother, Empress Hetmi of Aggem."

Niren, and the rest of her court stared at Hetmi as she was finally introduced, and at least partially calmed down. At last, she remembered proper etiquette and curtsied. She greeted Niren with a high and very nasal voice. Upon closer inspection, it could be seen that her nose had once been broken, and poorly set.

"In the name of the Empire of Aggem, I greet you, my future daughter-in-law. I have come to help plan my son's wedding. I certainly hope that none of this nonsense will be repeated during his wedding. Now that I am present, we can begin at once with preparations for the ceremony and ball. Ulst and I will both wear blue, and you ..."

Lyru scowled at Hetmi's audacity, and waited for her sister to react to this ridiculous woman. Instead, it was the imperial prince who reacted. Ulst took his mother firmly by the arm, stopping her before she could utter another word.

"Mother! Please! All of that can wait until you are rested from your journey. I know you must be very tired. All of this will be much easier when you aren't tired and out of sorts." He never explained the 'troll' comment, and thankfully, Hetmi did not bring it up again.

Arrangements were made for accommodation, and Empress Hetmi was escorted to her suite by her son. Once they were alone, Prince Ulst set the record straight.

"Mother, really, as lovely as it is to see you, I never expected you to arrive like this."

"What, then, did you expect? Did you think I would allow, my dearest, youngest, handsomest son, to be wed without me? I should think you would know better than that. Did Princess Niren put you up to it? Such a backward little country. I think perhaps she dreaded my coming, knowing how I would overshadow her. Now, tell me, why did you interrupt me and whisk me out of the throne room so hastily?"

"No, Mother, I stopped you because you were being rude. Niren hasn't put me up to anything. You would have been invited when the time was right. Now you have stormed in here, and upset everyone. And to top it off, you were prepared to stand there and dictate to the future queen of this country how her wedding should go! We aren't betrothed yet. In fact, there are still four other princes in attendance here, courting the princess."

The empress flicked open a blue lace fan, and rapidly waved it back and forth to cool her flushed face.

"Four other princes? Why are there still four other princes? NOT BETROATHED? What ever can you mean? Your letters indicated..."

Hetmi sounded as if she were about to cry. Ulst interrupted her again.

"My letters indicated exactly and only what you wished to hear, Mother. This is precisely what I wished to avoid. I can only imagine what Niren is thinking of me, now." Ulst drew a deep, calming breath. "But content yourself in the knowledge that there is no cause to worry. Prince Stohl is... well, he's lacking. In more ways than one. Depri has already stormed away once, taking his brother with him. Princess Niren cannot seriously entertain the thought of marrying anyone so mercurial. His younger brother poses no threat to my suit. And Sheikh Lyttogun is an ass as well as a thief. The princess clearly favors me, but we cannot act like ogres in an outhouse. There are rules here, Mother. There is a way to get what we want. People want to be made to feel important, and you always made certain that I was trained to do just that. I understand what I must do to win Midmun and the future queen. You must allow me to continue this courtship without any of your interference. I really ought to insist you return home, at once."

"Ulst! I've never heard you speak to me, or anyone else, this way! Why, your late father..."

"My late father is likely enjoying the silence of his grave! Mother, I never spoke to you this way in your castle, precisely because it was yours. This castle, Wayhall, and Midmun and Niren are all soon to be mine, and I will not have you spoil it with your overbearing ways. You will show respect for me and for the others here... or mark my words, I will have you returned home at once."

"Ulsty, my dear boy, please don't say such things to me. All I have ever wanted is what's best for you. A kingdom of your very own. There were so many princes born in your generation, and scarcely any princesses. I can't stand to think of you marrying a mere noblewoman. What would your children be, then? Half royal? You are young, and Midmun is rich. Such a coup! Your children might even be born with magic! I suspect they have never told other nations everything about the Great Spell. Have you seen magic while you've been here?"

Ulst rubbed his finger over the scar on his cheek.

"I think perhaps there's more here than they've let on. All the more reason to let me finish this as I see fit. I have seen how Niren reacts to being forced one way or another. It is far more effective to cajole and flatter her. I'm already her sister's favorite, she's half in love with me, herself. Think how much that will count for, Mother. Niren is all alone, but for her sister. Will you agree to my rules, Mother?"

"Yes, yes. Of course. I'm sure you know best. You'll have her charmed and married in no time. Then you and your brother can work together to expand the empire! This is a dynasty in the making!"

"Yes, Mother, we will do just that. I have accounted for everything. Calm yourself, and watch as I work. Midmun is as good as mine."

Chapter 33
Lokum and Lace

"Newrose, oldrose, Queen Anne's lace.
Water, river, stone and sun.
Wind over hill, under tree.
Past the border none can see.
Climbing into dark for you
Will you wait in stars for me?"
   -- Ally Condie, Reached

Later, alone in his workroom, Gojen fretted about the arrival of Ulst's mother. How would she affect his plans? He couldn't spare the mana to maintain yet another spell. Eventually, he decided that he could do nothing but watch her. Much to his delight, the Aggemite Empress put on quite a show.

Meals, which of late had become tiresome battles of wit and will between Ulst and Lyttogun, soon took on a new flavor. Often Depri and Edger just sat back and enjoyed the entertainment as the others worked to destroy one another.

At first, the Empress' attention was directed solely at her son. She heeded his warning to steer clear of pushing Niren around, and indeed, found the princess so dreadfully dull and boring that she had little desire to interact with her at all. With Ulst, she was still overbearing and manipulative, but gradually her focus shifted to Lyttogun.

Here, she thought, here was a young man who knew how to go after that which he wanted. He was bold and striking, and never at a loss for words. He made it clear that he wished to gain the princess and the kingdom.

Meanwhile Ulst continued to smile, not only at Niren, but at every other female in Wayhall. He acted almost as if Depri and Edger were his friends, his equals. As if anyone else was of any importance! Lyttogun's game was all sweeping moves from the bishops and strategic plays by the knights, while Ulst wasted all of his time on the pawns. Hetmi decided to change the game. She soon spent most of her time chatting with the Sheikh. She contrived to sit next to him at meals, or during the evening entertainment. She began to touch his arm briefly during conversation.

At first, Lyttogun was a little leery of the attention paid to him by the empress. He thought that perhaps she was like her son, prone to flirting with anyone, but soon noticed that she had singled him out. While strolling in the gardens, one day, seeking to 'accidentally' encounter Niren and Lyru, he was instead approached by Hetmi. Her servants fell back out of earshot. As they ambled along, she stopped at a bend in the pathway, and laid her hand over Lyttogun's, where it rested on his walking stick. Together they admired a plant with long, slender orange blossoms, each with a single dark blue berry at the center.

"Your favorite color, and one of my favorite flowers. It's poisonous, you know, and known in some places as 'Devil's Bush', but I find I prefer the Aggemite name, 'Lover's Knot'. After all, my dear Sheikh, what's poison to one may be bread and broth to another, don't you agree?"

"Oh, indeed, Empress. Tell me, is it poisonous to the touch?"

Hetmi indicated that it was not, and Lyttogun plucked one from the stem, and placed it behind her ear. It clashed terribly with her blue hat.

"Beautiful."

Henceforth, meals were no longer a series of verbal contests between Ulst and Lyttogun, but instead a display of growing affection, or at least infatuation, between the Empress of Aggem and the Sheikh of Melloss. Certainly they were both prone to sweeping gestures and loud voices. They seemed to suit each other very well. Prince Ulst was beyond disgusted by his mother's behavior. The Socran brothers found the situation hilarious, but encouraged Lyttogun to continue to pursue

Hetmi. After all, that was one fewer prince to compete with, just as Hetmi had intended.

Niren, when she noticed anything through the fog of the spell, was a little put out that the prince, who had come to Midmun to court her, was now clearly pursuing a woman twice his age, but mostly she was relieved to have one fewer princely problem.

Chapter 34
Stone Cold

"You buy land, you buy stones. You buy meat, you buy bones."
  -- Chinese Proverb

Hatred bloomed and grew in Prince Ulst's heart. His frustration increased, both at the lack of progress with Niren, and the growing fondness between the wretched Sheikh and his mother. Hetmi was an embarrassment to Ulst. She now spent all her time in the company of Sheikh Lyttogun. Ulst tried to convince himself that, as Empress, she was acting politically. Perhaps she was seeking not to win Lyttogun's heart, but to ally her empire with his, not to mention removing the sheikh from the field of princes seeking to wed Niren. Ulst recognized the gleam in her eye when she looked at her new lover, having seen it before, and he failed to convince himself that it was strictly business.

Just after the midday meal, Imperial Prince Ulst sat in his chambers. He had pulled his chair up to a window which overlooked the garden walkways. He watched as Lyru and Niren strolled, wondering what they were saying to one another. He also watched his mother flirt and flounce along another path, burrowing deeper and deeper into the affections of Sheikh Lyttogun. Flouncing! A woman of her age and station!

Just then, a chamber maid entered his suite, unaware that he was in his room at that unusual hour.

"Oh, Your Highness! Forgive me, please. I should have knocked, but I never guessed you would be here. Please, I ..."

The Imperial Prince rose from his chair, with a smile.

Ulst closed the distance, padding over the broadloom rug in his bare feet. Even without shoes, he towered over the maid. She shivered, nearly in tears as she looked up at his scarred face.

"Here, girl, listen. Please try to stop sniveling. There's no need to cry. Have I given you cause to fear me?"

"No sir. Of course not, sir. Only, some of the other princes..."

"I am nothing like those others, girl. Tell me your name"

The young chamber maid backed toward the door, looking panicked.

"My name, sir? Why? Oh, please, please don't report me to the housekeeper and Chancellor Gojen!"

"I have no intention of reporting anything to anyone. What have you done, other than your job? But I cannot keep addressing you as 'girl'. Now, tell me your name. Please?"

The maid curtsied again, and replied, "My name is Brigga, sir. Thank you for asking."

Ulst reached down, and took her hand in his own. The girl shivered again, but seemed unable to pull away, perhaps out of fear of losing her place at the castle. Or perhaps she was falling under the sway of the amulet, which Ulst could feel pulsing on his chest.

"There, that's better, thank you, Brigga. What a lovely name. That wasn't so bad, was it? I am so glad you came in, while I was here. I have been so very, very lonely, you see... and everyone else is busy at the moment. The princesses are together, and Sheikh Lyttogun is with my mother. Prince Stohl is with his dear little bottle."

Brigga giggled at the reference to Prince Stohl and his infamous leather flask. She looked into his brilliant blue eyes, and began to relax a little, at least enough to stop trying to withdraw her hand from that of the prince. He really was as charming as they said.

"Oh, yes, my dear Brigga, I have been feeling very lonely of late. But now, here you are. I don't need to remain quite so lonely, do I?"

An hour later, Ulst stood, washing his hands in the bedside basin. Brigga lay quite motionless on his bed.

Chapter 35
Ulst-terior Motive

"Lay me down like stone, oh God, and raise me up like new bread."
 -- Leo Tolstoy, War and Peace

Several servant girls went missing from the castle staff. Rumors spoke of another fever, or even the return of the dragon, though it had only been spotted at a great distance from the castle, in the time since Misk's death. Scholars claimed that the dragon could be likened to a snake, who could eat a large meal and then go for great periods of time without eating again.

"Clearly," the chief scholar said, "The dragon hungers once again. The fact that only maidens are missing points to the dragon. The fevers struck young and old, male and female, noble and common. The dragon only took young women. It killed Prince Misk, yes, when attacked, but it did not eat him, nor did it kill and eat the squire."

Rumors spread that the princes would go and hunt the dragon, but of course, they did nothing of the sort. Only Prince Ulst, and Gojen, knew the truth. The dragon was not snatching these girls, the prince was. Each time he killed, he was filled with an elation that pushed his frustration and misery aside for a little while. Between the kills, he was filled with remorse and dread.

Questions plagued him, constantly. What was becoming of him? Where had this monster inside him sprung from? And perhaps most importantly, where were the bodies?

A convenient stairwell led from Ulst's corridor to an exit near the kitchen midden. Behind the heaps of compost, there was a corner where no one ever went. There he had hidden each of the corpses. His intent was to return in the still of the night, to dump the bodies in the river. But each time he returned, surrounded by stench and decay, the midden was devoid of dead maidens. There was no corpse, no evidence of his depravity. Ulst spiraled into madness. It was growing less and less satisfying to kill the young women. The elation, the rush of the kill lasted for a shorter period, each time. The stink of death seemed to follow him, everywhere, and he doused himself in his signature scent. He had never felt anything like this before. He found himself in a state of panic between the killings, trying to stop the urges which were overwhelming him.

One evening, after having seduced and strangled a young woman from a low ranking noble family, Ulst stared at the cooling, bruised body with horror. Turning away from the bed, he caught sight of himself in the looking glass. Naked, as he was, the amulet which lay on his chest caught his eye in the reflection. Disgusted by the sight of the beautiful object on his sin-tainted body, he grasped the silver chain and snatched it up and away, attempting to break it. Before he could snap the chain, the links grew hot, and the smell of scorched flesh reached his nose as pain seared all around his neck. Panicking, he dropped the chain and poured the water from his pitcher and basin over his head. The links cooled, but suddenly he had more problems than he had charm to escape them.

Gojen felt a shock of sick elation, through his link to the amulet, each time Ulst killed another young woman. He felt the prince's satisfaction fade to despair.

Another blow was dealt to Ulst when his mother and Lyttogun approached Niren. The two of them planned to travel together to Aggem, and the sheikh wished to officially end his courtship of Niren.

"Oh, Princess Niren, please try not to be sad. It could never have worked between you and me. You do see that, don't you? You are lovely, but so very quiet. I am afraid that while you held your peace, Empress Hetmi has quite taken hold of my heart. I am so sorry to hurt you, but my dear Niren, it was not meant to be."

Hetmi smiled at Niren, looking like the cat that had captured the canary.

"Now, do take care of Ulst for me. I fear he isn't looking very well, of late. He'll be happier, now, that I'm taken care of. He worries too much."

The princess granted her leave for travel through Midmun with some relief, knowing that she would never consider marrying the crass, selfish sheikh, and certainly happy that Hetmi would be going away as well.

She did wonder, along with Lyru and the rest of the country, what was going to happen next. Prince Stohl was still in residence in Wayhall, but he rarely made himself known. Depri showed some promise, but she still wasn't sure she could trust him. What if he up and left, again? Prince Ulst, in some ways, had been the best choice from the start, but some inner instinct warned her that there was something amiss with him, something beyond being flirtatious. Duke Edger was knowledgeable but unknowable. She hadn't the least clue as to one personal detail about the man, other than his love of the color yellow. He might be good for Midmun, but she doubted he would be good to her.

"I will have to make an effort, now, to know all of them better." she told her sister. Lyru was more than a little concerned at the thought of having any of them as her brother-in-law and king, but Ulst especially unsettled her. Although she thought him repulsive, she sometimes felt compelled to touch him, to put her hand in his. She resisted, and made sure not to stand near him.

"Perhaps Stohl isn't as bad as we think, Niren. Perhaps, with Lyttogun gone, he will step up, and prove himself worthy. I think he may just be overly shy. Perhaps that's why we don't see much of him. At least he doesn't offend nearly everyone who meets him."

"He offends me. He falls asleep when I speak to him. He pays more attention to his flask than he does to me. If you wish it, I will attempt to draw him out. But, like it or not, I must make a better acquaintance with Ulst, as well as Edger. If only I could trust Depri, I might consider him the best choice. I don't think I can. How can I have a husband and a king I don't have any faith in?"

Chapter 36
Reaping Their Own Harvest

"Let twenty pass, and stone the twenty-first, loving not, hating not, just choosing so."
  -- Robert Browning, Caliban upon Setebos

Niren tried to do as she had said she would, to become better acquainted with the princes who remained in Midmun. The stone's grip on her heart and her spirit made this difficult, but from time to time she broke free of its grasp.

Duke Edger, with his genius for finance and trade, could be an asset to the kingdom, she knew, but she never felt she had his full attention, or any chance at his affection. If she could robe herself in gold, real gold, perhaps she could capture the attention he lavished on her treasurer.

Stohl, despite the one-on-one attention, remained as apathetic as ever. He was apparently uninterested in either the kingdom of Midmun or its future queen. Each time she strolled or dined with him, Niren had to fight back the urge to ask why he was there at all.

Depri had been a little less arrogant since their conversation in the garden. He still assumed he was Niren's natural choice, but he seemed more inclined to work at listening to Niren and responding to her, rather than just assuming he knew what she wanted. She appreciated the change, but she could not bring herself to commit to making him King of Midmun, while she still distrusted the level of his dedication.

Ulst had grown thin over the course of the last several weeks. His face was pale and drawn in a near constant frown, which made the scar on his cheek stand out. He did not take the news of his mother's departure with Sheikh Lyttogun at all well. When Niren spent time with him, he appeared distracted and agitated, and not at all like the charming prince he had been, when he first arrived in Midmun. Her decision was not growing any easier.

The princesses discussed the princes while the strolled through the garden, or sewed in the solar. Since Niren was still unable to make her choice, her sister proposed a plan.

"Niren, what if you reopened the Harvest Festival this year. There's just enough time to prepare for it, and the people have missed it. We aren't in mourning any longer. And the best part is that it may help you to choose."

"I know very well that mourning is over, Lyru, but I'm not sure that there is enough time for the preparations. And I don't understand what you mean. How will the festival help me choose? I don't think anything will help with this choice!"

"The gifts will help you choose. Not those silly, showy things they brought from their homes. Or the ones their mothers sent with them from home, anyway." Lyru giggle, and Niren grimaced at the memory. "The sweet, handmade gifts of the harvest. Do you remember the ribbon crown we made for Mama one year?"

Niren smiled sadly.

"I do remember it. She wore the silly thing. She loved it. Do you think even one of these princes is capable of a real gift like that?"

"I don't know... but wouldn't it be fun to find out. Let us have the festival this year. The people deserve it, and so do we."

Niren agreed to consider it for a few days as she continued her efforts to get better acquainted with the princes.

Despite the increased opportunity to court Niren, Ulst had begun to spend increasingly large amounts of time away from her and the court. Instead, he was generally in his chambers, sometimes seducing warm bodies, sometimes disposing of cold ones.

This behavior continued as a servant came into his suite one morning to clear away the breakfast dishes. She found Prince Ulst struggling to roll up a large broadloom carpet, which had lain before the fireplace. It had been too early in the day to take the body to his hiding place without being noticed.

"Your Highness," she said from the doorway, "What is the matter with the carpet? What are you doing, sir?"

Ulst looked up from the rug, and wiped the sweat from his brow.

"Wine," he said after a moment. "I spilled my wine, last night. It's a bloody mess, this stain, and I couldn't stand to look at it for another moment."

"Oh, Your Highness, you needn't have taken it upon yourself. I shall summon the steward. He will have this taken away, at once. A replacement will be brought for you, by this evening, at the latest."

Ulst smiled down at the young woman.

"You are kindness itself to see to it. Despite all appearances, I am in no particular rush, and any time today will be acceptable. Come in, please, away from the doorway. I haven't quite finished with my breakfast, will you wait a moment?"

"Certainly, sir, if you wish it."

"Thank you. I do indeed wish it. Now, come in, and tell me, what is your name?"

Chapter 37
The Pen is Just as Mighty as the Sword

"Thoughts are scribed in pencil but actions are carved in stone."
-- Carl Henegan, Darkness Left Undone

Back in Beklen, King Hastho and Prince Jenan fretted over the situation in Midmun. They tried to keep their worry from Queen Margam, but she could tell that something was terribly wrong. Eventually, she pressed them for information, and they told her what they knew to be happening in Midmun, and what they suspected. She took all this in her stride, having regained most of her strength in the time since Prince Misk's death. From that moment, she set aside her grief and went into action, becoming one Gojen's most insidious enemies.

Her first strike against Gojen was a long letter written to Queen Ilme of Parelm. The two queens were distant cousins, and had grown up visiting one another. After exchanging the usual news, Queen Margam reached the crux of her letter, inviting Ilme's younger son, Prince Ander, to visit Beklen. A courier left with the letter that very evening.

From then on, Margam attended all the meetings that took place regarding Gojen and Midmun. She read all the correspondence from Danj, and took an active role in the plans to aid Niren. For the first time since Misk's death, she felt herself to be connected to him, and to the world of the living. She had a purpose.

Prince Jenan chafed at being tied to Beklen, unable to go to Midmun and run Gojen through with his sword. His mother recognized his dismay.

"We are all anxious and unhappy, but we have Danj there, seeing to our interests. He is wise, and he will do everything necessary. Soon we will have good news. Have faith and be patient, you will be rewarded for it."

Prince Ander of Parelm arrived in Beklen not many days after Queen Margam's letter reached his mother. He bowed deeply before the king and queen.

"I apologize for not coming sooner to pay my respects and to offer my condolences. To my great sorrow, I have been unavoidably detained in Parelm, beholden to remain there, this past year, attending to matters of state. It saddens me that I could not help you grieve my cousin. My obligation was only barely lifted when my good mother received the invitation. She and my brother send all their best, and hope that my state visit will rekindle the friendship and alliance between your country and ours."

King Hastho nodded, knowingly.

"We know, too well, that the life of one in a royal house is never one without obligations, which are sometimes heavy to bear. We have found that these burdens are lighter when we share them. There is no cause to rekindle a flame which has never gone out, Prince Ander. Parelm is ever our ally."

Prince Jenan showed Ander to the guest chambers, and told him more about Misk, and about the current state of affairs in Midmun. After a year of near isolation in Parelm, Ander was suitably shocked.

"Why is he doing these things? Why is this Gojen so bent on taking the throne? On killing? Isn't there enough death?"

Jenan shrugged, looking sad.

"Death doesn't seem to bother some men. Perhaps his life is so wretched, he believes that every other life is the same, and is of no consequence. Or perhaps he believes himself to be better than other men. That is a frightening thought, isn't it, that there are worse than him?"

Ander frowned at the thought.

"It sounds as though Otyk was every bit as bad, if not worse than Gojen. Is it possible that he was some sort of follower or pupil of Otyk? How has he gotten so close to the throne? It's unthinkable, someone so awful becoming regent! And what's being done about him?"

STONE

Jenan explained that Danj, the Beklenese court magician was currently working from inside the kingdom of Midmun, and that General Ytef and troops were garrisoned near the border.

"Do you and your father think military involvement is wise against magic? Or, if it comes to a battle of magic, will your one magician be enough? Magic can kill so quickly. It can all go so wrong."

"The military is a last resort. As for the sufficiency of the plan, we must trust Danj. We do trust him. He is wise, and his magic is strong, though I'm not sure he is capable of hurting anyone. He will find a way to use the tools and the people there in Midmun to defeat Gojen and save the princess."

Ander sighed.

"How can you stand it? Sending a magician, instead of going yourself. Sitting and waiting to hear if your brother is avenged? How do you abide being helpless?"

"Here, now! Listen! I'd go to Midmun in a moment, if I weren't bound here. But I am. My mother would be frantic if I left Beklen. She nearly lost her health when Misk died. I could never allow her to go through that kind of pain again."

Ander shook his head.

"I'm sorry, Jenan. That isn't what I meant at all. I didn't mean to offend you. It's just that so often, I feel that same frustration and helplessness. Being a prince and a knight ought to mean you have the freedom, and the power, to do anything. To do everything! Or, at the very least, the power to stop some diabolical beast from doing horrid things to others. To stop unnecessary deaths. But our swords pin our sleeves to our thrones, and we can't even stand, let alone fight. Perhaps there's a bit of power, but there's no freedom, none at all, to use it."

Jenan replied with a sigh of his own.

"You've got more freedom than I have. First born. Crown prince. Heir to the throne. Duke of This, Lord of That, and Earl of the Other. All of it is code for being forced to stay when I would rather go. Please, don't misunderstand me... I love my kingdom, and I serve with pride. But Gojen killed my brother, and there's not a thing I can do about it except wait for word that someone has killed the scoundrel... or that he's killed someone else."

"What about all of those princes in Midmun. Seven of them? That's bit of overkill! Are none of them the least bit suspicious of Gojen?"

Jenan shrugged.

"Apparently not. He has them all under his control, more or less."

"How could you have all of them there, together? I've met several of them, over the years... it must be like trying to mix oil and water."

"Yes, apparently it has been a bit like that, from what Misk's squire told us. Three of them have stormed off and gone home."

"Stormed off! Abandoned a chance for a throne of their own? It must be worse there than I imagined. And what of Princess Niren? She just lets them go, she lets all of this happen? I cannot fathom the amount of control Gojen has over all of them, and no one is the least bit suspicious?"

"Well, Princess Lyru has seen what's happening. And one of the princes was a bit suspicious, at least about some gift he was given. That was Daegun Vyne, of Gunmar. I'm guessing you did not know him, since Gunmar is so far away. By all accounts he was quite unpleasant, but Gojen killed him, horribly. He used the gift he'd given to Vyne to kill him. Princess Lyru witnessed that murder. She needs help... and here I sit, with no help to give."

Chapter 38
Dear and Departed

"Become dust - and they will throw thee in the air; become stone - and they will throw thee on glass."
-- Sir Muhammad Iqbal

Queen Margam watched with genuine and growing satisfaction as Prince Jenan formed a friendship with Prince Ander. His loneliness and frustration had not gone unnoticed. She knew how much he missed his younger brother. The two princes grew steadily closer.

In just a short while in Beklen, Ander had bloomed. Away from the stresses and strains of his home in Parelm, he grew more relaxed and more confident. King Hastho invited him to join the council debates. He and Jenan practiced swordplay and jousting together, and the queen watched them with a mixture of sadness and affection. In the span of a week or two, Ander had become part of the family.

At last a day arrived, one which the royal family of Beklen had been anticipating and dreading. Prince Ander announced his intention to travel to Midmun.

"I have to go. I cannot stay here, enjoying your hospitality, being safe and useless. Sometimes a chance comes to make good some wrong. I have a penance to pay, and this may be my opportunity to pay it. Perhaps I can make a difference. I feel I must go, and at least try to help to dispose of Gojen."

A flurry of activity followed Ander over the next two days. Beklen outfitted him with all he needed for the journey, as he did not intend to return home to Parelm before he set out for Midmun. Letters and packages were sent with him for Danj and Lyru. King Hastho also sent him off to Midmun with more than a little advice.

"Above all else, be watchful, and constantly aware. Gojen will certainly see you as a threat, an unknown, and you must protect yourself if you mean to rescue the princesses. Accept no gifts. Even if they come from the hands of one of the princesses, they may have been tainted by the magician. Take anything you are offered directly to Danj. You can trust Squire Eto, as he seems to have prevented any magical influence over him, when he rejected the sword. Princess Lyru, too, seems to have overcome his spell, but she is still a prime target. She remains second in line for succession to the throne, and will always be a threat to Gojen."

"I do not have the least desire for any magical gift, from anyone. I don't mean to accept anything from Gojen."

The king nodded, and continued.

"The future queen is still crowned by a magical aura and robed in regret and fear. As of the last reports I received, no one has been able to find whatever object Gojen has invested with his spell. Whatever that is, it is how he is controlling her. You must find that secret, and help Danj to dispel it, or Niren will never be free."

Prince Jenan shook Ander's hand, and wished him well on his journey. He tried to squelch the small fire of jealousy which flared up inside him.

"Take care, Ander. I have no wish to lose a friend, especially one who has come to feel like a member of the family."

Queen Margam did not speak, but simply kissed the young prince on the cheek as he departed.

Chapter 39
Strolling and Trolling

"I am powerless to resist it and am being turned into stone, devoid of all knowledge or feeling."
  -- Miguel de Cervantes Saavedra, Don Quixote

Eto and Lyru cautiously continued meet together at the castle, and Eto went to the Bell House as often as he thought it safe to do so. Lyru kept up her loving campaign to draw Niren out of her lassitude. At least, now, she felt she had a few small advantages. Ulst was often nowhere to be found, and Stohl made no effort to keep Niren to himself.

As they were strolling through the gardens, Niren told Lyru she had decided that she would announce the reinstatement of the Harvest Festival. Lyru was elated. Niren was less so.

"I am not feeling very festive. It's just another burden, to me, but as you say the people will enjoy it."

"They will! I hope you can find a way to enjoy it as well. Everyone is worried about you, you know. They want you to be happy. The festival is always a happy time. They will love you for it."

Niren snorted in a most unladylike manner.

"Love me? I think you are the only one who loves me, now. Tell me the truth, Lyru. Am I such a troll? Am I an ogre, that all these princes have fled Wayhall, rather than be wed to me? It's true that I didn't care a bit for any of them, but they came here for a reason. Surely... I cannot be so awful that the kingship of Midmun, with me as the queen, becomes so intolerable a thought that the princes feel they must run away home, or into the arms of that grotesque empress!"

Lyru looked at her sister in surprise. This was the most Niren had said to her in months. She smiled gently, and placed her hand on Niren's shoulder.

"You're no troll, nor an ogre either! Don't say such things! Lyttogun wanted the Aggem Empire, not the empress, surely you can see that? Well? Let him have it, an empire of cabbage fields! They speak only of growing orchids, but most of what they grow doesn't smell as sweet."

That got a small laugh from Niren.

"What about the others, then? Stohl would only be interested if I were shaped like a flask. For Edger, I would have to wrap myself from head to toe in gold. I know I should have acted as though I was more interested in them from the beginning, and shown more gratitude for their gifts, but they're all so horrid... not a bit like Misk. It's not fair to compare them, I know that, but I can't help it. Not one of them reached me. They leave me as cold as a stone in winter."

She sighed and began walking again.

"How I long to be warmed by sunshine and light again. But instead of warming me, they fight amongst themselves, and ignore me. Depri speaks well, since his return. He says the right things. But does he know me? Does he really see me? Perhaps they think of me as... as a hard little lump of something, but if I am, it's wax, Lyru, not stone. I have to think that the right prince could find a way in. He could help me. As frightening as it is, I want to let someone in, but sometimes I feel powerless to do it. Is it hopeless, Lyru? Am I hopeless?"

Lyru was so overwhelmed by the cracks in Niren's facade, she reached out and hugged her. While Niren didn't return the embrace, she did relax, just a little, in her sister's arms.

"Of course it isn't hopeless, Niren. You aren't powerless. You've been so strong, through so many hardships. You helped me learn to be strong. You can make a life with one of the princes, I know it. Of course, he won't be like Misk, but..."

As Lyru mentioned Misk, something changed with Niren. The openness of the last few minutes faded, and she became closed off again, hard and tight and unreachable.

When the sisters parted, Lyru went to find Eto. She told him of the progress that she seemed to be making with Niren, and then fell to tears at the end.

"She's so tormented, Eto. She thinks she's unlovable, and not worth loving. It breaks my heart."

"Don't fret, Princess. Obviously, there's still something left of the old Niren, something Gojen's magic can't change, and she's fighting back."

Chapter 40
The Thought that Counts

"What you leave behind is not what is engraved in stone monuments, but what is woven into the lives of others."
   -- Pericles

Chancellor Gojen had objected to the idea of holding the Harvest Festival when Niren and Lyru discussed it with him.
"It is too ssoon, Your Highnesses. Perhaps next year, when you are wed, and the country is sstable once again. Midmun needs a king. The country is sstill feeling the loss of your parents. And what will the mothers of the missing maidens think when you declare the festival open? You will appear very callous. The people fear the dragon. They come to me every day, asking what's being done."
"I would like to know what's being done, as well. You say you are watching the dragon. When will we do more than watch it?"
"We will do more when the ssigns are favorable. Would you ssend another to his death, Your Highness? I will remind you, this is a dragon. There is more to it than..."
Niren interrupted Gojen, furious.
"I know very well the danger! How dare you imply that I would send Midmun's knights to their deaths? I would slay the dragon myself, if I were a man. If I were a man, I would be the king this country needs, and you, Regent, would be dismissed. But I am a woman, and there is little I can do, but I will do that much. I can show Midmun we are still strong, and that joy can still be found. Princess Lyru is correct. The people need this. The festival will go forward."
Niren disappeared into her room, and didn't come out for the rest of the day, spent as she was by mustering the strength to break

through the stone's hold on her. Gojen scowled and sulked, and foul smells issued from his workroom, for several days.

Niren might have reconsidered her decision, but she found it impossible to do so, in the face of disappointing Lyru. She stood upon the dais with Lyru beside her.

"We are pleased to announce that the Harvest Festival will take place in one month's time. Princess Lyru will take charge of the preparations for Wayhall Castle."

The people gathered for the announcement cheered as Lyru stepped forward and smiled nervously. This was the first time she had been put in charge of an event of this scope. She addressed everyone in the hall, but most of the information was for the benefit of the princes.

"This festival has taken place for hundreds of years, with... only a few exceptions. Once the harvest is safely brought in, we celebrate a year of plenty with small, handmade gifts. The materials for the gift may be purchased, but you must make something of them. A gift of your hands and your heart, for the harvest."

The princes looked at each other. Most of them had never lifted a hand toward the making of anything. Lyru noticed these looks with a grin.

"There will be artisans in the market who will open their workspaces, and they will be happy to advise you. They will show you the way, but no one will make the gift for you. This is a long-standing tradition in Midmun. Harvest gifts don't have to be fancy, or perfect. They can be fun, and charming. I know that you princes will come up with something wonderful for Princess Niren. You should try to have fun while you do it."

The marketplace and castle were abuzz with activity for the next several weeks. Many nobles took advantage of the open forges and kilns and looms. It was well known that an extra coin could buy extra help with the gifts, though no artisan would finish a gift. Only the giver could add the final touches, such as silken ribbons tied to a wool cape. Commoners generally made their simple harvest gifts at home.

While the other princes wandered from shop to shop, Ulst prowled like an animal. He watched where they went, and slipped into the shadows when they came near him. He was racked by nerves and a guilty conscience, and he was convinced that someone would soon associate him with the missing women. The missing bodies plagued his mind. Someone must know what he was doing... why didn't they confront him, or report him?

Almost in a daze as these thoughts churned through his mind, he entered a shop where he purchased a canvas and frame, as well as some brushes and paints. When the owner asked if he needed any help with his gift, the Imperial Prince growled that he knew what he was doing, and he left as quickly as he had come.

Duke Edger resented being told to make something as a gift. He muttered to himself as he explored the marketplace. "As if I was some common craftsman. Why must I dirty my hands making a gift? That's what craftsmen are for." It went against the very fiber of his being. Well, it wasn't as if he were really wooing Niren at this point. He would make something to 'show willing'. The sooner he and Depri were in charge of this backward country, the better. He decided that he could not go far wrong with gold jewelry, and eventually found a jeweler who was willing to do most of the work, for a significant fee, which Edger was happy to pay.

Prince Stohl went from stall to shop, and made nothing except a nuisance of himself. The shopkeepers were appalled at the thought of this man becoming the king of Midmun. At last he sat at a potter's wheel, poking and prodding the clay ineffectively. The potter shaped a small vase for him, and allowed Stohl to dab some blue glaze onto it before it was fired in the kiln.

Depri took almost two weeks to begin making his gift. He could never make something to rival the jeweled egg he'd given the princess when he arrived in Midmun. How could he hope to make an impression on her? He was convinced at first that he should make some sort of jewelry for her, perhaps some gold and amethyst ear-bobs to remind her of the egg. There were several jewelers who were prepared to instruct him, but he held back, unsure, for the first time he could remember.

In a small building, next to one of the jeweler's shops, there was a woodcarver's business. Depri looked over the goods, at first with a bit of a sneer, until he noticed that while the wooden disks on display weren't ostentatious, they were beautiful.

He came every day for two weeks. The shop owner had shaped the disk from a thin section of linden wood, but it was Depri who smoothed the edges, drew the design, and carved the surface with chisels.

Edger entered the shop while his brother was working.

"My gift is done... I had to pay the jeweler a pretty penny. Why are you still working at this? Offer the man a coin, and be done with it."

"You paid for the gift? That's not how this is supposed to work, Edger. Can't you for once enter into the spirit of something?"

"Enter into the spirit of some archaic, outdated and sentimental tomfoolery? Why should I? Niren will get a gift either way. Why do you care, Depri? What's gotten into you? Let me see what you're doing."

Depri shook his head and put the disk in its box.

"No, Edger. You'll have to wait to see it, like everyone else. I won't show it until it's done, until it's perfect for Niren."

Edger arched his eyebrow, looking displeased.

"I thought we were working together. Do you want my support, or not?"

"Of course I do. This is different. There's nothing to be gained by your seeing it before anyone else. As for what's gotten into me, it will make an impression on Niren, and I find I am enjoying this. It's every bit as good as the perfect sword thrust, or arranging a tricky diplomatic contract. There's a thrill to it. If I don't care about what I've made, how will Niren?"

When the carving was done, he rubbed linseed oil into the wood, and buffed it with a cloth. The owner told him how impressed he was by the work. Depri was pleased by the result, as well. He'd never created anything before, and he happily anticipated giving it to Niren.

While the princes and princesses and the people of Midmun were preparing gifts for one another, Gojen was often out of the castle. He said he was seeking information about the dragon, which had been drawing nearer and nearer to Wayhall. He entered the marketplace from time to time, trying to find the cause of the decreased levels of mana available to him. No one there seemed capable of producing anything more magical than herbal cough syrup. He checked the Thaumery as well, but it was as empty and abandoned as ever.

Chapter 41
Perfect Pitch

"Every charitable act is a stepping stone toward heaven."
    -- Henry Ward Beecher

Before Niren had noticed, the month of preparation had almost passed. She was at a loss as to the gifts she should make for Lyru and the princes. With little time to spare, she decided on something she could easily replicate with slight variations for the four princes, a small drawstring bag. She stitched each with a symbol which brought the recipient to mind for her. The choice for Lyru's gift was even more difficult for her.

Preparations continued throughout Wayhall Castle, under Princess Lyru's careful eye. She was determined that Niren should not regret the decision to allow the festival to go forward.

On the day of the full moon, the castle gates were opened wide, and booths were set up in the outer ward, selling sweets and pastries and hard breads hollowed out and filled with soup. Children ran and laughed, and adults stood in clusters, and laughed just as much, if not quite as shrilly. Jugglers threw their balls and batons over and around people. Puppet shows were performed throughout the morning. There were foot races and archery competitions outside the gate.

Niren and Lyru watched from a balcony.

"This was a good idea, Lyru. Thank you. You've done well."

Lyru beamed. The two of them parted while Lyru went to retrieve the gifts she'd made. Everyone gathered in the Great Hall. Everyone, that is, except Gojen. No one minded his absence.

Niren, as the future queen, was the first to give and receive gifts. She took an embroidered cloth cover off the basket sitting beside her, then called Prince Stohl forward first. He bowed, and presented her with the blue glazed vase.

He parroted the traditional greeting he'd been told. "Happy Harvest, Princess Niren."

"Happiest of Harvests to you, Prince Stohl. Thank you. What a lovely shade of blue."

Niren lifted a drawstring pouch, embroidered with a tree which resembled the one on his flask. He glanced at the bag, and thanked Niren. He bowed slightly again before he wandered away to sit and watch the other princes give and receive their gifts.

Next Niren called Duke Edger to come forward. He held out his hand, and offered her two tiny, delicate ear-bobs with yellow stones wrapped in a spiral of gold wire.

"Happiest of Harvests, Duke Edger. Thank you. These are so delicate. Why, even a jeweler couldn't make anything finer."

The Duke's gift was a similarly embroidered bag, this one with a chartreuse frog with a golden coin in its mouth on the front. He noted the weight of a gold coin inside, something which Stohl had apparently missed.

"Thank you, Your Highness. I see that in Midmun you share the tradition of never giving an empty pouch. And the frog is a symbol of accumulated wealth. I am impressed that you were aware of it."

Niren smiled as politely as she could, while thinking of how well the frog represented Duke Edger.

"You are welcome. We pray you never go without, and we wish you to share in the riches of Midmun."

Edger went and sat beside his brother, who rose and approached Niren as she summoned him. Depri withdrew the wooden disk he'd finished just the day before, and presented it to the princess. She studied the carving, two crowns, one masculine, the other feminine. The crowns were angled, touching at the bottom, so that they created the image of a heart when viewed together. As she ran her thumb over the carving, Niren flushed.

"While we appreciate the fine workmanship, the implication is a bit presumptuous, Grand Duke! Interlocking crowns and a heart? Such a thing might serve as a wedding gift, but I assure you there is no certainty that you will ever wear a crown with me."

Depri's eyes widened, and he flushed as well, not in anger but embarrassment.

"Oh, Your Highness, I should have spoken my thoughts before I let you see the gift. I did not mean to presume that you and I would serve together as king and queen, though I hold out that hope. The medallion is meant to memorialize King Thowin and Queen Jaynn. Their love for one another was legendary."

Niren returned her gaze to the wooden medallion, chagrined.

"Forgive me, Grand Duke Depri. I never imagined you would choose such a gift. You have surprised me and blessed me on this Harvest Day. I wish you the happiest of harvests."

The image on the pouch she gave to him was a mountain, embroidered with gray and lavender. At the top, white ridges of snow capped the rock, and at the bottom, shades of green picked out the trees.

Grand Duke Depri ran his finger over the delicate stitches.

"I've never paid much attention to embroidery, Your Highness, but this is beautiful. It is remarkable that you can create such things out of a bit of thread. I am impressed, and I thank you for it."

As he bowed, he raised Niren's hand to his lips for a kiss. As he returned to his seat, Niren blushed faintly. With a deep breath, she summoned Imperial Prince Ulst to the dais. As he approached, she noticed that Ulst was not the man he had been when he arrived. His hair was unkempt, and his face was pale and haggard.

Ulst uncovered the painting he'd made. Niren and the others stared at it. Depri and Edger whispered to one another. There were several murmurs from those gathered to watch the royal gifts.

There was no form, but only a chaotic swirl of blues and purples and lurid pinks on a black background. Niren, who had always appreciated art, had never seen anything like it. There was beauty there, but it was buried in chaos and pain. Her jaw went slack for a moment before she recovered her poise.

"What a remarkable painting, Prince Ulst. Thank you. I wish you the happiest of harvests."

Niren dipped her hand into the basket, and pulled out the last of the coin purses. Ulst muttered his thanks, scarcely looking at the image of an orchid, which she'd sewn onto the cloth in various shades of blue. He returned to the other princes without wishing Niren a happy harvest in return.

Seeing the mood turning dark, Princess Lyru stepped forward, eager to keep the ceremony light and pleasant. She brought her gift for Niren, and gave it to her.

"Happy Harvest, Niren."

Lyru held a circle of golden wire, wrapped and tied with gauzy lavender ribbons. Three longer lengths hung down from the back. Niren swallowed a lump in her throat at the sight of it.

"A ribbon crown."

"Like the one we made for mama, so many years ago. I hoped you might like it."

"I do like it, Lyru. I like it very much."

Lyru placed the crown on her sister's head, settling it over the golden circlet of the heir to Midmun's throne. Niren reached up and adjusted it with a smile.

"Thank you. I wish you the Happiest of Harvests."

She reached once more into her basket and brought out a bit of ivory lace. Silver threads ran through the design, and made it shimmer slightly. Once it was unfolded, Lyru could see that it was a fine, ornate collar.

"I believe it's time you wore your hair up, so you'll need a collar. It won't suit any of your gowns, but you may meet with the dressmaker, and until your new gowns are ready, there are several in my wardrobe which I believe may fit you. You've gotten tall, without my noticing it. The dressmaker will have to make your gowns full length from now on."

Lyru's cheeks were flushed with excitement. The day had gone so well, far better than she might have dreamed it would.

Once all the gifts had been given, they dined together on more elegant versions of the foods being sold in the market. The meal opened with stuffed squash. Venison stew was served, then roasted pheasant with plum sauce and baked potatoes. Wine flowed freely, and the mood was as festive and light as it had been at any harvest festival in the past. Dessert was apple tarts served with sweetened cream.

When everyone had eaten their fill, the evening's entertainment began. The princesses and princes and a few nobles sat before a stage. A choir of children from the village stood at the rear of the hall, and began to sing as they walked, single file to the stage. They sang of the rich harvest and the gifts of the heart. As they passed, Duke Edger noticed what the children were wearing. Each boy and girl wore a short surplice in yellow silk. The boys had large brown bows at their throats, and the girls had orange ones. They finished their song just as the last little girl stepped onto the stage. They began a second song, but Duke Edger interrupted them. He stood, and glared down at Princess Niren.

"This is what you've done with my gift? SMOCKS for grubby little children? Brats, in MY SILK."

Niren also rose, to face him. Her face and voice were as chilly and distant as his were hot and angry.

"Your silk? No, Duke Edger, you gave that silk to me. Once the gift is given, the recipient has the right to use it as she sees fit, and the giver forfeits all say. So I think you will find that the silk was MY SILK, and now it belongs to the lovely choir, whom you have interrupted. Now be seated, or be gone."

Duke Edger chose the latter option, and stormed out of the hall. He went and found Lord Barin, and they left immediately for Socra. Depri watched his brother go with a look of disgust.

Niren sat once again, and at a signal from her, the choir began to sing again. While the children's voices soothed the princess, and the others, Ulst found them unsettling. He slipped away, followed discretely by a young noblewoman who had been watching him.

Section 3
The Advent of Ander

*"Let them not make me a stone
and let them not spill me,
otherwise kill me"*
   -- Louis MacNeice, A Prayer Before Dying

Ander made his way across the mountains between Beklen and Midmun. These countries were very different than his home. Parelm was low-lying forests and farmland. Many of the villagers made their livings as fishermen or woodsmen. Their magicians worked with the woodsmen, selecting trees which would suit their purposes. They carefully maintained the forests health, as well. In similar fashion, they told the fishermen where and when to fish.

In Beklen, many magicians used their magic for arts and pleasures. Musicians and entertainers often had gifts which aided them in their art. Children were taught to recite and sing and dance, as well as act out legends and folk tales. They also aided their farmers and vintners and all the people who produced the food and spirits. They saw to the health of the crops and the quality of the final product. A wine which had been watched over by a magician was almost always much more potent and appealing than one which had been made without aid.

Midmun had once been the strongest of the three countries, both in military might and in magic. Their ability to heal had always been unsurpassed. And, while their magicians were in control, no other country could forcibly cross their borders. Magical barriers were added to the mountains and shorelines.

Ander wondered how they've been managing for twenty-five years with such a little bit of magic remaining. He smiled grimly to himself. A country without magic might be just what he needed.

One question remained. Could he be what that country needed, in return?

Chapter 42
Ander Abroad

"A rolling stone gathers no moss, but it gains a certain polish."
   -- Oliver Herford

   Prince Ander arrived in Midmun several days after his farewell to the royal family of Beklen. He went directly to the Thaumery, as instructed by King Hastho. He searched there for Danj, but instead found the magical epicenter of Midmun to be abandoned by all but the caretaker, who was clearly not the man he was looking for. The air in the building set his skin tingling, raising the hairs on his arms and the back of his neck. Just as he was about to give up, a little boy appeared from the shadows between two nearby buildings.
   Jobias beckoned to him, crooking his finger, and trying to look nonchalant.
   "My Gran said you'd come soon. She sent me looking for you. Again! You are the prince, aren't you? You're the one who was coming to help us, and the princesses?"
   Ander smiled down at the eager boy, who had dark hair and eyes.
   "May I ask, who is your Gran? How did she know that I was on my way here? And most importantly, young man, who are you?"
   Jobias grinned and announced his name.
   "She's my grandmother, Debran. I'm her translator. You'll see when you meet her... If you come with me, if you ARE the prince. You ARE the prince, aren't you?"
   Ander bowed.
   "Well, Master Jobias, I am 'a' prince, if not 'the' prince. I am Ander of Parelm, and I am pleased to make your acquaintance. Will you take me to your Gran? I very much wish to meet her."

"Thank the stars and the bells! They just kept sending me back here, my gran, and Danj, looking for you. Every day! And you never came, at least, not till now. It's not so far to walk, because I'm nearly grown, now, but I'll be glad to stay home."

Ander listened, greatly amused by this young man, but taking care not to show his mirth.

"I'll take you home. That's where Gran is, now. We stayed here a while, but Danj decided we could go home. I didn't like staying here at the Thaumery, anyway. It just stinks of ghosts, I don't mind saying."

It seemed that young Jobias did not much mind saying anything and everything on his mind as they walked to Debran's cottage. He'd grown a little precocious, being privy to everything Danj and Debran discussed, and he wanted to make a good impression on this prince.

"Anyway, you're a good bit better than that other fellow. He was named Vyne, like plants on an old house. He called himself Daegun Vyne, whatever that means. I didn't like him a bit. But he's dead now. Anyway, we're here. This is the Bell House."

Jobias ushered the new arrival into the small and tidy cottage. The rows of bells and hooks took all of the prince's attention for a moment, then he remembered himself. Debran curtsied and Danj bowed, and Prince Ander introduced himself. All the while, Jobias made himself useful with translations.

The four of them settled around the little wooden table, and exchanged information, while they sipped tea and ate pastries. Danj was glad to get a first-hand account of the state of affairs in Beklen. Margam's returning strength and resolve were especially welcome news to him.

"I am so relieved that it is you who has come, and not Prince Jenan. When Debran first heard of the coming of a new prince, I feared he might come to avenge his brother, without regard to the fact that he is the only heir remaining in Beklen."

"Jenan wishes he could come to avenge Misk, and to stop Gojen."

"He'll be needed before long, to play his part, but now is not the time."

"He can't come. He doesn't want to hurt Queen Margam. We'll have to do the best we can without him. I only hope my presence here is for the good, and that somehow I can make a difference. I will try to avenge Misk for Jenan, and I will be honored to lend my sword to the cause."

Debran gestured to Jobias, who turned to the prince.

"She wants to know, what about your magic? Will you use that for our cause, too?"

Ander put his tea down, and frowned.

"Only if I absolutely must, and only as a last resort. Enough of that. I don't wish to speak of my magic. Please, tell me more about Gojen. How did he come to be regent, and why is he the only one who had access to magic for so long?"

Danj told Ander what he knew.

"Thowin was a young king, and one who had never expected to rule. In his first years on the throne, he sought advice from many quarters. At first, Gojen was one of many who guided him, but over time, his support and council edged out that of all the others. Nothing about him seemed amiss, while Thowin was alive."

"Where did he hail from? Is he Midmunese, or a foreigner?"

Danj sat back in his chair, thinking before speaking.

"I suppose he is from Midmun, he sounds as though he was born of a noble family near the capital, but I could be wrong. He has a bit of a speech impediment, and that plays havoc with an accent."

"Then Thowin would have known him before the Great Spell? I just don't understand how someone like him was named as Regent. Aren't there other noblemen who rank higher? For that matter, we don't even know his rank? Was he part of the Great Spell? Did he earn his rank there? I don't mean to press you, but I feel I must know whom I am up against, if you wish me to... to do whatever I can do to aid the princess."

This time Debran answered, with Jobias translating for her.

"Gran says she's lived here all her life, and she never knew a thing about Gojen, not until a couple of years after the Great Spell. He's not from any noble family, not here in Midmun, anyway. She can't tell you about his accent, of course. It could be that he's from Rand, or even Beklen. Neither of those is very far away, and they speak about the same as we do."

Danj shook his head.

"I'd know if Gojen was Beklenese. None of our nobles are unaccounted for. Perhaps he is Randish then, but it strikes me as strange that none of the visiting princes recognized him, either. I suppose they would be too young to remember him."

Prince Ander sighed.

"We are still in the dark. Is there nothing else we can do to learn more of him? Or must we simply guess at it? I feel ill prepared to face him, as it stands now."

Danj explained that this was the very reason they had left the Thaumery.

"We came back here to prepare. Firstly, because it is likely he watches the Thaumery for magic use, and might be able to detect a larger spell there, especially if he is the focus of that spell. Even with wards in place, we couldn't ensure that we would remain hidden. Secondly, Debran needed access to all of her bells, not just the few she could carry with her to the Thaumery."

"Anyway, that place is haunted! And I wanted to come back home."

The three adults smiled at the outburst from Jobias, and went on to discuss the spell they were planning.

Chapter 43
Ulst Undone

"The proud, the cold untroubled heart of stone, that never mused on any sorrow but its own."
    --Thomas Campbell

After the harvest festival, Ulst's tenuous grip on sanity slipped again. He killed three young women in as many days, and each time he tried a different hiding place. This was to no avail as the bodies were missing, just the same as they had been from the midden.

Standing in the graveyard, where he'd hidden the third body, some final dam of reserve broke. He grasped the chain around his neck, determined to be rid of it. He tried to snap it, but as before, he failed. He ran into Wayhall Castle. Tears traced the path of the scar on his left cheek. He pushed people out of his way, ranting and raving as he went. At last he arrived at Gojen's workroom and burst through the door.

"Enough! Lift this curse! What have I done to deserve this? Lift it at once, or know the wrath of the Aggemite Empire!"

Gojen looked up from his work bench, sliding several of the replica gifts to the side. He covered everything in a length of white cloth before turning toward the Imperial Prince.

The prince ripped open his dark blue doublet, sending brass buttons flying in every direction as the threads holding them snapped under the strain. The sight that met Gojen's eyes was horrifying and grotesque. The chain of the amulet was buried in Ulst's neck in a ring of red welts, having burnt its way into his flesh as he attempted to remove it. Worse than the chain was the amulet itself. Almost all of it was shrouded in the bright, puckered flesh of the prince's chest. Only the tip of the sapphire protruded from his skin, the clear, bright blue a startling contrast to the putrid and charred flesh beneath.

"Lift this killing curse from me! It won't come off! Help me!"

Finally, Ulst stopped screaming, and stood panting and clawing at the sapphire. Gojen stared at him, apparently nonplussed. He arched one eyebrow, and at last raised his eyes away from the sapphire to the prince's face. As he spoke, he ran his fingertips over his beard. Ulst could still see some of the wounds, still unhealed and covered in an amber ointment.

"A curse? I daresay it does look as though you've been cursed, but how would I go about lifting it, Prince Ulst? You know there is very little magic here in Midmun. I can send for help, perhaps from Beklen. Meanwhile I can produce a healing salve, or some medication..."

"A salve? Look, you fool! Look at my chest! My neck! What good will a salve do? You laid this curse on me when you gave me this amulet!"

"Again, my prince... I do not possess such art, nor the access to the level of magic required to place such a curse. The amulet is a gift from Midmun, not from me. Have you taken it off, and let it fall into the wrong hands?"

Ulst closed his eyes and trembled with rage.

"I have not taken it off, since you gave it to me. I CANNOT take it off! I am trapped in it! What is it you want? You want me to leave Midmun? I will leave at once, just lift the curse! I won't marry Niren, you have my word. Please. PLEASE!"

"I don't have that sort of power, Your Highness. You understand that magic was eradicated in the Great Spell..."

"The Great Spell was years ago, and you, you... demon, you have found a way around it! Ever since you laid this chain over my neck it has been choking out the good in me, and making me do... Never mind! Never mind what I have done! I will give you one chance more. Lift This Curse From Me!"

Gojen stood, listening to the prince rave. He reached beneath the cloth, and took the amulet's twin. He held it aloft, and the amulet slid down the chain. Ulst grabbed for it, but Gojen closed his hand over it and shook his head, dismissively.

"I cannot do that. But before you go, I must thank you for the bodies you've been providing. You're right about the Great Sspell. I have found a way around it, and the magic requires sso much mana. The ssteady ssupply of newly killed maidens has been just enough to fuel it, of late. Their terror, your elation, and yes, even their bodies. I knew the amulet would drive you mad with desire, but I've quite outdone myself! You're correct. There is a curse, and you have been feeding it."

Gojen laughed as Ulst ran from the room, screaming that he would find a cure, and revenge, once he reached the Aggem Empire.

He went straight to the stable, where he saddled his own horse, tears streaming down his face. Grooms and stable hands stared in shock at his ripped clothes and the wound on his chest. He laid his spurs into the horse and left at a gallop. His shrieks could be heard echoing between the castle and the stone wall which surrounded it.

Chapter 44
Dragon It Out

"Deep in the shady sadness of a vale,
Far sunken from the healthy breath of morn,
Far from the fiery noon and eve's one star,
Sat gray-haired Saturn, quiet as a stone,
Still as the silence round about his lair."
   -- John Keats, Hyperion

   Gojen packed each of the gifts away in his vault. He removed a cloth-wrapped item before closing up the vault, with a chant under his breath. He cleared a large space on his table, placing bright oil lamps on either side of the space, but he left the center clear. Slowly, carefully, he unwrapped the cloth.
   Gojen examined the green dragon scale. It was slightly shorter than the palm of his hand, with serrated edges and a hooked point. His fingers trembled as he stroked the pitted surface. So much power lay within the scale that it seemed to pulse with its own energy. So much power, but so very difficult to control.
   Taking a soft brush from a container on the table, he swept away any dust the surface, as well as several white threads which clung to the rough edges. He tested the sharpness of the hooked point against his thumb and took special care at the base, which was as sharp as any knife.
   Gojen walked through the castle and out onto the wall, far away from the gate or any of the guard houses. He rolled up his sleeves and began to chant over the scale.
   "Fierce fiend, full of fire,
   Fear and panic to inspire

Breath hot, heart black
Born to bring me what I lack
Wings, talons and teeth employ
Take to the air, hunt and destroy
Carve away this human sshell
And sstoke the fire none can quell!"

    With that, Gojen ran the sharp, hooked point down his forearm, tracing the scars of previous transformations, some barely healed. He trembled as he allowed blood from the cut to cover the dragon scale completely. With a deep breath, he thrust the base of the scale into the cut.

    Gojen screamed, a sound of bitter pain, but also of elation, of triumph over the spell, then the noise was transformed into the bellow of a beast. Between one breath and the next, the magician's form shifted and expanded. The long broad sleeves of his robe became leathery wings, and his skin darkened as it transformed into scales. He was now the dragon, perched on the wall. His talons dug into the stones, leaving long scars, while his great wings began to flap. He pushed off the wall, and glided downward, pulling up at the last moment. His head lifted, and his wings beat the air as the tip of his spiked tail grazed the ground.

    Gaining height, the dragon circled the castle several times. He reveled in the screams which reached his ears, trumpeting and spewing flames into the air. After he completed another sweeping circle, he turned northward, following road which Ulst had travelled. In the distance, he could see dust being kicked up by Ulst's galloping horse.

    As a dragon, he flew much more quickly than any horse could run, even a horse being spurred on by a rider gone mad. Soon no more dust rose up from the road, but instead a plume of black smoke polluted the sky. Lying on the ground, at the base of the plume, was a perfect silver chain with a sparkling blue amulet surrounded by ash and char, and nothing more.

Chapter 45
The Bell Curve

"You will find something more in woods than in books. Trees and stones will teach you that which you can never learn from masters."
   -- Bernard of Clairvaux

   Preparations for the seeking spell were under way at the Bell House. The table was laid with a padded white cloth, and Debran selected a variety of bells, which Jobias placed on it. Danj asked several questions, and made suggestions. He had learned a remarkable amount of hand signs in the time he had spent with Debran and Jobias.
   Ander had grown up with magic in Parelm, but he had never seen anything quite like this. Jobias grinned at him, once again feeling smug and smart. The prince couldn't help but grin back at him.
   "Gran always says she learns more from the bells that don't ring than the ones that do. Does that make sense, anyway? All of them sit there, all the time, not ringing."
   "I suspect she means she learns from the ones that don't respond when she is actively using them, asking them to ring. Think of it like this... If you are lying in bed, late at night in the dark, and you can't fall asleep, is that the same as not falling asleep while you are running down the road?"
   "Oh! I like that! Anyway, it makes sense. What kind of magic do you do? Are you going to help Gran and Danj? I can't wait to see it!"
   The grin fled Ander's face. His whole body stiffened, and he sat up straight in his chair. He frowned and shook his head.
   "No. I intend to help them, but not with magic. Not unless I absolutely must."

Jobias looked disappointed, but only for a moment.

"Anyway, you never did tell me what kind of magic you have. Do you have six toes, like Danj does?" He wrinkled his nose, and pinched it closed at the thought of stinky feet. He laughed, then launched back into his high-speed speech. "I can tell you're not blind, and both of your eyes are the same color... blue. Maybe you have an army of ghosts. Oh! I bet you can make weapons do more damage. I heard a story, once, about a soldier whose sword never got dull, and he was the best soldier in the king's army, but then the king got scared of him..."

"No, Jobias, my magic isn't like any of those things. It isn't something I want to talk about. Be a good lad, and go outside to play for a bit. If your gran needs you, I'll come and find you."

Jobias sighed dramatically, and went out to the garden as instructed.

A little while later, Prince Ander called him back into the Bell House. Debran and Danj were prepared to begin the seeking spell.

"Galangal is used to aid those who seek justice. Vervain allows for truer divination."

Danj scattered the table with a fragrant mixture of the powdered root of galangal and dried vervain leaves, then joined Ander and Jobias to watch.

Debran began ringing the bells. Sometimes she would ring the bells individually, and sometimes two or three together. To Ander and the others the bells sounded musical, but not magical. Some of them were high pitched, light and tinkling and bright. Some were deep, sonorous and resonant. Debran handed most of the bells back to her grandson, who put them neatly back in their places. She rang different combinations of those which remained on the table, pairing and re-pairing them until she was satisfied. At last, she stepped back.

Ander watched intently, fascinated and perplexed.

"What does it all mean? Did your bells tell us more about who Gojen is? Or how we can defeat him?"

Debran paused for a long moment, reviewing the positions of the bells, before she began her explanation.

"Most of the metals, tin and brass and bronze, didn't do much good." Jobias translated. "But gold sure did. See that little gold one, right in the center. She says it rang out, loud and clear when she asked it about Gojen. He likes gold plenty, but who doesn't? Anyway, she says he doesn't get along with steel, at all. I guess that's why he's a magician, not a soldier. The rest of the metals aren't as strong, but none except gold and silver tolerate him. China and wood and stone are so-so."

Debran signed again, and Jobias blinked. He signed back, and she repeated the gestures with a nod.

"She says he's afraid of glass. Isn't that strange? Who's afraid of glass? Anyway, she can't tell much else, he's got too many wards."

"How can a metal like a person?"

Danj looked askance at Ander.

"Everything in nature has affinities. A magnet is drawn to iron. Red wine gives some women a headache. Pollen makes young Jobias here sneeze. These are not random occurrences. The universe has rules, both magical and mundane. Didn't your tutors teach you these things?"

"They may have. I'm afraid I tended to ignore my tutors when it came to magic. I've never liked having my 'gift'. I wanted to be a knight-prince, not a spell caster." Ander blushed, looking embarrassed, "I mean no offense to you."

"I take no offense. You may always speak your mind with me."

Ander rubbed his hand through his hair.

"So, for all of that work, we haven't learned a thing."

Debran began to sign, but Ander interrupted.

"No. We don't know anything more than we did, before. He's a magician, and he seeks gold, he wants the wealth of the kingdom. We knew that. I hope I haven't come here in vain, raising your hopes, only to find I am certain to fail."

A flurry of activity between Debran and Jobias began as Ander ended his melancholy speech.

"Gran says you stop it, and stop it right now! You came here for a reason, and nothing is ever certain to fail! She says that if you want to turn tail and run away, you'd best do it right now. If not, if you're staying, if you're going to help the princesses and stop Gojen, then you have to be willing to do everything you can. And she says that everything includes your magic, because her bells tell her that's what it will take."

Debran stopped signing. Jobias fell silent. Danj just watched the prince.

Ander walked to the door, but not through it. He stood there, with his arms wide, grasping the posts so tightly his knuckles turned white. He took several deep breaths with his chin on his chest. It looked as though he was fighting back either angry tears. After another moment, and a breath that shook his entire body, he turned and faced them. They were watching him with concern on their faces.

"I hate my magic. I hate how it feels as it goes through me! I hate what it does! If you knew how it felt, if you knew.... You wouldn't ask me."

Danj went to Ander and put his hand on his shoulder. After long years as a teacher and friend to Jenan and Misk, he naturally fell into those same roles with Ander.

"You hate your magic, so you refuse to use it. You don't use it, so you don't know how to control it. You fail to control it, so it controls you. It controls you... so you hate it. Now is the time to end this cycle. You must learn to use it, just as you learned to use your sword. Debran and I will help you."

Ander let go of the door posts and shook Danj's hand off his shoulder.

"I don't know what good learning about it can do, my magic only hurts, it only destroys. No good can come from it."

Jobias darted forward to catch Ander's attention.

"My Gran says you're wrong. Magic is a tool, like a saw, or a sword, and the user decides if it's good, or not..."

"Your Gran is wrong! You don't understand! You don't know what I've done! Do you want to see? Everyone wants to see me use my magic? Well, then, LOOK!"

Ander's whole body began to tremble and shake. With a violent gesture, he raised his left hand toward the ceiling, and pointed with his right index finger at the huge brass bell in the corner. The air around him buzzed, and was filled with an acrid smell. Bright white sparks gathered in his left hand and traveled over and through his body, and then went arcing across the room to the bell.

The bolt hit the Great Bell, and it pealed as though it had been hit by the hammer of the gods. Several other bells rang, as well, in response to the vibrations, but the sound of the great bell went on and on. Debran screamed and covered her ears.

Chapter 46
For Whom the Bell Tolls

"As soon as stones can swim, leaves will sink."
   -- Japanese Proverb

As the peal of the Great Bell faded, Debran slowly drew her hands away from her ears. Tears were streaming down her cheeks. Jobias ran to her side, frightened by her reaction. He started signing at once, asking her what was wrong, but she placed her hands around his smaller ones, stopping him.

Removing her hands from his, she signed two words. *Speak.* *Quietly.*

He looked up at her in wonder, shaking his head.

"I don't even know what you want me to say, anyway."

"Oh!"

She hand-signed and spoke at the same time. Her voice sounded thick and heavy, like syrup.

"Oh, Jobias! I did not think I would ever hear your voice!"

Ander stared at Debran, startled and confused.

"I don't understand. The bell was loud, yes, but... how could even the loudest bell make you hear again, and allow you to speak?"

It was Danj who spoke first, as Debran was still clearly too overwhelmed to answer the prince.

"This is the Great Bell, isn't it? It was constructed and consecrated for the Great Spell. I recall my father speaking of it, but I never put two and two together. Surely you've sounded it since then?"

Debran held her hands near her ears, but not quite over them, as if she was afraid of another loud sound.

"We have tried to ring it, many times. There was no magic left in it. All the other bells, I could hear... I could hear the magic in them, even with the magic in Midmun diminished. The Great Bell was dead. It only sounded like a wooden mallet hitting a wooden block. There was no peal. No echo. No magic."

Jobias ran over to Prince Ander and wrapped his arms around the prince's waist.

"Why don't you like your magic, anyway? When you can make it do a miracle like that! None of the healers could cure her! No one else had magic that could fix her ears! I wonder what will happen the next time you use your magic on the Great Bell."

"Don't ask!" Ander cried. "Don't ask it of me. I won't use my magic again. Don't you see, it could just as easily have harmed her? It could have killed her. It could have killed any or all of you! It's better not to use it at all."

Debran frowned, swallowed hard. Then she found her voice again, and spoke with growing confidence.

"I must disagree with you, Prince Ander. I have three reasons for doing so."

Ander grunted and looked skeptical, but did not interrupt.

"Firstly, I disagree with you out of my great gratitude, for that which you have done for me. You have accomplished what no other could do. You have performed a wonder. I have never heard my grandson's voice, until your spell, today."

Jobias nodded, and went back to Debran's side, to hold his Gran's hand, since she was no longer using it to sign.

"Secondly, it is wrong and dangerous to refuse to use your magic. It will fester inside you, and may soon go afoul, wreaking havoc, the very thing you fear. You must control it, not conceal it. It is as much a part of you as your lungs. If you feared the air, and held it in, you would die. Your magic is no different, you must take it and and let it out, just as you do with your breath."

"Better I should die than chance another's death!"

Debran continued, ignoring the prince's outburst.

"Thirdly, my prince, I disagree because today we have gained a great amount of knowledge. I heard more in the peal of the great bell than just a loud sound. I heard a name. Two names which are familiar to us, one old and one new, but both of them tied to the magic of the Great Bell. Otyk, for whom the bell was created, in order to drive him out of Midmun, and Gojen, who seeks the same throne that Otyk sought. You asked where he came from, and you have received your answer. In fact, they are one and the same. Gojen is Otyk."

Jobias and Danj stared at Debran, stunned by her revelation. Ander refused to look at her, instead keeping his eyes on the Great Bell.

In Wayhall Castle, far out of the range of the sound of any mundane bell, Gojen lay on the stone floor of his workroom, writhing in pain.

Chapter 47
The Practice of Magic

"Patience can cook a stone."
   -- Fula Proverb

Ander was working in the garden of the Bell House. After a great deal of argument, he had finally consented to practice his magic. Danj placed wards around the garden to protect Debran and Jobias, then arranged rows of targets on poles. These were made of many different materials
"Brass. Oak. Coal. Elm. Shell. Gold. Bread. Bone."
As Danj called out, Ander gathered power from some unseen source and let it flow through him and out into the target. The air around the cottage had a sharp, metallic tang, and the faint smell of charred wood.
Outside the wards, Eto stood with Jobias and Debran. As they watched Ander, they explained their recent discovery. He was dumbfounded by the news of Otyk, and thrilled by Debran's recovery of voice and hearing. At last, Danj spotted Eto, and relented. He dropped the wards, scuffing the herbs with his foot, and breaking the circle. Ander stood with his hands on his knees, panting and frowning. He wiped the sweat from his brow, and joined the group.
"Prince Ander of Parelm, allow me to introduce Squire Eto. He was the messenger who bore Princess Lyru's plea to King Hastho, which brought both of us here to Midmun."
Eto bowed, and smiled at the prince.
"Well met, Your Highness. You are very welcome here. Princess Lyru will be so glad to have your help. I hope you don't think it too

forward for me to speak for her that way. It's not that I don't know my place, I assure you, it's just that with everything happening as it has..."

Eto broke off his nervous train of thought as Ander held up a hand to stop him.

"Indeed, well met, Squire Eto. I pray I can assist the princesses. I understand that Prince Misk chose you from amongst all the candidates from Midmun, to be his squire."

"Yes, Your Highness. It was the greatest honor of my life."

"I have heard that you served him well. You have shown estimable courage and loyalty to both princesses. I would be pleased and honored to have your help. I will need someone whom I can trust inside Wayhall."

Eto was nearly overwhelmed with relief. He'd been so worried that the prince would not approve of him. At least one weight was lifted from his shoulders.

"You can count on me. I think I'd better try to prepare Princess Lyru, to tell her that you're coming. She can help Princess Niren accept you."

Together they arranged that Ander would go to the castle in two days' time.

"The truth is, you got here just in the nick of time. The dragon's been seen again, much closer to Wayhall than ever before. And just about that time, Prince Ulst went mad. The grooms in the stable haven't stopped talking about him. They say he had horrible wounds around his neck, as if he'd tried to hang himself. He rode away, screaming about curses."

"Did anyone go after him? Try to help him?"

Eto took a deep breath.

"No one's been able to find him, since. Duke Edger left too. Princess Niren took the silk he'd given her, and had robes made for the children's choir. He said it was wasted on the brats. He stormed off and took the treasurer with him. With them gone, that leaves only Stohl and Depri at court. Depri isn't too bad. He did give Princess Niren a wonderful Harvest gift. He's already left court once. No one knows if he would stay and challenge the dragon, if it came to that. And Prince Stohl doesn't lift a finger. Well. He lifts one finger. He taps his flask and falls asleep."

"That flask sounds like a curse as well. Gojen has had all the princes under his thumb. It sounds like the ones who've left have been the lucky ones."

"Gojen says we've all been lucky that the dragon has stayed away so long. Well, I know better. I know it isn't luck at all. He's using magic to summon it, to call it from its den. He's never around when it comes out, I'm sure he's in his workroom, casting some spell to control it. He says he's in there working on a way to stop the dragon."

Eto trembled.

"That dragon killed Prince Misk, and I swear, I will kill it before I allow it to hurt Princess Niren, or Princess Lyru."

Danj placed his hand on Eto's shoulder.

"I am certain you are correct Squire Eto. He is tied to the dragon. He must hold some charm over it, allowing him to control it. He must think he is very near his goal, with only two princes remaining in Niren's retinue, and Stohl not a very likely one at that. But no one is to face him or the dragon, alone. We must work together. Prince Ander, you will certainly cause Gojen to panic. That could be dangerous, for everyone. You must take great care once you are at court."

Chapter 48
Something Other than Love

"Something there is that doesn't love a wall,
Where they have left not one stone on a stone."
  -- Robert Frost, The Mending Wall

"Prince Ander of Parelm."

Ander bowed as the herald announced him. He stood and smiled up at the future queen and at her younger sister. Having recognized Gojen from the descriptions he had heard, he nodded his head to acknowledge of the acting regent.

Niren watched the new arrival from her throne. She had been surprised by the announcement of yet another prince, here to try for her hand. She thought she had exhausted the West Whitsen's supply. Grand Duke Depri frowned deeply at the sight of the newcomer. When Ander made eye contact with him, he replaced the frown with a blatantly false smile. Prince Stohl barely noticed what was happening around him.

"We welcome you, Prince Ander, though we fear your arrival is nearly too late. We in Midmun value promptness and punctuality. You may present your gift to my lady-in-waiting."

"I beg your pardon for my tardy arrival, Your Highness. My obligations in Parelm were quite unavoidable, and lengthy in their nature. I came here after my travels had led me elsewhere. I do not have a gift for you. I hope to win your friendship, affection and respect, not to buy them."

Niren stood, her cheeks reddened, and her eyes flashed with annoyance. Her anger broke through the stone's influence.

"My friendship, my affection and my respect cannot BE bought! I resent the implication that I can be won over as easily as that."

"Your Highness, I fear I misspoke. Of course those things can never be bought. I believe gifts should come later, when both of the people involved are more certain of one another's feelings, and motives. Please forgive me, and allow me a new beginning."

Niren took a deep breath, and the color drained from her cheeks as anger turned to embarrassment.

"I see." Her voice took on a chill, and she returned to her throne. "It was impolite of me to assume you brought a gift. Your princely predecessors all believed that they could procure an advantage over the others with some trinket or bauble."

"Perhaps I can visit the marketplace, if a gift is truly required."

"It's a bit late now, much like you."

Ander took a steadying breath, and turned to a less fraught subject.

"I have brought greetings from Parelm, Where my brother King Dulas and my Lady-Mother, Dowager Queen Ilme wish you joy and peace. Also, from my cousins in Beklen, where the king, queen and prince have asked me to make it known to you that their great love for you has not diminished, and never will."

Niren quietly thanked Ander for the messages, and ordered a suite of rooms to be made ready for him. Gojen showed the newly arrived prince to the suite. There, he questioned him closely.

"Prince Ander, we are thrilled that you have come to Midmun. We are honored by your presence here, but at the ssame time, I am curious. At that time of Prince Misk's unfortunate death, Queen Jaynn and I began researching the sstatus of princes throughout West Whitsen, or the near the nearby islands. Your brother was ineligible because he held the throne of Parelm. And you were also ineligible, due to a betrothal. I can tell you that Princess Niren will not take kindly to news of you breaking off an engagement to come here for a chance at a throne of your own."

"Chancellor Gojen, your words border on the insulting. I have done no such thing."

"I will require an explanation of the termination of the betrothal. You sseek the hand of the future queen, and the highest position in

Midmun. I don't know you, and I don't know if I can trust you. I must protect the throne of Midmun. It is my primary function in my role as Regent."

"Lord Gojen, whether you trust me or not, I have no intention of anything other than coming to know the princess. She was more than just a means to an end for my cousin, and I hope that she can be as happy as circumstances will allow. She has been through a great many tragedies, and I think I understand a bit about that, so perhaps she can find a sympathetic friend in me. If I am the best choice, then so be it. If I am not sufficient to the task, then it will be she who makes the choice, not you. She may judge my character, my motives, and my intentions for herself."

Static electricity set Ander's hair on end. Gojen felt a twinge of pain, reminiscent of the agony which had recently incapacitated him. Muttering excuses, he left and beat a retreat to his workroom. He rifled through his possessions, looking for an item he could spell for this problem of a prince, on such short notice. He needed something to counter or contain Ander's magic. Just the hint he'd sensed set his teeth on edge.

Jewels and jewelry were out. The prince wore none, and did not appear to be the sort inclined to do so. Food and drink were possibilities, but without proper research, how could he know what would best suit Gojen's need to exacerbate Ander's faults? What WERE his faults? What were his strengths?

Gojen sat at his desk, holding his throbbing head. As tempted as he was to answer the call of the scale, to feed the hunger that was gnawing at him, he needed to conserve mana to perfect the spell on Ander. Hopefully, he could force the prince to leave before he interfered too much. Soon he could feed as much as he liked.

Chapter 49
These Boots are Made for Walking

"Any stone in your boot always migrates ... to exactly the point of most pressure."
  -- Milton Barber, The Physical Laws of Backpacking

After a great deal of deliberation, Gojen decided he would give Ander a pair of boots. The boots were constructed of supple brown leather, and stitched with a pattern of swirls and whirls. The tops, meant to reach almost to the knee, were folded down several inches. Below the fold, brass buckles held the sides of the boot neatly together.

  "Boots of leather, ssturdy and sstrong,
  Lead you astray and lead you wrong
  When you sset your foot upon the track
  These boots assure you won't come back
  Each sstep confuses and confounds
  Carried away, and out of bounds
  Caused to falter, sstumble and sslow
  Forget where you are meant to go"

Gojen had the boots delivered by a castle page, knowing that the prince was already suspicious of him. A note proclaimed the boots as a welcome gift from Princess Niren. Prince Ander, expecting just such a visit, allowed the page to enter his rooms and place the boots by the door. Thoroughly warned by King Hastho and Danj, Ander never touched the tainted gift, although he found his eyes continually drawn to the complex spiral patterns.

Knowing that Gojen now thought he was under control, he smiled grimly to himself. He left his chambers with one last longing look at the boots. As he walked down the corridor, he rubbed his hand over his eyes. The further he got from the boots, the less they impressed him... the less they called to him. For the first time he felt a smattering of sympathy for the other princes. Without magic of their own, they had little chance to resist. No one had warned them not to accept the gifts from Gojen. No one had told them that Gojen was there, not to choose the one prince most suitable for Niren, but to kill or eliminate each of them.

Walking through the gardens, next to the reflecting pool, he took deep breaths of the cool air, and cleared his head. The boots had thrown him. He hadn't prepared himself for something simple and subtle. He'd come expecting jewelry or a weapon, something more impressive than footwear. Well, now that he knew a bit more about Gojen, he felt better prepared to face him.

Facing Niren was a different story altogether. She was beautiful, yes, but that wasn't what gave him pause. Beauty was only a small part of her attraction. Far more evocative was her manner, her refusal to be regarded as a prize at a fete. She must be feeling so cheapened, to be offered again and again as an accouterments to the throne.

In the distance, he saw her strolling with her sister. He cast a coin into the pool, wishing for an opportunity to dispel the princess, whether or not that included an opportunity to win and woo her. He rejected the idea of following the princesses, or arranging a meeting along the path. Instead he returned to his room, determined to get the boots to Danj and Debran as quickly as possible for study. He was more than a little surprised to find that the boots were not beside his door, or anywhere in his suite.

While Ander had been in the garden, Eto had gone to look for him. He was curious to find out what gift Gojen had given the newly arrived prince. When he knocked on the door, there was no answer except the sound of someone kicking the door. Worried that Ander was in trouble, possibly gagged and bound, Eto burst into the room. As the door opened, the disembodied boots stopped kicking, and walked themselves down the corridor. Mystified by this, the squire followed.

The boots wound their way through the castle's halls and passages, and then led Eto out through a seldom used door, into the garden and up to the rear section of the wall. From there, they jumped, landing on the outside of the wall, and ran down the path leading northward. Eto lowered himself and dropped to the ground, then followed the boots for several miles. Finally, the boots stopped in a pile of ash and char, with something blue just showing. Eto prodded the ash with a long stick, and uncovered a long silver chain, and Ulst's amulet. The boots remained where they were, unmoving, looking as if they had been left there by someone who walked away barefoot.

Carefully, using his long stick along with a shorter one, Eto carried the boots and the necklace directly back to the Bell House.

With the boots delivered to Ander, Gojen was satisfied that the prince would soon be under his control. He glanced at the vault holding the spelled items, but instead of renewing any of the spells, he withdrew the dragon scale, prepared to indulge in the consuming need to transform and feed on fear and flesh.

Chapter 50
Flesh and Fire

"... if there were no dragons of flesh and blood and fire, whence would come the idea for these stone carvings?"
  -- Robin Hobb, Assassin's Creed

Gojen went out into the farmlands which supplied the castle and capitol with wool and leather as well as beef, mutton, pork and produce. Once he was well away from any inhabited land, he spoke the spell, and plunged the scale into his arm. When the transformation was complete, he began to feed in a meadow of sheep, consuming a ewe and her lamb. He was about to move to the place where the sheep had scattered, when he spotted a shepherdess, crouched and trembling behind a formation of boulders. The hunger for a maiden had been growing since he'd killed Ulst. Her slingshot and staff offered her no protection. With his appetite sated, the buzz and chatter of the dragon scale in his mind had quieted. He flew over the hills and meadows for hours.

Upon his return, he found the castle in an uproar over the return of the dragon. Their terror both pleased and agitated him. He assured everyone that he was busy working on a plan to rid the country of the beast once and for all.

"You must trust me. Allow me time to continue to sstudy the ssituation, and to find the ssolution. I am well aware of the dragon's flight. I have been afield, trying to learn more about it. You will not need to fear the dragon for much longer. Unless ssome of you wish to go and dispose of it? No?"

Back in his workroom, he lifted the long sleeve of his robe, and retrieved the dragon scale. His blood had turned the iridescent silvery green almost black. He cleaned the scale and wrapped it in the protective cloth. He went to his vault to stow it, and retrieve the other spelled objects.

    As he began to work, he realized the scale was still there, in its cloth, on the table. Its buzz was already growing loud in his ears, again, and he hadn't put it away at all.

Chapter 51
Alone

"And He's kneeling in the garden
As silent as a stone
All His friends are sleeping
And He's weeping all alone."
   -- Andrew Peterson, The Silence of God

    Having found himself alone, unable to find Squire Eto, and without the boots to take to Debran and Danj, Ander returned to the gardens. He found a bench, shaded by a tall oak. As he watched the sun setting, he contemplated the twists and turns which had led him so far from home, and from everything he had ever imagined his life would become.

    He suddenly felt overwhelmed by sadness. He missed his family and his former fiancée He missed the certainty of knowing who he was and where he belonged. He yearned to be back in a time and place where his value was determined by his skill with a sword, and his honest good nature, not by his ability to defeat an evil magician.

    Yet he was here because he was drawn to Midmun, and to Niren. Something here called to him, and had done so since his mother had received the letter from Queen Margam. There had never been much doubt in his mind that he would come. All the doubts were about his abilities, not his intentions.

    Now he was here, and he was determined to make a difference. Prince Ander stood, suddenly resolute. He would find a way to win the battle, and to win the princess' hand and heart. He would not fail again.

On the other side of the garden, near the reflecting pool, Niren sat under the shade of the pavilion, watching the sunlight glint on the water, and on the coins beneath the surface. She sighed, but no one heard it, because she was alone. She had strolled for a while with Lyru, but sent her away after a bit. Niren's ladies-in-waiting were chatting with one another a small distance away, waiting to be called upon.

Niren was pensive as well. One by one the foreign princes had paraded past her. Each of them made her feel more isolated, and forlorn. This new prince, Ander, spoke well, and said the right things, but that didn't endear him to her. Several of the princes had started by saying and doing the right things, and had failed to be the right person. And where had he been, why wasn't he amongst the ones her mother had spoken of? What was his explanation for his tardy arrival? Where could he lead her, were she willing to follow? Was he any better than the others? She sighed unhappily.

Lyru was alone in her room, working on her embroidery. She felt so helpless. What good was sewing, dreaming of her trousseau, when at any moment she might be made Gojen's concubine?

Gojen too was alone at his workbench. The white cloth was spread out on his table, once again and the dragon scale lay upon it. The vibration was so pronounced, he could see it. In fact, he could barely take his eyes off it. He was compelled to have it within arm's reach. Grand Duke Depri was packing his brother's belongings to be sent back to Socra. Stohl was resting in a comfortable armchair in his room, tapping his flask.

Chapter 52
A Slip of the Tongue

*"Snake glides among stones, coils and loops and hisses,
Forked tongue darts as fast as an arrow, aims and misses."*
   --Moira Andrew, Snake

   Control. Gojen longed for control, over the kingdom, Niren, the princes... But he was losing control of his own mind and body. He woke at night with the dragon scale next to his head on the pillow, although he was certain he'd locked it in the vault. He could hear its call all the time, now, hissing in his head. It never relented.
   He left his chambers, seeking to put physical distance between the scale and himself. He couldn't transform nearly as often as it seemed to demand. As he neared the great hall, he came across Ander, returning from the garden.
   "Ah, Prince Ander. I ssee you have been making yourself at home, here. Isn't it kind of the princess to allow you to court her, even as late as you've arrived?"
   "It is very kind. I hope it will benefit her. Are you going to keep baiting me about that, Chancellor?"
   "I would not ssay baiting, My Lord Prince. I would ssay I am concerned, and I would not have to continue to ask, were you to answer the question, once and for all."
   "That information is privy to the King of Parelm. I was required to remain there, in mour... in my brother's service. I am here. Let that suffice."
   Gojen frowned, and rubbed his chin through his beard. The wounds had finally scabbed over, but none were completely healed.

"And the boots from the princess? Do they fit? Is there any problem with them? I ssee you aren't wearing them."

Gojen sounded a bit desperate, to Prince Ander.

"I thought it rather odd that she sent a gift after our discussion. Of course, it was generous of her. They're exceptional boots, but I have no cause to wear them yet. Such a fine pair is for combat, and I have no enemies here."

"The generous princess may take exception to the fact that you are refusing to wear her gift."

"I am hardly refusing when I say I will wear the boots only when the occasion calls for it, and not while strolling through the gardens of Wayhall. Any warrior would know when to wear boots such as those. Obviously, you are not an expert on such things. If the princess wishes me to wear the boots, then I am certain she will ask that I do so."

"I sshould make you aware, Arch Duke Depri is very near to winning Princess Niren's hand. Prince Sstohl is sstill as much in contention as he was when he arrived. I would not let ssuch a thing come between the two of us, if I were you. "

Ander's hair was all on end, and Gojen could smell the magic in the air around him.

"Thankfully, Chancellor, you are not me."

This prince was as bad if not worse than all the others. He was even more arrogant that Depri! Now Gojen could practically taste Ander's magic. It was actinic and bitter.

"Prince Ander, you sspeak as if you mean to insult me. You ssay you have no enemies here. If you continue to sspeak to your hosts in that fashion, you may ssoon earn enmity."

Gojen's voice grew louder, not shouting, but trying to be heard over the buzz of the scale. Why was it so loud, at this distance? Surely he'd secured it in the vault? But no. No, here it was in the pocket of his robe.

"And you, Chancellor, speak to me as though you were my equal. You are the regent, not a prince. Watch your tone, perhaps the other princes were lenient, but I demand respect. I could almost believe you were trying to drive me away."

Irate, Gojen's pale face reddened. His hands were balled up at his sides. Suddenly, a bright flow of blood coursed over his left fist. The self-inflicted wound in his wrist had opened and was bleeding freely. Although Prince Ander could not see the cause of the bleeding beneath Gojen's long, broad sleeves, he could not help but notice the blood.

"Take care, Prince of Parelm. You are not royalty here, either, but only a visiting dignitary, unless Princess Niren chooses you. I can ssee to it that sshe considers you a prime candidate, or that sshe does not consider you, at all."

Ander watched for a moment as the blood dripped down, and puddled on the stone floor. Gojen didn't seem to notice the blood, but his odd speech was growing more and more pronounced. That made Ander look up. Just as he did so, he saw the chancellor's tongue flick out between his lips. Twice, or perhaps three times, and almost so quickly that he doubted what he'd seen. Gojen's tongue was forked!

Gathering his wits, Ander returned his gaze to Gojen's left hand.

"Chancellor, you are bleeding. Don't allow a discussion about the appropriate footwear to stop from seeking the attention you need."

Gojen's eyes flicked down to his left arm.

"This is nothing but a sscratch. I was handling ssome plants with rather lengthy thorns, this afternoon."

He reached around his left wrist with his right hand, holding his sleeve tight against the wound. Soon the fabric was stained.

"A scratch? Plants here in Midmun must be as deadly as dragons. Perhaps you'll want to get that bandaged and cleaned. It never pays to let a small wound fester."

Chapter 53
About the Boots

"When nothing seems to help, I go look at a stone cutter, hammering away at his rock, perhaps a hundred times without as much as a crack showing in it. Yet at the hundred-and-first blow it will split in two, and I know it was not the last blow that did it, but all that had gone before."
   -- Jacob August Riis

   Eto arrived at the Bell House, with the boots slung over his shoulder on the stick. Jobias let him in when he knocked. Under the curious eyes of Danj and Debran, he placed the boots on the table, and put the amulet beside them.
   "The three of you won't believe the tale I have to tell you. In fact, I'm not quite certain I quite believe it myself."
   Debran could see that Eto was shaken.
   "Sit and tell us, and I'll pour out the tea." Debran spoke and signed at the same time, her hands habitually forming the shapes after all the years. Jobias, freed from the duty of translating, sat on the floor and played with wooden blocks and carved figures. He had built a castle from the blocks, surrounded by carts and wagons.
   "I had gone to Prince Ander's room to find out what kind of gift Gojen had given to him. I was curious to see if perhaps he'd tried another sword. When I got there, I heard kicking at the door. I thought the prince must have been hurt, or bound, so I rushed in. Only... he wasn't in the room. There was no one in the room at all. There were only these boots, kicking the door. The moment I opened the door, they strolled out, on their own. It looked as if they were being worn by an invisible man, or a ghost."

Jobias, long used to listening to adult conversations, stopped playing and rushed to the table to hear the rest.

"What was it? Was it someone invisible, or was it a ghost?"

Jobias made silly "OOOoooOOOooo" sounds until his Gran silenced him with a stern look, so that Eto could continue.

"I still don't know what it was. I suppose it must have been some sort of magic. I followed along, after the boots, just a few steps behind them. They went through the passages of the castle as if they knew just where they were headed. They kept going downward and toward the back. They went out through the kitchen garden, and up onto the wall."

Jobias risked his grandmother's wrath. "Did they stop there? Or did they float away like a ghost?"

"They stopped for a moment. There were six huge gouges in the wall, there. Then the boots jumped down off the wall. I'm sorry, Jobias, they did not fly or float. I lowered myself to the ground. When I caught up to them, they were walking north, at that same quick, steady pace. I am glad the road was empty. I don't know what I would have said if anyone had seen me following the boots, like a hunter follows his hounds. After a few miles they stopped again. I watched for a bit, to see if they'd continue, but they stayed there. Just in front of them, there was a pile of ash and char... And there, at the center, was this amulet."

Danj used Eto's stick to lift the chain. The amulet was not scorched or broken, not damaged in any way.

"Do you recognize this, Eto?"

"Yes, it belonged to Prince Ulst. I never saw him without it. And none of us at the castle have seen him, for a while. Another servant girl has gone missing as well. There's some talk that they went off together."

Debran and Danj spent the best part of the next hour examining the amulet and the boots, he with his herbs and charms and she with her bells. Jobias grew bored and went outside to catch frogs and climb trees. At the end of their studies, Danj confirmed that the magic of the amulet was Gojen's, not Ulst's.

"The magic matches that which we found on your sword, Eto. The sword didn't tell us much, since you rejected it quickly and completely, its magic became inert. Be glad that you did so. If you'd handled the sword, and used it, especially if you'd used it to draw blood, the consequences would have been dire. The stain of that same magic is on the boots as well."

Eto whistled an all clear signal, one used amongst knights to signal that some danger had passed.

"You said that the sword unbalanced you, and tried to pull you along after it? I think the boots were made for a similar purpose. They were meant to keep the wearer on certain set paths, or off certain other paths. Had Prince Ander worn them, or even tried them on, he would almost certainly have been led astray, to somewhere he had no wish to visit."

"I don't understand how and why they went where they did, without anyone in them! You can't imagine how unnerving it was, watching them walk away, empty. Following them was bizarre. It still has me spooked!"

"I am certain it was very unsettling for you. The spell on them was very strong. It may have even influenced you to follow them. When their intended 'victim' refused to wear them, they followed the path of their maker's most recent magic. It is clear to me that Gojen sent the dragon to kill Ulst. The amulet is marked by death. Not just Ulst's death, but the deaths of many. I believe that Gojen spelled the amulet to lead Ulst, as the sword would have led you, or the boots would have led Ander. It took him down a very dark road."

"Do you mean that Prince Ulst was killing people? What people? The missing servants? Could Gojen have made me kill people if I'd used that sword? I think I liked Midmun better without any magic. What chance does Ander stand against him? Or Princess Niren, or Lyru or any of us?"

Danj rested his hand on Eto's shoulder, calming him.

"Remember what I taught you. Magic can't do everything. It can never change the very essence of who a person is. That is why you rejected the tainted sword, and why Ander never tried on the boots, though I am certain they were spelled to draw him to them. Gojen wished to be rid of him, and quickly. We should thank our lucky stars, as well as King Hastho, that the prince was well warned."

As Eto finally calmed and settled, Debran changed the subject.

"Has Prince Ander met with Niren? Tell us, is there any hope of a match?"

Eto related what he'd seen of Ander's first meeting with Niren. As he did so, Jobias came back inside.

"Are you done talking yet? Gran, I'm hungry, can I have my supper? Anyway, I want a piece of white cloth, so I can make a ghost for my castle."

Chapter 54
Snap and Sizzle

"We should build with the stones we have."
-- Swedish Proverb

After his unsettling encounter with Gojen, Ander found his way through the streets of Wayhall Village to the Bell House. There he found the missing boots as well as Eto, still discussing the boots and the amulet. Over the next half an hour, Debran and Danj filled the prince in on all they had surmised.

"So, if I had worn the boots, I would have gone to the place where Prince Ulst died? That seems counter-productive, so far as Gojen is concerned. Why would he want me to see that evidence?"

Danj shook his head.

"Where they would have led you is hard to guess, Prince Ander. I am certain you would have found it difficult, if not impossible, to resist their lead, once you were wearing them. Even with your magic, they would have overwhelmed you. I am glad you were well warned."

"I wanted to wear them. To touch them. I could scarcely look away from them. That's why I left the room. I thought perhaps I could find Eto, and we could bring them here, together. But I am glad that I did not, for I have yet another strange log to add to this fire."

Debran bustled around the kitchen, and served her guests tea and ginger cookies. As they ate, Ander revealed Gojen's secret.

"I came across him in the corridor near my room. I rather got the sense that he was checking to see if I'd already worn the boots and to find out what happened when I did. Of course, I didn't let on that they were missing. I told him that I would only wear such fine footwear in combat. Well, if I wanted combat, I found it in him. Gojen questioned me over and over about the boots and my intentions. He said I would earn Niren's wrath and enmity by not wearing them. He sounded desperate... almost frantic."

Debran smiled, slightly.

"You've got him worried, dear prince. He doesn't know what to make of you, and you're already resisting him more than any of the others managed to do. None of the others has their own magic... they hadn't much chance of resisting his gifts. "

Ander ran his hand through his short, brown hair, making it stand up around his head like the white fluff of a dandelion weed. Those in the room with him could hear the snap and sizzle of static electricity.

"I almost feel sorry for them. They were lured here to their death and destruction. However much I dislike it, at least my magic saved me that fate."

"You might not feel that way, if you'd known them, my lord. They weren't worth much, especially not compared to Prince Misk."

"Eto, I did know them. At least I had met a few of them. Several years ago, Depri and Edger of Socra came to Parelm, as part of a trade and diplomacy mission. Of course, Edger was far more interested in trade than diplomacy, but every country needs someone like him, even if he makes a dreadful dinner companion. Depri could be abrasive, but so can many commoners. I met Ergan of Rand in his home. I can't say the two of us were ever likely to become friends, but he was passionate and brave. That is more than I can say of myself this last year. The effects of the spells from Gojen must have caused far more damage to their personalities. And Squire, the time will come when the people of Midmun will have to cease in comparing everyone to Prince Misk."

Eto was immediately ashamed of himself. He apologized at once.

"All is forgiven, Squire. At any rate, I have much more to tell all of you. As the two of them argued about the boots, Gojen became more and more agitated. That lisp of his kept getting worse and worse. He told me I was not royalty here! I reminded him that he, too, was not royalty. He grew so furious, he balled his hands into fists... and then his arm began to bleed. He didn't even notice, but blood was dripping onto the floor and pooling there. And just as I drew attention to the blood, I looked up at his face. Can it be that none of you have ever seen it? The man has a forked tongue! He was so irritated that it flicked out from between his lips. I thought I was facing a demon."

Debran's face paled. Danj placed his hands over his face. Eto just stared at Prince Ander in fascinated horror.

Danj recovered himself a little more quickly than the others.

"Does he know you've seen it? Is he aware that he showed it?"

Ander considered, for a moment.

"No," he answered, "I don't think he knew that I had noticed it. Really, all the blood was just as unsettling. What does it mean?"

"It means that we were wrong about him. He isn't controlling the dragon. He is becoming the dragon. And if he is as unstable as you are telling us... the dragon form is winning, and the human form and nature are diminishing. Soon there will be nothing left of the man, however awful he is, he will be easier to best as a man than as a dragon. We must not delay."

Debran cleared away the dishes and cups.

"Then, Danj, it is time for you to return to Beklen. The bells won't be silent, we need Prince Jenan. I will pack some supplies for you."

"Jenan? No! I know he'd wish to slay Gojen with his bare hands, to avenge his brother, but how can you ask him to come? He is all his country and his mother have left?"

"My lord prince, the bells, or rather the magic in them, tell me that we require Jenan. Would you, like Misk, face the dragon, Otyk, alone? Will you, like him, die alone?"

Chapter 55
Along the Primrose Path

"With aching hands and bleeding feet
We dig and heap, lay stone on stone;
We bear the burden and the heat
Of the long day and wish 'twere done.
Not till the hours of light return
All we have built do we discern."
   -- Matthew Arnold, Morality

Since Ander's arrival in Wayhall Castle, Depri had been blustery and dismissive. Stohl had ignored him as he ignored everything. Ander spent most his time avoiding Gojen and gently pursuing Niren. He spent what time she allowed him with her by speaking quietly of those things they had in common. They discussed policy and politics often. She was worried that trade and diplomatic relations with the countries of the rejected princes would deteriorate. It was hard to dispute that this might occur, but Ander attempted to reassure her as they walked through the sunlit garden.

"Each of the princes knew they stood little chance, with seven of them here. Their elder brothers or fathers knew that as well. You can only choose one prince."

Niren picked a late blooming flower from beside the path, and smelled it, thinking of Prince Misk. After a minute or two of silence, she turned to him again.

"And what about Parelm, Prince Ander? Will our relations there remain friendly, if or when I do not select you as my husband? How will you and your family treat with us?"

"My brother is a fair man. He will not punish you when, or if, you do not choose me. I would like to think I am a fair man too. I would never ask that he punish you, and all of Midmun. Still, I hold out some small hope."

Niren blushed a little and shivered as the wind increased. Soon she excused herself and started off to find Lyru. Ander bowed, and watched as she walked away with her ladies-in-waiting. Before she was halfway back to the door, Niren thought better of fleeing, and she turned back to continue her discussion with Ander. She was determined to choose a prince, soon. Stohl had continued to fail to impress her... so... the decision was down to Depri or Ander. She would force herself to make the choice, then the others could move on, and she could begin her reign.

As she approached, she noticed that Depri had joined Ander. He must have been waiting for a chance to speak to him, alone. She stopped, just out of sight, but near enough to hear their conversation.

"How is it that you, who were both late and last to arrive here, get more time with the princess than any of us? What's your game? I nearly had her convinced that she should choose me. Do you know how hard I worked on the gift for the Harvest Festival? Do you know how many days I spent covered in sawdust and linseed oil? How many little cuts and scrapes I got on my knuckles? Of course you don't. You weren't even here!"

"Listen, I wish..."

"Then she was upset! She said I was presumptuous! It took a little quick thinking, to make her think I'd made a gift to honor her parents. But she believed me, and she was nearly mine. And then you stroll in, and she's unsure, once again. She may not be sure, but I am. I am sure she is bound for great things, with me as her husband. I am sure I want to wed her, and be king of Midmun. And I am sure you are in my way. So, Prince of Parelm, what would it take to send you back home? My brother left a great deal of gold behind when he went back to Socra. Name your price."

Ander bristled, running his hand through his hair, making it stand on end.

"Are you mad? You're every bit as greedy as your brother. Princess Niren can't be bought and sold!"

STONE

Princess Niren herself appeared from behind a tree. She'd overheard every word. The spelled stone could not begin to dull her outrage.

"Grand Duke, we require that you quit these premises at once. We will send your possessions and your precious gold to you in Socra. You are no longer welcome here, and if you are still in my castle in one hour's time, I will have you returned to Socra in chains and without your gold and without your ridiculous hairpiece!"

"Princess..."

"Go now, or with a little quick thinking on my part, and you will be mine. My prisoner! GO!"

"You would not dare."

"Depri, all the things I would dare would amaze you. Many things about me might have amazed you, had you once bothered to look beyond the end of your own nose. Now, GO!"

Depri turned on his high heeled boot and stormed down the garden path.

"Princess..." Ander began.

"Please, don't say anything. Not another word. You cannot imagine how tired I am of the voices of princes. You're all so clever! 'One so sharp, he'll cut himself!' Well, I've been cut, too, and the wounds run deeper each time. The stone isn't WORKING!"

Niren ran off, in the opposite direction from that which Depri had taken. Ander was left reeling. He called out for her.

"Princess! Wait! What stone?"

Niren did not stop or answer him.

Chapter 56
I Was Drowning, and You Threw Me a Brick

"But which is the stone that supports the bridge?"
-- Kublai Khan

The princess ran along the garden paths until she was exhausted. When she stopped running, she went to find Gojen.

"This stone of yours... this chalcedony is failing, Chancellor. These princes are getting too close! They're hurting me. Well, Depri has hurt me for the last time! And Prince Ander... I fear him. He stands to hurt me more than all the others, combined."

"Ander is a fresh face, that is all. There is nothing sspecial about him. He arrived and was ssimply a bit of a welcome change."

Niren shook her head. She still had tears in her eyes.

"That isn't it at all. Is the stone worn out? Has it been too long since you created it? Or is your spell not strong enough to protect me from a real prince? Perhaps none of the others even tested it."

"Princess," Gojen drawled, his voice oily and condescending, "How could you know whether or not the sspell was working? It worked perfectly with all the others. I feel ssure that it has been tested with each of the sseven princes. It has kept you ssafely distant from every prince who came to woo you. Each of them has felt it. That is why you cared not one bit for any of them. It has not failed you, and it is not failing you now. You are overreacting."

"Gojen! I am not overreacting. I order you to check and renew the spell. It is failing. I can feel it. It must be at full power... I must make my choice soon, before there are no more princes left to choose from."

"As you desire, I will check on the sstone. Sspeaking of your choices, I also find Prince Ander a bit unsettling. You would do well to continue to consider Prince Sstohl, and Grand Duke Depri."

"Depri! He thinks I can be bought and sold. I will never choose him. You needn't mention Depri ever again, unless it's an order for his arrest. I have ordered him out of the castle."

Gojen assured Niren that he would see to it that Depri was escorted to the border, and that he would check that the spelled chalcedony was functioning.

Niren was not wholly satisfied by Gojen's reassurances, but she was unable to rouse herself further, exhausted by the day's emotions. She went to her rooms to rest, ignoring an invitation to stroll with Lyru in the garden.

Once Niren was gone, Gojen opened his vault. Oh, yes, he intended to check and strengthen the spell on the stone. This sort of emotional upheaval should not have been possible in the princess.

First, though, he wanted to touch the dragon scale, and enjoy the rush of power he felt when he held it. He emptied the vault, searching for the scale. It was not there. Dread and panic began to take hold...

No. There it was, in his pocket, safe and sound, but not at all where he thought he'd placed it. He unwrapped it and held it on the palm of his hand. He was instantly soothed, but soon he felt the gnawing need to transform and feed. With great difficulty, he put the scale down.

He placed the blue chalcedony next to the dragon scale, and chanted the spell over it. Everything went just as it had before, the stone was still working. It hadn't exploded, no pain came rebounding back at him. Niren had been fighting the effects, but she could not hold out much longer. He was so near his goal. Edger and Depri were gone again. He would drive Ander off, and see to Stohl.

The people would see that Niren was unable to make a choice, and was therefore not fit to be queen. A few whispered rumors would see to that. Princess Lyru was too young, too weak, too childish to be a threat to him. The charade would soon be over, and the crown would be on his head. He'd keep both princesses alive. Killing them would upset the kingdom, and they would make suitable concubines. Once he had his heirs, he could rid himself of his nieces.

Chapter 57
Sunlight, Shadows and Stone

"Laughter went on and on, like sunlight and stone, even if the human beings who laughed did not."
    -- Robin McKinley, Chalice

Niren avoided Ander, and everyone else, for several days. It was easier to dismiss her feelings, and the depth of her emotions while she was isolated and alone.

Ander approached Princess Lyru, and they discussed the incident with Depri. Lyru had never gotten the whole story, and she was pleased that Ander would include her. They talked for some time, and Lyru grew cautiously hopeful that he could be a real help to her Niren.

"Princess, your sister said something which puzzled me. After Depri left, she went, too. As she walked away, she cried out that the stone wasn't working. What stone? Do you know?"

Lyru shook her head.

"The stone isn't working? How perfectly bizarre. Could that be what we've been looking for? A stone? How could he use a stone to control her?"

"I don't know, but we'd best keep it in mind. Perhaps Danj and Debran will have a better idea."

Eventually, with coaxing from her sister, Niren emerged from her rooms again. As she and Lyru were strolling they found Ander sitting near the reflecting pool. As they approached, he rose to meet her. Lyru and the ladies-in-waiting fell back. Determined to see if the stone was once again in full effect, Niren invited him to walk with her. The two of them spent several minutes in silence, then Niren turned to him.

"You've never said why you came. Or why you came so late. I do think I deserve to know, if you wish to continue to be considered."

Ander chose his words carefully, neither lying nor revealing the whole truth of his purpose in Midmun.

"I came because my cousins suggested that I should do so. They had heard that you had not yet made your choice. Perhaps they thought we would be well suited. Perhaps they only wanted something for me to do. They hoped I would understand some of what you have endured. They continue to wish for your happiness."

"What about your happiness? Is there nothing for you to do in Parelm? You are a prince. Surely you are important there, and have work to do? "

Ander sighed, and ran his hand through his short hair, a habit of his when he was upset or agitated, she had noticed.

"My brother, Dulas, has been king there for three years. He had been nominally in charge for two years before that, after my father had a stroke which paralyzed his right side. Dulas is comfortable in his role. The work of the kingdom is well seen to. Our borders are clear and not in dispute. In a few years, I will take my nephew as squire, as is customary. Currently, I am not assigned to any specific task. I went to visit my cousins, in Beklen, and then I came here. I am glad I have done so."

Niren smiled a little.

"I see. But why have you waited so long to come? I don't recall your name ever being mentioned when we began to discuss princes."

Ander hesitated for a moment, and frowned before he answered.

"I was beholden to remain in Parelm for a year. I believe your custom demands that mourning lasts a year as well? It is as simple, and as complicated as that. I could not have come sooner."

With a quiet "Oh", Niren turned back to the path.

They continued to walk together for a while, in silence. The weather was turning cooler, and the trees lining the path were shedding their autumn colors. The sun shone through the branches, and leaves blew gently across the stepping stones. Niren's foot caught an edge, and she stumbled. Ander steadied her, taking her elbow for a moment, until she was safe and sound on her feet. A shiver went through her body at his touch.

After a moment, she pulled her elbow free of his hand.

"Thank you, Prince Ander. I believe I will return to the castle."

When he turned to accompany her, she shook her head.

"Alone."

As she walked away from him, she shivered again at the memory of his touch. She paused and looked back over her shoulder.

"I suppose you must think that because you are a better candidate than Prince Stohl, or Depri, or any of them... that I will have to choose you! I wish I didn't have to make this choice at all! I wish I could be queen alone. I hate this law. I hate that Misk is gone! Well, perhaps I must... must make the choice, and perhaps I must choose you, but that doesn't make you anything like my first choice. Not anything like as good as Misk! I would still rather have him than you!"

Chapter 58
Inches and Miles

"Not an inch of our territory, not a stone of our fortress."
  -- Jules Favre

Danj returned to the Bell House with Prince Jenan, having again used his magic to speed the journey. There they met with Ander and Eto. Together they planned the final assault on Gojen. Lyru bristled at being excluded, but there was no safe time for her to leave the castle.

Danj spoke firmly, detailing his thoughts to those gathered around Debran's table.

"When the time comes to confront the dragon, the battle will not be fought by one man. We know, too well, that one-on-one combat will fail. Prince Jenan, you will be responsible for the physical attack. Squire Eto will assist you, and follow your lead. Debran and I will do all we can to shield you with our magic, and to heal you, if necessary. Remember that the mana pool is very limited, and Gojen will be drawing on it as well. We will have to pace ourselves, and to keep some mana in reserve. Prince Ander will head our party, and use both his sword and his sorcery. Magic cannot do everything, a fact which Gojen appears to have forgotten. Neither magic nor physical force alone will win this battle."

Prince Jenan sighed.

"I wish I had my own magic to use against him."

Ander scowled at Jenan.

"Please don't wish that, my friend. Magic comes at far too great a cost."

"As great a cost as your only brother?"

"Yes! No! You don't understand!"

Jenan shook his head.

"I understand that if Misk had a magical gift, perhaps he'd be alive. But you are correct... I don't know how you can hate your gift so much."

"Gift! Better to call it a curse. Be thankful you don't understand it, Jenan. Please. I cannot explain it, but if you were in my shoes..."

Eto was feeling uncomfortable in the growing tension in the room. He cleared his throat, and changed the subject.

"How do we draw him out? We won't want to fight anywhere near the castle. Enough people have been hurt by Gojen."

Debran smiled, grimly. She walked to the bell in the corner.

"We will use the Great Bell to draw him out. I think he must have heard it, when Ander first revealed his magic to us. It's a mercy that he hasn't come looking for it. I do know that if we use it intentionally, as we did twenty-five years ago, it will force him out of the castle. It will bring him to us. We will take the bell to the clearing, a few miles west of the castle."

Eto looked concerned.

"Will he hear it? I think I know the clearing you mean. I rested there... when I was bringing Misk back."

"Squire, he will hear this bell if he is in the air, or beneath a mountain. He would feel its vibration, even if he were on another continent. He could, perhaps, hear it on some other planet. This bell is crafted by magic, and is imbued with his names, his character, his faults, and his ambitions. While we have been waiting for Prince Jenan and Danj to return, I have been adding to it, replacing that which was meant to cast out with that which will draw him to it. We cannot break the original binding on the Great Bell, it can never be used, directly, to kill him. King Johnel ensured that, at the time of the Great Spell. Your magic, Prince Ander, and your swords must see to that. And this time, though it pains me to say it, only death will do. Casting him out will never be enough. We must kill or be killed."

The group was silent and solemn. Ander went outside with Jenan and Eto, where they practiced and sparred together, getting to know one another's strengths and weaknesses. They created signals, and agreed on how best to pace each other.

Then the three of them settled into a quiet meditation. Debran and Danj prayed with them, once they had finished preparing the bell. Even Jobias joined the circle, sitting as quietly as an eight-year-old boy is able, caught up in the pensive, expectant mood.

Chapter 59
For Misk

"I honored the fallen enemy by placing a stone on his beautiful grave."
-- Manfred von Richthofen, The Red Baron

Morning came at last to Midmun, and found the five who sought to destroy the growing evil ready to go to work. They were gathered in the clearing, miles beyond the western gate of Wayhall Castle. The Great Bell had been carted there with them. Jobias returned to the Bell House with the donkey, after he had begged to stay, and had been denied permission. He carried several letters to be delivered if the spell failed.

Danj described the three circles he would cast, and why he was using the herbs and artifacts he had chosen.

"The outer circle is a shield circle. As the earth element, I will scatter dried sage and sweet grass. At the compass points, I will place a piece of amber, because it is a stone known for its ability to safeguard. These will keep out all influences, and all people but those I have named. No outsider will be able to interfere. No help will come for Gojen, if indeed he has anyone he can call on for aid."

"The middle circle is a ward circle. For the water element, I will pour vinegar, in which I have distilled knot weed, on this circle to keep the magic contained within the circle. I will place opals on this ring as well, to absorb magical energies. These wards will not allow errant spells to escape. No innocent man nor beast will be harmed by his magic, or ours."

"The inner circle is a binding circle. For the fire element, I have burnt osha root, which repels snakes and hopefully dragons as well. I have added crushed glass, which is sand which has fused together in the heat of a volcano, because Gojen fears and loathes it. These are so that once he is in the circle, he will be bound inside, not able to walk nor fly out of it, so long as my magic holds."

Once the sun was well up from the horizon, Danj walked an enormous circle three times, casting herbs, drizzling vinegar, and placing the other items on the ground, as he had described. He chanted as he walked.

"*Osha root to bind the drake*
Hissing, coiling, as a snake
Turned back again by fine crushed glass
This inner sphere, you shall not pass"

Danj stepped back one pace, and cast another circle, a little wider than the first.

"*The middle ring, a ward of power*
Knot weed, in vinegar most sour
Opals keep the spells contained
No errant ray shall come unchained."

When he returned to the point where he had begun this ward, he closed the circle, and again stepped back one pace.

"*The outer circle forms a shield*
A wall of amber will not yield
Sweet grass dried, along with sage
Protecting warrior, squire and mage"

As soon as Danj had completed his work, Debran began to strike the Great Bell. Three times she struck it, each time calling out. Her voice had become clear and strong since her hearing had been returned to her.

Clang

"Otyk, miscreant prince. By your faithlessness and false pretense, murderer of your mother Queen Kyran, and many magicians and citizens of Midmun. Practitioner of black magic. Banished by King Johnel in the Great Spell. Come to the Great Bell, and meet your fate at last!"

Clang

"Gojen, unworthy regent, and would-be king. By fear and fever, murderer of your brother, King Thowin, his wife, Queen Jaynn, Daegun

Vyne, and many more. Betrayer, deceiver, and usurper. Come to the Great Bell, and meet your fate at last!"

Clang

"Dragon, beast which bears no name, but instead carries all the guilt and depravity of one man. By fire and flame, murderer of Prince Misk, the maidens of Midmun, Imperial Prince Ulst, and many more. Brute, beast, and behemoth. Come to the Great Bell and meet your fate at last!"

Debran stood next to the bell, and Danj came to her side. Prince Ander took up his position at the westernmost point on the circle, gazing toward the east, waiting for a glimpse of the dragon. Prince Jenan stood at the southeast and Squire Eto to the northeast. They too watched for signs of the dragon's arrival.

In Wayhall Castle, some three miles away, Gojen was in a fit of agony. Each of the bell's soundings had shaken him to the core. He could only stand by gripping the edge of his workbench and pulling himself up. Clutching the dragon scale, trembling with pain and rage and indignation, he reopened the long wound on his arm. He hastily chanted the transformation spell and thrust the scale into his arm as he leapt from his window.

In dragon form, he felt less pain, or perhaps the pain was the same, but there was more of him to absorb it. However, his compulsion to find the magic was far stronger. No matter how he tried to do otherwise, he could fly only toward the west. Who could be casting this spell? Who could create magic that could compel him? He was Otyk! He was the Dragon! How dare they!

The spell drew him onward. It took only a matter of minutes until the purple blaze and the sizzle of the magic in the clearing showed him his destination. He circled in the air, flying slowly, lower and lower, trying to catch sight of those in the field. Instead of sight, he became more aware of scents. Gold. Gold was good, but it shouldn't hold this kind of sway over him that he was experiencing. Steel, too, lots of steel. So they meant to fight? That was fine, he was in a mood for a good fight. A trace of wood and glass. There was more as well, but none of it mattered now. He landed, and noticing the wards around him, but he did not fear them. What were mere human wards to a dragon?

Sweeping his silvery green head from side to side, he found he could only see one, or sometimes two of the warriors. There in front of him was that wretched Prince Ander. Was this all his doing? Gojen had underestimated Ander, and discounted his magic. Ander was no match for his own power. And there was that squire, Eto. He should have killed him when he killed Misk. That mistake would soon be rectified. He did not recognize the third warrior, and he couldn't quite make out the man and woman just outside the circle. Never mind, he would kill them all.

He flapped his great leathery wings as he prepared to take off, planning to sweep in again, leading with his flames. He gathered his strength and leapt... or at least he tried to do so. Some barrier kept him earthbound; he could not take off. He bellowed in rage and charged at Prince Ander. Ander stood just outside the third circle of herbs and stones, and Gojen found that for all his brute strength, he could not break through the barrier. He ricocheted off the unseen boundary, no more able to go out than up. Whoever had cast these circles had skill, and full access to the mana in Midmun. No wonder he'd been finding the supply diminished.

When he breathed fire, he found that the flames could not breach the magic, but instead spread out, arced along some unseen sphere. As the flames dissipated, Eto leapt into the circle and heaved his sword at the dragon's tail.

"For Misk!"

The blow sliced under the dragon's scales and into his flesh. He shrieked rage and defiance, and turned to blast his fiery breath at the squire, but just then Ander and the other man both fell on him, slashing at his long, scaled neck.

They were quick, these three, and they worked well together. It was a challenge to keep track of all of them, but now they were trapped in the circle with him. His tail was nearly useless, which hindered him. Wounds to his tail, or wings, body parts he did not possess as a man, should have simply disappeared, as they had when he fought Misk.

Still, he had teeth and talons... and fire. He turned his head and flamed at the bearded man, who fell back onto the ground as the flames brushed his hair. Just then, Prince Ander ran in from the other side, and pierced his shoulder. The tip of his sword slid between his scales, into his flesh. Gojen turned his attention to the prince.

Eto helped Jenan extinguish the flames in his hair. At the edge of the outer circle, Danj chanted continuously, and Debran rang bell after bell.

Gojen snapped at Ander, who ducked and sliced up at the dragon's rib cage as he ran beneath him. This action was more distracting than destructive. While the dragon tried to find Ander, Eto rushed back and sliced through the membrane between the spines of his right wing, causing him to list to that side. Even when not flying, his wings were essential to his balance. Jenan recovered from his tumble and rejoined the fray, singed hair and all.

Gojen turned his focus on Eto, who deflected the fiery breath with his shield. As he did so, he failed to see the dragon's great foreleg in motion. The blow sent him flying through the air. He landed on his left arm with a sickening thud.

Eto struggled to his feet. He stumbled and weaved back and forth, unable to walk in a straight line. The dragon's laughing roar was just as sickening as the pain of his broken arm, but Eto would not stay down.

While Prince Ander remained behind Gojen, Prince Jenan rushed forward to distract the dragon's attention from the young squire.

"Dragon! Gojen! You fiend! You killed my brother! You will not kill his squire as well!"

Ah, that explained it. This man must be Misk's brother, here for his revenge. How charming, and how foolish! Who would rule Beklen when both of its princes were dead? He'd have to annex it to Midmun, once he was king.

Eto stumbled toward Prince Jenan. He shoved the squire out of the way. Before the dragon could scorch the disoriented squire, Jenan rammed his sword straight up, lodging it securely in the underside of the dragon's jaw.

Ander came around the dragon's damaged wing, and let loose the bolt of lightning which he had been gathering, striking Jenan's sword and sending his electricity coursing through the steel, into the dragon's skull and body. With a squelch and a thud, Gojen, in human form, dropped to the ground. He was no longer able to control the dragon form, with his arm, back and jaw bleeding freely. He stood between the three men, reeling from the magic and blood loss.

As Gojen swayed, he gathered the blood flowing from his left arm in his hand, and flung it at Jenan's face. The blood burned him, causing more damage than the flames had. The prince fell back into the barrier, and stayed where he had fallen.

Now the battle was between Gojen and Ander. The squire and the other prince were incapacitated, and he could kill them later. Outside the barrier, he could hear chimes and chanting, but he would take care of the magicians there once these three were dead.

As they faced each other, Gojen began to chant.

"Sshrink and harden
Constrict and kill
Turn to sstone
Both dead and sstill
No hope, no help
No heart to beat
The queen falls now!
Her doom complete."

As he finished this last, deadly spell, he pulled a small blue stone from the pocket of his blood soaked robe, and swallowed it. With this bit of magic in place, they would never be able to undo the spell and save the princess. Even now, she must be fainting, falling, slipping into a coma. Perhaps she was already dead.

Ander was shocked, and unable to stop Gojen from swallowing the stone. The act was complete before the prince could begin to comprehend just what Gojen was doing. He gathered his wits and held his left hand up as high in the air as he could reach.

Gojen smirked. Was the fool trying to make himself a better target? So be it... Gojen summoned the mana, but found that Ander had already gathered the majority of it.

Ander's body began to glow and twitch. The hair on his head and his body stood out from his flesh. Over and over, outside the circles, Debran sounded the small gold bell. Just as Ander let the electricity free, as it arced from his body to Gojen's, Debran turned and struck the Great Bell. While the magic of Great Bell could not be used to kill Gojen, Debran had reworked it to bind him and hold him perfectly still, while Ander's electricity flowed through his veins like blood and gathered at the base of his brain, dropping him to the ground like a rock.

Danj broke the circles, and ran to Jenan. Debran assisted Eto, splinting his arm, while Danj quickly applied herbal salve to the blood burns on Jenan's face and hands. In a matter of moments, the injured men were prepared to travel.

Chapter 60
Breaking Point

"I have seen a medicine
That's able to breathe life into a stone
Quicken a rock, and make you dance canary."
   -- William Shakespeare, All's Well That Ends Well

Danj transported the three warriors and Debran into the castle. From the courtyard where they appeared, Eto led the way, holding his broken arm close to his chest. A terrified maid pressed herself against a wall as the five sweaty, bloody people ran urgently toward the royal chambers. As they approached, they heard Princess Lyru calling out for help.

"Please! Please, someone! Please help Princess Niren, help my sister!"

Quickly they found the princesses. Lyru was seated on the floor, shaking and sobbing. Niren lay beside her, where she had fallen, her body at an awkward angle. Lyru had lifted her sister's head onto her lap, her face was so pale one could see the blood in her veins, causing her to appear slightly blue. She made no sound.

Ander watched to see if Niren was breathing. It was difficult to tell, with Lyru holding her and trembling, but he didn't think so.

Before the rest of them were through the door, Lyru was shouting at them.

"She collapsed! Do something, please! Help her! Save her!"

Danj lifted Niren's head gently from Lyru's lap, while Debran straightened the princess' arms and legs. Eto caught Lyru's hand in his good one, and pulled her up and away, so that the magicians could begin to do their work. Jenan sat slumped against the wall, shivering.

Danj crushed herbs from his pouch, and held some of them up to Niren's nose, and laid others under her tongue. He chanted quietly. Debran struck a long, narrow stone chime, over and over.

Niren did not move. Her eyelids did not flutter. Her fingers did not twitch.

"Is my sister going to die?"

Danj turned his attention from Niren to Lyru for a moment.

"Not yet, Princess Lyru. With my magic, I can hold her here, at least for a short time, but... I cannot bring her back from this place without help."

He turned back to Niren and began chanting again.

"How short a time?"

Danj didn't waste his breath to answer Lyru. She hid her face against Eto's chest, and began to cry again.

Debran approached Prince Ander

"Now is the time for you to use your magic. I told you it would come to this. The bells spoke of it very plainly, and now the time has come. You must use your magic, and break the stone around her heart. You heard Gojen's spell. It was a killing spell, and one cast with his death magic. Only a very great power can counteract such a thing."

Ander took a few steps back, toward the door.

"I can't do it. I cannot!"

Danj looked up, very briefly.

"You can, Prince Ander. You have learned so much in our time together. I have faith in you. You can control it, now. Your magic will serve you, now."

"What if it won't? I will not take that chance with her life. Find someone else! The court has healers, call them. There has to be some other way."

Debran shook her head, with her eyes full of tears.

"No healer in this land will be able to help her, Prince Ander, even if they were able to arrive in time. They are weak, their gifts have atrophied too long. The bells told me that Niren needed you, before we came here today, before we went to the clearing this morning. Killing Gojen will be for nothing, unless you destroy the stone which has grown around Niren's heart. Gojen swallowed its twin when he cast the curse. If she had not been fighting the spell all along, the stone would have killed her instantly. It is blocking everything that must enter her heart, and everything which must come forth from it. Do you remember what I told you about magic and breath? There must be an exchange. The stone must be broken, or her heart will."

Ander rubbed his head, causing sparks to form in his hair.

"If I use my magic, it will kill her. I will KILL her. I cannot be responsible for another's death! You don't understand!"

Lyru broke free from Eto's one-armed grip, and turned to glare at Ander.

"You will save her, or I will kill YOU!"

Chapter 61
Monsters and Memories

"This memory, this pretty little stone, I examine it with my eyes closed tight, turn it over in my fingers."
   -- Joseph Boyden, Three Day Road

Eto tried to pull Lyru back, but she broke away from him, and returned to the floor. She glared at Prince Ander, and sat again with Niren's head in her lap. She continued stroking her sister's long brown hair, and Debran kept her fingers on the princess' wrist, monitoring her pulse. Occasionally, she rang the stone chime. Danj continued to chant quietly.
   Everyone stared at Ander, expectantly. He began to tell the story he'd kept secret for so long.
   "I didn't want to ever tell this to anyone, but you have to understand why I can't do this. I was betrothed, and should have been married over a year ago. My fiancé was Lady Lizzu. She was a water-mage, of high birth, the daughter of a well-respected baron. I never cared that she was not of royal birth. A lake on their land was infested with monsters known as the afanc. She'd been working for some time on the problem, with little success. She couldn't spend more than an afternoon away from the shore. The afanc were ruining the fisherman's business, and hurting anyone who tried to swim or wade in the lake."
   "After trying for weeks to rid the lake of these monsters alone, Lizzu came to me, and asked for my help."
   "I put her off several times, and flat out refused to help her for a while. I have never considered myself a magician. I have never been interested in exercising my 'gift'. I was a prince and a knight. That was

good enough for me, and I told her she would have to let it be good enough for her."

"Lizzu continued to pursue the idea. She was stubborn and relentless. She felt that perhaps my magic could be the key. It grew harder to resist her, if only for the opportunity to see her working her magic. As much as I disliked my own powers, hers were a joy to watch, and she was beautiful while she worked."

"She appealed at last to my sense of duty. This was an opportunity to practice our work together. Whether mundane or magical, someday we would each have important work to do in the kingdom of Parelm, and we could learn to do so together. Some day we would be raising children together. 'It might even be fun,' she said. 'You hardly ever dust off your magic. What harm can it do to try to help me?"

Both Debran and Danj shuddered a little at this last tempting of fate.

"It was clear she would not take no for an answer. Besides, I wanted her to be happy. I wanted her to defeat the afanc, so she could return to the castle, and we could concentrate on our wedding. I agreed to go."

"We returned to the lake together, and she began to work her magic, trying to purify the water. The monsters were shrieking, stirring the lake into a frenzy with their thrashing. When she signaled to me, I began my own spell. I called down a great lightning bolt from the sky. As it hit the surface, she laughed, delighted at the power. Her face shone as brightly as the lightning on the water. She was so lovely."

Ander ran his fingers though his short hair. After taking a deep breath, he continued, sounding tortured.

"It seemed to be working. The afanc were overwhelmed, and disappearing or dying. Lizzu asked me to strike the lake once again, to be certain that the work was complete. She was elated at the thought that the problem was solved, and that she could return home. I wish that had been the case."

Danj continued quietly chanting, while the others listened. A bead of sweat ran down the side of his face. Debran stood, and placed her hands on his shoulders, lending what strength and mana she could.

"I had ignored my magic for most of my life and refused to practice it. I had always disliked it, even before... before what happened next. My magic escaped from me. The power overcame me. I felt it coursing through me, and then I must have passed out. When I came to, Lizzu was lying beside me, with her feet in the lake, and she was dead. She had been electrocuted."

Tears streamed from Lyru's eyes. Debran dabbed at her face with her handkerchief. Ander was almost as pale as Niren. He sat in a chair, almost motionless, but for a slight tremble.

"Can't you all see that this is too dangerous? There must be someone else, some other way. She could die. She Will Die! I'll kill her...too, like I killed Lizzu."

He buried his face in his hands.

Lyru rose, gently laying her sister's head on a pillow, and went to Ander. She prized his fingers from his face and took his hands in her own.

"She's going to die if you don't do something. Look at her. Look at her face! Can you let that happen, without even trying to help? How can you just sit there? Don't you care for her, at all? Prince Ander, listen to me! Who else is there? Do you think Prince Stohl is going to save her?"

Lyru let go of Ander's hands.

"Please, Ander, listen to Debran and Danj. Save her, please. She's all I have, my only family."

Eto went to Lyru's side, but instead of wrapping his arm around her shoulders again, he held her chin with his good hand, and made her look into his eyes.

"No, Princess Lyru, you're not alone any more. That much, I can promise you, no matter what comes next."

Swallowing hard, the squire then approached the prince, and spoke ardently.

"Prince Ander, you'll have to forgive me for speaking out of turn, but the ladies are right. They both are, the princess and Mistress Debran. If you could have saved Princess Niren, if there was even a chance, and you haven't as much as tried, all the doubts and fears that have hindered you for so long... they'll cripple you. They'll bind you up tighter than that stone on Niren's heart. It will turn you as dark as Gojen was. You don't have to hear bells to know that."

Ander stared at Eto, his face blank with horror at the thought of turning into someone as evil as Gojen.

Prince Jenan broke his silence with a groan of pain. "Ander, I know you. You must do this, for yourself as much as for the princess. And for my brother. For Misk. Please."

Danj, who had not paused in his chanting over Niren this whole time, looked up, and spoke to the tormented prince.

"It is time. She is fading, minute by minute. I cannot hold her this way for much longer, Prince Ander. Make your decision. Act now, while there is mana to do so or let her die."

Ander ran his hand through the halo of his hair, and sparks crackled. With a shudder, he finally conceded.

"I will try. I can only pray that we will not regret the attempt."

Eto took Lyru by the hand and led her to a corner of the room while Danj laid slivers of white willow bark down around Niren and Ander, forming a circle of protection and healing. Debran rang several of her bells, her face solemn. She rang glass for Lyru, for the clear, pure love of her sister. She rang steel for Eto, for his support, forged in the fire. She rang a wooden bell for Danj, that his knowledge and wisdom would be sufficient. For Prince Jenan, she rang a brass bell, a strong sound which filled the room with its echo, and with the echoes of Prince Misk, his brother. Her own bell was made of porcelain, pure white, and small.

At last, she began to ring the bells for Ander and Niren. Ander's bell was surprisingly small. It was made of gold, and its tone was rich. The last bell, selected for Niren, didn't look much like a bell at all. Instead, it was a long, narrow slab of gray stone, slightly larger at the bottom than the top. It hung from a leather cord around Debran's left hand, and she struck it with a small wooden hammer. The note hung in the air, and she nodded for Ander to begin.

Ander stood over Niren, as she lay, her pale face pinched in a grimace. He raised his left hand toward the roof and called down the magic, through the stone walls and ceilings of Wayhall Castle. He let the lightning flow through him and out again, into Niren, straight to the stone around her heart. Lyru, who had not been at the Bell House when Ander first revealed his power, gasped. Niren groaned, once, as her arms and legs flailed about. Another pulse of magic made her twitch again, then she fell still. Lyru would have rushed into the circle, but Eto held onto her, hugging her to his chest.

Ander called his electricity again, and sent it surging through Niren, causing her muscles to twitch. Outside the circle, Debran struck the stone chime, and the princess became calm. Still, she frowned, and did not wake.

"Prince Ander, you must stop holding back. Your fear is killing her. You must find your courage, and act on it now. Half of your magic will only electrocute her. Half your magic will never be enough."

Ander glared at Danj, then called down the lighting again, and allowed it to build inside him. His whole body trembled. His hair stood out from his head, and fairly sizzled. More lighting appeared around him, covering his body, seeking a place to join with that which already seethed within him. He cried out, struggling to contain so much power. Debran struck the gold bell, and the magic found its place.

When his magic had filled every inch of him, when he could not hold it, and could kindle it no longer, he let it flow out of his hands and into the fallen princess. This was nothing like the other attempts.

This time it was much, much worse.

First came the sound, a clap of thunder so loud and startling that Lyru screamed. The noise was followed, so quickly it appeared to happen at the same instant, by a force which threw everyone standing outside the circle into the walls.

After they righted themselves, everyone turned to look at the prince and princess. Ander's head hung low to his chest. He was covered in sweat, and trembling violently. His hair still crackled with current. Niren trembled too, and then she stilled. For a moment, no one in the room even dared to breathe.

As Ander sunk down onto his knees beside Niren, a horrific crack sounded from her chest. Lyru hid her face against Eto's chest, but he forced her to turn around and watch. Niren was breathing again. She was alive. The grimace faded from her face. With a gasp and a cough she opened her eyes, and smiled up at Ander.

Chapter 62
Love, Made New

"Love doesn't just sit there, like a stone. It has to be made, like bread, remade all the time, made new."
   -- Ursula K. LeGuin, The Lathe of Heaven

Later that evening, while Niren was sitting up in bed, Ander came to visit. Lyru and Debran chaperoned the visit, sitting across the room, embroidering. Niren insisted that she felt quite well, and asked to be allowed to stroll in the gardens, but everyone refused her request.

Debran had clucked over her like a mother hen.

"Tomorrow will be soon enough although it may feel none too soon. Your body's been through a storm, right enough, and I don't mean just at the end. Rest now. Visit with your young man, while you have the luxury of doing so. The people will be wanting to see you, and hear your story, and there's plenty of work to do to set things right, but that will come later. Right now, you must rest."

Ander sat in a chair beside her bed, looking uneasy. He had combed his hair down, but soon it was in disarray, again.

"Princess Niren, I am glad you feeling well, and honored that you would see me. I know you must still be feeling very weak."

"I rather wish that everyone would stop telling me what I must be feeling. You can't know what a relief it is to feel anything at all. What a fool I was to swallow that stone!"

"Princess, please don't say such things. You couldn't have known what it would do to you. You didn't know that Gojen was your enemy."

"I did study magic, though, you know. From HIM! He taught me about stones which could affect emotion. Why! That's the very reason

I sought it out. I was afraid, so afraid that I would fall in love again... and be hurt, again. I thought I would prefer to feel nothing. I played right into his hands... I gave him exactly what he needed to be certain I would never marry. I will say it again, I was a fool."

"If you were, I was too. I refused to study magic, though I possessed my own. I thought I could keep it stowed away... like an oil cloth to protect you from rain.... while you travel through a desert. I thought I would never need it, and I never dreamed I would want it."

He hesitated for a moment.

"I want to tell you about Lizzu. She was my fiancée. She is the reason I was not on the first list of princes, and the reason I could not leave Parelm. I was in mourning for her. I loved her. I killed her."

Niren reached out, and took Ander's hand in hers, stopping him.

"I don't know how, but I heard everything you told the others, while they tried to convince you to use your magic on me. I know what happened to her. I don't believe you killed her... it was an accident."

Ander looked down at his hand, as Niren held it.

"Part of why I loved Lizzu was because she was out there, in the world, every day. She was doing the magic she loved, in the place she loved. That's why she wanted me there with her. Because she loved me, and she thought having me work with her would make it perfect. She even convinced me. But I'm not perfect, Niren."

"No one is perfect, Ander."

"I thought she was. Even if I didn't think it when she was alive, I built her up in my memory. Does that make sense? She was perfect, living a perfect life. She was about to marry a prince. She was wonderful with her magic, and it was beautiful when she worked it. She was beautiful when she worked it. She loved every moment of it, and she did so much good with it."

Ander paused to take a breath.

"That is, until she drug me into it with her. You see? I've been afraid for so long that everything would have gone differently that day if I wasn't there with her. I've been so unhappy."

"It's not wrong to be unhappy. I've learned that much, at last. It has a place."

"You're right. It's not wrong to be unhappy, it's only wrong to hide from it. We've both done that. I've done a lot of hiding. I can't hide from my magic any more. You can't hide from heartache. And I won't hide from the fact that I love you."

"Oh."

Ander shook his head in wonderment.

"I tell you that I love you, and you say 'Oh'".

"I'm sorry. I didn't expect you to say it quite so soon."

"Quite so soon? Soon? Wait... you knew it was coming?"

Niren smiled.

"I've known since the moment your lightning struck my heart. I felt you. I really saw and heard you, for the first time. I saw how patient you'd been with me, even when I told you that you could never be like Misk. I saw how determined you were to spend time with me, but never to push me too hard. I saw that you loved me."

"Oh."

They both smiled at that.

"Could you tell what happened when my magic met yours, then?"

Niren looked puzzled, her brow wrinkled.

"My magic? I don't have magic. What do you mean?"

"You're wrong. You do have magic. When I let my magic fill me, completely, and I sent every last bit of it out into you, something changed. I let go of my fear, then. There wasn't any room for it. My magic found yours, and together, they wrapped around that evil stone, and when the stone cracked, some of the magic returned to me. Mine and yours, too. But I'm not afraid of it. Not anymore. I can control it, now. Your magic grounded mine. I won't kill anyone else. It will never get away from me again."

"Oh."

This time they both laughed out loud. Debran and Lyru glanced at them from across the room, then returned to their embroidery.

"Magic isn't much different from love, Niren. Half measures won't do. It's got to be all or nothing. Otherwise it's unpleasant, at best, and unsafe, at worst. It's better to be sold out to it. To let the magic... or the love... own you completely."

Ander took Niren's hand in his, and held it. He rubbed his thumb over her palm, much as King Thowin used to do to reassure her. She choked back a sob at the memory.

"It is time to live again, Niren. A new love doesn't make your disloyal to Misk. Nor I to Lizzu."

Ander left his chair and knelt down beside the bed, still holding Niren's hand.

"You thought, when you invited all of us princes here, that you could have a wedding and have a husband. You'd be married, fulfilling the law. You'd be safe, without wanting or needing or feeling or giving anything. But it is not about having... it's about doing. Marriage has its very own magic, and it's active, not idle. I'm going to ask you to feel things. I'm going to ask you to let my love fill your heart so that there is no room for fear. Take a chance, it might not be safe, but I will never hurt you."

Niren trembled at intensity of the feelings churning in her breast. Raw emotion, and something more. Magic. Ander's magic, and when she concentrated... some magic there that belonged to her, as well.

"I'm ready to start. To start living again, and loving again. A fresh start is important, for both of us."

"You are important. You. Niren. Not as the princess or the queen. Not as someone with new magic. You must be important to yourself... as you've become important to me. I loved Lizzu first... but I didn't love her better, or more. I won't say there was some fate, or destiny, which caused us to come together... because that means that it was fate that our other loved ones died. And it wasn't destiny, it was their choices. They chose to try to save others, both of them, and it cost them everything. I honor them, but I love you."

He raised his head, and looked Niren in the eye.

"I love you, now. Truly. And forever, if you'll have me. Will you marry me, Niren?"

"Oh," she said as her smile lit up her pale face.

"Oh, yes!"

Chapter 63
Coronation and Consecration

"When a king reigns, it is thanks to the people, when a river sings, it is thanks to the stones."
-- Malagasy Proverb

For a month and a day, Wayhall Castle bustled with activity, as everyone readied themselves for Niren's wedding to Ander, and their coronation. Guests poured in, more every day, filling all the rooms, both in the castle and at the surrounding inns. People opened their homes as well. None of the rejected princes came, except for Prince Stohl, whom everyone agreed hardly counted.

Of course Daegun Vyne of Gunmar and Imperial Prince Ulst of the Aggem Empire had never returned to their homes. Their families received long letters from Princess Niren, explaining that Otyk had returned to Midmun. In his plotting, these princes had fallen victim. Their personal effects were returned, along with substantial grave gifts. Only a select few in Midmun ever knew how gruesome their deaths were, and fewer still knew of Prince Ulst's crimes. Condolences and monetary compensations were sent to the families of his victims as well.

Once that grim work was over, Niren and Lyru spent most of their time together, each sewing for her trousseau, or strolling with Ander and Eto through the gardens. Together, they listened to the commoners who came once a week for judgments and legal rulings, and to see for themselves that Princess Niren was once again the wonderful young woman whom they had always loved.

Niren shocked almost everyone when she announced that her coronation would take place the day before the wedding.

She wore a full-skirted lilac silk gown, with a fitted bodice. The sleeves hugged her arms and ended in triangular points at her wrists. The ivory lace collar at her throat was shot through with thread-of-gold, but she wore no jewelry. Her dark hair was bound up in a series of intricate knots. To finish the lovely ensemble, she wore the ribbon crown which Lyru had made for her.

"I am not breaking the law, I have chosen to change the law, for the good of my country and for my descendants. My daughters and granddaughters will not be forced to marry in order to rule Midmun. They will be held to the same conditions and requirements as future princes. None of them will be forced to forfeit the throne, if no suitable spouse can be found for them."

"Under the old law, I was Midmun was nearly destroyed, and I was nearly killed. My mother and father were murdered, but the damage extended well past our royal family. Gojen killed farm girls and shepherdesses. He killed three princes, Misk, Vyne and Ulst. If he could not rule Midmun, he would have destroyed it, as well as Beklen and Parelm. Who knows how far he would have extended his reach, to satisfy his greed and lust and envy. He took advantage of the law which I am changing, to do these things."

"Therefore, I now decree that henceforth, and evermore, the Daughters of Midmun may rule with or without a husband. In the same way, the Sons may rule with or without a wife."

Not even the most conservative, staid nobles dared to grumble about the new protocol. With that bit of business seen to, Niren relaxed a little. She stood with her head held high and her shoulders back, confident and beautiful.

"Fear must never rule us. I lived in the fear of what others could do to my heart, and my beloved lived in the fear of what lay within his heart. Each of us let fear blind us and bind us, and we made unwise choices. We are blessed to have another chance, to make wiser, more courageous choices."

Niren looked out over the crowd which filled the throne room. Nobles, ambassadors and commoners mingled together. The people hung on her every word.

"Gojen was filled with hatred, so full of loathing that there was no room inside him for anything good. Some may say that hate is the opposite of love, but I believe it is fear which is the opposite of love. Love frees us, and fear binds us. Love strengthens, while fear weakens. Love brings life, and fear ushers in death. It very nearly brought me to my death."

Murmurs ran through the crowd, as people made the sign against evil, crossing their hearts.

"Listen to me! If fear is the opposite of love, then it is love which opposes fear. Love drives fear out of the heart. There is not room enough for both. Let love fill your hearts, good people of Midmun, allies and friends. Let love make fear tremble and flee. Let love rule us all!"

A cheer rose from the lips of those closest to the dais. "Let love rule us all!" Soon everyone in the hall had taken it up. "Let love rule us all!"

Niren waited for silence, smiling down on her people.

"I will honor the love of my parents for each other, for my sister and me, and for you, our great country. I humbly accept the crown of Midmun."

Lyru stepped forward, standing in for her parents, as the last member of Niren's family. As her sister bowed her head, Lyru lifted away the ribbon crown, smiling and crying at the same time. On the pedestal beside the throne, lay Niren's new crown. It was similar to the crown Queen Jaynn had worn, three intertwined golden strands. It differed from her mother's crown in that three golden chains hung down from the back, reminiscent of the ribbon crowns. Lyru lifted it into place on Niren's head.

Niren and Lyru kissed each other on the cheeks. They each cried as the people cheered.

"My first act, as your queen is to name Lyru as my regent, if such should ever be needed, until such time as my first daughter or son reaches the age of majority. Princess Lyru has already served you, keeping you safe, making arrangements for help to come while I was bound and incapacitated by Gojen's spell. She acted with authority and love. She did not let fear rule her."

Lyru wore a simpler version of her sister's gown, in pale yellow. Her collar was the very one which Niren had made for her for the Harvest Festival. She curtsied to her sister, then to her people.

"My second act is to declare Eto, formerly Squire to Prince Misk, a knight in his own right. He served Misk for the year of the royal progress, and further served King Hastho of Beklen. He made the journey to Beklen to get the help I so desperately needed. He has been loyal and brave. It was only with his help that Gojen was slain."

At her summons, Eto stepped forward, elegant in his burgundy doublet and hose. Lyru thought he had never looked more handsome. He knelt before Queen Niren. He offered her his sword, (the old, battered one he'd used against Gojen, declining offers to have a new one forged for him) and lifted it toward her on his palms. Taking it, she touched each of his shoulders.

"I dub thee Sir Eto, Dragon-Foe, Protector of Midmun, and consort of Princess Lyru. I further grant my permission for the betrothal of Princess Lyru to Sir Eto, and I say truly that no finer match could be made. In the presence of grief, treachery and fear, these two have found friendship, embraced bravery and embodied selfless love."

The assembled crowd cheered wildly as the younger princess went to stand beside the new knight.

"Prince Jenan of Beklen, there is little we can offer to you, by way of titles or privileges. Our gratitude, friendship and love will be yours forever. We honor you, and your brother, Prince Misk, as well as King Hastho and Queen Margam. I declare you to be my brother, if not under the law, then under the bounds of respect and fealty. I wish you every joy in this life."

Jenan bowed to Niren, and she curtsied to him, and then they embraced.

"Prince Jenan has granted permission for Danj to remain in Midmun. He is released from his position as adviser to the court of Beklen, and shall henceforth be our Magister. We shall need a great deal of knowledge to undo twenty-five years of a lack of magic, and its study. We can think of no better source of knowledge, and we bestow this chain of office, marking Danj as one to be revered and respected."

Danj stepped forward and bowed his head, and Niren lifted the chain and medallion, settling it on his neck and shoulders. He also embraced Prince Jenan.

"Debran, Mistress of the Bell House, we would heap honor after honor upon you, would you but accept them. At last, we must respect your refusal of any title or position, and accept your offer of friendship and your willingness to use your bells as you see fit, in our aid. Your grandson, Jobias, will never want for anything. Should he choose it, he may serve as a squire when he comes of age, or study under Danj in the new school which he means to found in the Thaumery. Thus begins a new noble house in Midmun."

Jobias joined Debran on the dais, and together they went and stood with Magister Danj. Prince Jenan grinned at Jobias.

Niren turned at last to her beloved, dressed in gray silk. His blue eyes were bright.

"Prince Ander of Parelm, tomorrow we begin life together as husband and wife, king and queen. Tomorrow we become legally bonded, and enter a contract of commitment to each other, as well as to the people of Midmun. Tomorrow, you will be my husband, and the people's king. My father, King Thowin..."

At the mention of Thowin, the crowd cheered, loudly and with great feeling. As they quieted, Niren continued.

"King Thowin was well respected. His wisdom and care served Midmun well for twenty-five years. He feared little, and loved much. My mother, Queen Jaynn..."

The gathered people cheered again, just as loudly as before.

"Queen Jaynn was beloved to her people, as well. She was fiercely loyal to her subjects, and they to her. Tomorrow, you and I take up the task of living up to their legacy. Perhaps in twenty-five years, we will have accomplished that."

"Today, however, I seek to thank you for your role in my rescue. Today, I recognize that you undertook a task which was more frightening to you than facing a dragon. You faced yourself. You put fear aside, and by so doing, you allowed love in. I can offer no greater reward than that which you have found for yourself."

Ander and Niren exchanged the formal obeisances, but with such joy on their faces that more than one young woman in the crowd sighed and wiped away a tear.

"People of Midmun, my dear people. I stand humbly before you today, accepting the crown of the Queen. I would not be here to do so without the aid of these seven people. Princess Lyru! Prince Jenan!

Prince Ander! Sir Eto! Magister Danj! Mistress Debran! Master Jobias! Please help me to thank them."

The crowd outdid themselves. Their cheering could be heard from a mile away, carried by the breeze. Gold and stone bells rang out in every chapel, and fireworks lit the sky from every hill. All of Midmun rejoiced. The six heroes of the dragon battle, along with the new queen, her sister, and little Jobias waved and smiled at the people. Some of them cried, as well.

Chapter 64
The Wedding in Wayhall

"Our hearts are not stones. A stone may disintegrate in time and lose its outward form."
   -- Haruki Murakami, After the Quake

Rain threatened the morning of the wedding, but Danj pushed the storm away. Sun shone down on the chapel, illuminating the stained glass windows. Every pew was full, and people stood at the back, and along the side aisles.

Princess Lyru and Sir Eto served the bride and groom as their first friends. Lyru wore pale pink, which set off the blush of happiness on her cheeks.

Queen Niren elected Prince Jenan to escort her as she walked toward Ander, and he released her from her old life into her new one. He kissed her cheek, and reminded her that Misk had loved her very much, and would always have put her happiness first.

"I am well pleased that you have chosen Prince Ander. Now I have a new brother, as well as a new sister. Be blessed, and happy, always."

Both Prince Misk and Lady Lizzu were represented at the altar. Debran and Danj lit gray candles with black bands, which flanked the white ones representing Niren and Ander.

The young priest who presided over the wedding had been instructed to concentrate on all that the future held for the couple and for Midmun, and he did so. He did, however, take a moment to memorialize King Thowin and Queen Jaynn. They had left a legacy of great love, for each other, their daughters and their country. While Niren and Ander would have large shoes to fill, everyone was confident that they could do so.

The couple looked regal and elegant, each of them dressed in white and gold from head to toe.

Ander spoke his vows first.

"Niren, my queen, my love. Winding roads have brought me to your side, but I will follow them no more. Magic has bonded me to you, but magic, perhaps, is just another function of love. Both of them have great power, and must be held in the highest respect. They must each be practiced every day. Today, I swear my oath to you, to be your husband, and your king and your friend forever."

Niren wiped tears from her eyes, and then spoke her vows.

"Ander, my prince of many princes, my love. I once lived in fear of love. I once hid from even the idea of it. I thought duty, honor, and loyalty could be good enough to allow me to serve my country. I allowed myself to forget that without love, duty is slavery, honor is obligation, and loyalty is only a lack of other choices. With love, these three things are beautiful, and a joy to share. Today, I swear my oath to you, and I open my heart to love and be loved by you forever."

With that, Debran sounded a new bell which had been crafted especially for the royal wedding. This bell was a large stone chime, bound by gold along the edges. She struck the chime three times. Every guest at the wedding had been given a smaller version, and as the new king and queen came up the aisle and exited the chapel, the sound of the bells filled the air.

The people feasted that night, and drank to the health and prosperity of the newly married couple, as well as the country.

New wine and aged wine were served, along with beer, ale, mead, cider and other spirits. There were breads and cakes and pies. There was a table groaning beneath three roast pigs. There was roast chicken, and duck, and goose as well. There were vegetables and fruits, and jams and jellies. By the end of the evening, the menfolk were groaning (as the tables had been earlier) and their women were shaking their heads and tsk tsking. It had been a truly glorious day.

Ander's mother, Queen Ilme, was delighted by her new daughter-in-law, and promised to visit, but no more nor less often than once a year, so as not to make a nuisance of herself. Still, she would be waiting eagerly for word of grandchildren. Niren smiled and Ander blushed.

After the meal and these announcements, Glasyd the Bard stood. At the request of the new king and queen, along with the princess and her new fiancé, he had written a new legend.

"Bell, book, candle
Blood, sweat, tears
Stone, steel, sand
Loves, hates, fears
Use them all together
This is the place to start
Undo the wicked spell
And free the binded heart
No man is an island
No heart can beat in stone
No safety can be found
In a hiding place, alone
Come out, into the open
Let the enemy hear our cry
Today we are not divided
We stand, that you must die
No dragon can be bested
No enemy undone
Unless we work together
And stand the breach as one
Magic and emotion
Skill and knowledge, too
Victory and triumph
Love that's pure and true
This is how the scales are balanced
How justice shows its face
This is how we seek tomorrow
To find peace, and take our place."

Epilogue

"Therefore I tell my sorrows to the stones... For that they will not interrupt my tale."
  -- William Shakespeare, Titus Andronicus

During the wedding feast, Prince Stohl sat amongst the guests, tapping his damned flask. Of course, with Gojen dead, the magic had ended, and it failed to refill. Still, he stubbornly tapped it, over and over. He complained bitterly, to anyone within earshot, about the wretched unfairness of his life. Why! He'd never even gotten a proper chance to woo the princess. Soon he was alone in one corner of the garden pavilion, silent and sullen, and slothful as ever, as wedding guests ate and danced and enjoyed the royal hospitality to its fullest.

The next day, King Ander's first royal order was that the castle guards accompany Prince Stohl to the harbor, and seek passage for him on a ship bound for the island kingdom of Layant. Even as the ship sailed away, the guards could see Stohl's finger tapping the flask.

THE END

DISCUSSION QUESTIONS

Why did Misk go alone to face the dragon?
Do you think that Gojen had any influence over his decision to do so?
Misk truly believed in the Legend of Sir Halb. How do people let popular myths and legends affect their decisions?
--
What did you think of Niren?
Was she a hero or a victim?
Did Niren's fear about the prospect of finding a husband seem reasonable to you?
Did it seem fair to you that she had to be married in order to be queen of Midmun?
Should King Thowin have changed the law?
How else could she have dealt with that fear?
Did her apathy ever annoy you?
Did you, like Lyru, wish Niren would do more to control her own destiny?
How much of her attitude and actions can we blame on the stone?
--
The seven prince candidates were loosely based on the seven deadly sins. Did you notice?
(The seven prince's names are anagrams of the sins they represent.)
Which of them did you like or dislike at first?
How did your opinion of the princes change over time?
Did their various ethnicities, clothing and cultures help you form clear pictures of the princes?
With so many princes present, can you think of other effective ways to differentiate them?
What did you think of Depri when he returned?
--
Both Lyru and Eto started out as 'throw away characters', meant for a very limited purpose. Does that surprise you, given how important they became to the story?
How did each of them drive the plot?
Why were they able to do so?

Why were the five who fought together able to defeat the dragon and Gojen when Misk had failed?
Was their victory due to the inclusion of magic?
Was it due to the fact that there were five people working together?
Were there other factors?
How would the absence of any of them have affected the victory?
Why were Debran and the Great Bell needed?
Why was in necessary for Prince Jenan to come to Midmun?
Was Eto strong enough to be part of the battle?
Was he an asset?
What were Danj's main contributions to the victory?
Could Ander have used his sword and ignored his magic?
Would the five of them still have overcome the dragon?
--
Is Ander the hero?
Why or why not?
How do fear and regret affect him?
How did he overcome his inability to act?
Who helped him?
What fears hold you back?
What is the best way to move past regret?
--
Where do you think Gojen learned black magic?
Why was he so driven?
Why was he so impatient to gain the throne?
Did the magic he was using affect his will and patience?
What habit of yours negatively affects you and those around you?
--
How does magic in the world of Midmun and West Whitsen differ from that in other fantasy worlds?
What magic would you like to have?
How would that magic be reflected in your body?
--
What is the moral of the story?

GLOSSARY

Afanc - A lake monster from Welsh mythology, known for drowning people.

Brace - A pair of something, typically birds or mammals killed in hunting.

Crape - Fabric, usually made from silk or wool, most often in black. Typically refers to garments worn during mourning.

Crepes - Very thin pancakes.

Daegun - Korean term translated as Grand Prince.

Dance canary – An energetic dance, popular throughout Europe in the late 16th and early 17th centuries. Usually choreographed for one couple.

Drake - An archaic word for dragon.

Induratize - To harden the heart.

Lady-in-waiting - A woman who attends to a queen or princess.

Lokum - A gelatin based sweet, coated in powdered sugar. Also known as Turkish Delight.

Milady - Form of address for a noblewoman.

Nosegay - A small bouquet of flowers.

Obeisances – A bow or curtsy meant to convey deep respect.

Philtre - A magic potion, usually a love potion.

Pommel - A rounded knob at the end of a sword hilt.

Sophistry - Use of an argument that sounds correct, but is false, especially with the intent to deceive.

Stanch - To stop or restrict the flow of something, as in blood or power.

Staunchest - Most loyal and committed in attitude.

Subtleties - Fine, delicate desserts.

Torque - A neck ornament, consisting of a band of twisted metal.

Vainglorious - Filled with excessive elation or pride over one's own achievements or abilities.

CONNECT WITH NICOLE B HICKS

~

www.NicoleBHicks.com

NicoleBHicks@gmail.com

Facebook: Nicole B Hicks Author

Twitter: @NicoleBHicks

WATCH FOR THE SEQUEL "STONE & GLASS" COMING SOON

Made in the USA
Monee, IL
08 August 2021